T0342998

Beyond & Within
BLACK FRIDAY

Short Stories from Africa

Cheryl S. Ntumy

Foreword by Eugen Bacon

Beyond & Within

BLACK FRIDAY

Short Stories from Africa

Cheryl S. Ntumy

Foreword by Eugen Bacon

FLAME TREE
PUBLISHING

Publisher & Creative Director: Nick Wells
Senior Project Editor: Gillian Whitaker

FLAME TREE PUBLISHING
6 Melbray Mews, Fulham,
London SW6 3NS, United Kingdom
www.flametreepublishing.com

First published 2025
By arrangement with Future Fiction.
Copyright in each story is held by Cheryl S. Ntumy.
All other text © 2025 Flame Tree Publishing.
The Foreword author asserts their moral rights.

25 27 29 28 26
1 3 5 7 9 10 8 6 4 2

Hardback ISBN: 978-1-83562-302-2
ebook ISBN: 978-1-83562-303-9

All rights reserved. No part of this publication may be reproduced,
stored in a retrieval system, or transmitted in any form or by any means,
electronic, mechanical, photocopying, recording or otherwise, without
the prior written permission of the publisher.

Publisher's Note: This is a work of fiction. Names, characters, places, and
incidents are a product of the authors' imaginations. Locales and public
names are sometimes used for atmospheric purposes. Any resemblance
to actual people, living or dead, or to businesses, companies, events,
institutions, or locales is completely coincidental.

The cover image is created by Flame Tree Studio. Frontispiece illustration
and cover detail is based on *Vision* © 2025 Marvin Opuni Kwabia.

A copy of the CIP data for this book is available from the British Library.

Printed and bound in China

To my mother, who reads everything I write,
no matter how weird, and loves me even
when I'm impossible.

Table of Contents

Foreword by Eugen Bacon..8

Black Friday 15

Clickbait..39

The Way of Baa'gh: A Sauútiverse Story.....................57

Lady Abra's Butterflies 92

Armour 114

Sikami 128

Empathy 156

Easing In 172

Silverfish...202

Godmother 216

The Wedding Dress 247

Lest We Forget 257

The Feeding Grounds 279

The Storymage 304

The Ghost of Dzablui Estate 329

Wild 357

Dream State 386

The Mother 399

ABOUT THE AUTHOR 410

ACKNOWLEDGEMENTS 412

BEYOND & WITHIN 415

FLAME TREE FICTION 416

Foreword

by Eugen Bacon

Once upon a time, we were governed by the moon. Our bodies, water poured into skin, swirling around bone and sinew, were as drawn to her as the tides. After all, what were we but little oceans, waves cresting and falling against the coast of history?

'Wild'

EXISTENCES AGO when I started scribbling fiction in earnest, someone told me the short form is a dying art. Despite its looming demise and imprecise placement and definition, I found soaring captivation in the short story – it's one of the most elusive literary forms.

There are no cast-iron rules about short-story writing, even on word count. Author A.L. Kennedy in her essay 'Small in a Way that a Bullet Is Small', published in *The*

Short Story (2008) edited by Ailsa Cox, asks, 'Where do you draw the line formally between a novella and a long short story and a short-short story and a literary letter?' The enduring blurring of boundaries of the short form exhibit themselves in ranging award rules on word count on what posits as sudden fiction, shorter fiction or a novelette.

I am exhilarated today to see the short story, perhaps more so in speculative fiction, pulsing with vigour and accessibility, and with no mind to perish any time soon. In its capacity to allow extraordinary storytelling in the literal sense of the word – odd, unexpected – speculative fiction insists on an investment in worldbuilding. Remember the richly invented worlds and made-up languages of J.R.R. Tolkien in *The Lord of the Rings*, the visionary topography and ingenious perspective that teleport you to infinite possibilities inside the fictional realm of the author's originality.

Such inventiveness stands out in Cheryl S. Ntumy's disquieting collection *Black Friday* and its futuristic worlds and their hosting of rules, gatekeepers and possibilities. There's much to adore about these Afrocentric stories that showcase the ecstasies and dreads of community, as you question, together with the protagonists, what it means to be connected or 'unplugged'.

The miscellany engages with difference and reminds you of the power of storytelling, the measure of knowledge and the significance of belonging. Reading each narrative, you get a sense that this is an author who, like her characters, lives and loves deeply, who, in almost auto-ethnographical fictions, feels intensely and, in so doing, empowers herself and the reader to 'reach the impossible'. Ntumy paints a vivid world that's terrifying for the ominous cautions into the near future it casts. Characters find themselves inhabiting spaces that eradicate choice between coping and living, tradition and indoctrination, and those who insist on staying different get to fully realise consequences.

The writing is simulative – decentralised and offering new centres of meaning. It does this in the titular dystopian story, 'Black Friday', with its Protectorate and the Wretched, tanks and riot squads, placards and slogans in parallel protagonists – one obsessed with carnage, the other driven by stats, video footage and 'the experience'. The writing is clean, personal and inventive. It allows the reader to uncover meaning, as in 'Click Bait', a circular story on what it means to encounter knowledge in a near future new-new South Africa.

'The Way of Ba'agh' speaks to itself as an elegant dark horror in a ritualistic cannibalism that is also a cycle of living.

In this finalist story in the Nommo Awards for speculative fiction by Africans, Ntumy spotlights the uniqueness of the Sauútiverse, an Afrocentric world, and its use of song and sound magic. The poignant story, again, resounding in first person and this time from the perspective of a nonhumanoid, offers up themes of incarceration and sacrifice.

Hugging her Ghanian roots and reinventing the shades and silhouettes of new and old Asante cities, Ntumy plunges you into philosophical, yet stark, dystopian worlds, petrifying in their insistence of intolerable embodiment. *Black Friday* entices you with yams, cassava and okra, ushers you to meet characters named Edem, Fafa, Sese, Sebele, Yoliswa, Nene, Kodzo, Kweka, Misa, Aten, Zanele, Lindiwe… and buries you into an immersive experience of literary fragments that are not short-short stories but mostly long short stories at between 5,000 to 6,000 words, like 'Godmother' – with its Department of Authentication and an all-seeing AI.

Shorter tales arrive at about 2,000 to 3,000 words, and are just as cunning in their simulations, convictions, manipulations and fellowships, how they line you up to face ideals, trust, betrayal and a hunger to believe. You encounter 'Empathy' – that opens with a suicide, and

'Easing In' – with its tech, labs and 'organorugs', and they both leave you pondering how to guard those you love from conditioning worlds.

But there is no fear, only resolve and a glimmer of excitement. What we have is a half-life. There is nothing to lose. – 'Sikami' is a call to transformation magic for the greater good, as 'Silverfish' lusters a devouring light straight into your unblinking eye, and insists up close that you reconnoiter the arteries of human existence. 'Dream State' grinds you with existential questions, like what is the future, what does it mean to dream, who is family, what, why, where, when is belief?

Listen.

'The Storymage' yarns you to a water world where stories are truth serums, before 'The Ghost of Dzablui Estate' nudges you to plug into the Volta-Mind, and network into a connection with the self and other and the entombing world around you, to shore up a new allegiance to Ashanti-Mind as you honour the Meld.

Summer brings a sick, sweet heat, sticky and inescapable. – 'The Mother' arrives tiny and just as impactful in a story of tragedy and hope. Meet body walking and cocooned babies in 'Lest We Forget' that stretches your imagination. More radical dystopias and enforced contracts materialise in 'The Feeding Ground'. Ntumy buoys her protagonists with humanity, and you cannot help but root for them as they exhibit the type of curiosity that doesn't kill a cat.

'Lady Abra's Butterflies' opens with a readerly address in a metafictional story-within-a-story that is also an odyssey into the village of butterflies. There's more to a dress than meets the eye in 'Armour' that explores belief. Confront another luminous gown in 'The Wedding Dress', a benevolent tale that births itself from the sweat and blood of devotion.

Riveting stories like the titular 'Black Friday' accomplish – seemingly without effort – what one writer, Paul Ariss, says good short stories do: they 'come to visit for a while, take you somewhere you didn't expect and then put you back where you started before you'd even realised you were gone' (2015).

Amen to literary letters and the short form in all its palimpsests.

Black Friday shuttles you in transportive fiction from your chair to infinite possibilities inside this author's resourcefulness from unwanted occupation, birthright, to what is the colour of pain? In 18 stirring stories that are complete in their incompleteness, a perfect half of them original, Cheryl S. Ntumy gifts you with artistic constructions that are totalities. She magiks in mages, gods, hybrids, soldiers and ordinary people – mothers, fathers, sons, daughters, aunties, cousins – reminding you how very much alive is the beating heart of the short form.

Yesterday, today and tomorrow.

Eugen Bacon
British Fantasy Award-winner and Philip K. Dick Award finalist

Black Friday

"FOR TOO LONG, the Wretched Righteous have twisted things to suit their wicked purposes!" Boss points towards Protectorate Plaza as he speaks. "For too long, they have propagated an unequal system that benefits them and oppresses us!"

Elders nod. Women ululate. Someone shouts, "The devil is a liar!" Whatever that means. One guy is so moved that his eyes roll back in his skull, and his body convulses.

Sese lifts one foot off the searing cement, holds it in the air, then switches to the other foot. There's a small hole starting in the heel of her left shoe, and the heat goes right through to her skin.

Boss raises his fist. "Black People, not Black Friday!"

And everyone shouts, "Hai!"

"Black Power, not Black Greed!"

"Hai!"

"Black Masters, not Black Slaves!"

"Hai!"

Black Friday is a big day across the Protectorate. Sese isn't sure how long it's been an official holiday, but she knows it started long before her time, before the Diamond Tabernacle was built, back in the days of the Warning Signs. Rioters don't venture out of the camps much on normal days – it's not worth running into Bo-skwata patrols. But a rioter can't stay in on Black Friday while the Wretched Righteous celebrate the rape of the land. Black Friday is the day rioters push back with everything they've got, to remind the Wretched that they still exist.

Boss finishes being motivational, and everyone moves to get stocked. Sese grabs a placard and a slingshot. There are pangas, too, and metal rods and bats and stuff, but she's good with a slingshot. She has this recurring dream where she kills a Skwata by launching a stone through his skull, like that kid David in their scriptures. They don't know that they are Goliath and the rioters are David, but then again, you can't expect Bo-skwata to know shit.

"Long walk to freedom," one of the old men quips, baring his rotten teeth at Sese.

She smiles back. She hears this a lot and knows it's supposed to mean something, but she dropped out of the Centres of Indoctrination when she was twelve. Gripping her slingshot, she stops to pick up stones along the dirt roads that snake through the Protectorate.

"You're daydreaming again."

Sese jumps. Boss is next to her suddenly, and she has no idea how that happened.

"No, Boss, I swear."

He nods. Boss is big, which might be part of the reason he became Boss, but he's also clever. He knows how to do things like map the stars and tell the time using the sun and find secret ways through the Protectorate where Bo-skwata don't have cameras.

"You're eager, Sese," he says. "I want you to know how much I value that. But you're still young, and there are things you don't yet understand."

Sese bristles. Even though she's only fifteen, she's a seasoned rioter with seven (and a half) crusades to her credit. "I'm not a kid! I know that we're fighting for Justice and Equitable Distribution and the Rights of the People and the Sanctity of the Land."

Boss smiles. "Do you know what any of that means?"

"Yes." She has a rough idea, and a rough idea is the same as knowing, right?

He nods again. "Do well today. Make your parents proud."

Sese swallows. She always gets a lump in her throat

when people mention her dead parents. "Boss, can I ask you something?"

"Mmm."

"Why don't they just kill us?"

"They kill many of us."

She shakes her head. "Why don't they wipe us out? They could. Instead, they just arrest us and release us and arrest us again."

"Why kill us when they can torture us?" Boss touches her shoulder. "Don't get caught." He makes his way to the front.

He always says that. Don't get caught. It's not as though Sese is trying to get caught. Getting caught means getting tagged, and she would rather die than have a Skwata chip in her flesh. It's like he thinks she's stupid.

Sese pushes these thoughts away and focuses on the crowd, trying to get her energy up. Everybody is chanting and waving placards.

"Black People, not Black Friday! Black Power, not Black Greed!"

Sometimes, when the chanting goes on for a while, her mind wanders, and she follows the path until the words lose all meaning. Black stops being a colour and a race and a symbol, and becomes just a bunch of letters put together that don't signify anything, because really, at the root of it what does it mean?

To rioters, there's only one definition, and it's pure and precious but really, it's just a word like any other. Sese finds it hard to grasp that one word means so many things. When she looks at it in her mind's eye, she sees this: blkbbbbbbbllllllkkkkaaaaaaaaaaahhhhhhh.

Which means exactly nothing.

Sese quickly pulls herself back from that kind of thinking before somebody catches her. She chants like a good girl and thinks about Justice and her slingshot.

There is only one Black that matters today, anyway.

* * *

Officer Vee Phiri is not in the mood for Black Friday, known throughout the Order Squad Riot Division as End of Days. It's the loudest, busiest, and most violent day of the year. It's also the most profitable day for Riot officers, the one day no one can afford to be off sick.

Vee steps inside the station, ducks out of the way as two vagrants are marched down the corridor in handcuffs, and slips into the briefing room just in time to catch Commander Dube's pep talk.

"End of Days, ladies and gentlemen! Holiest day of the year, when the heathens are judged and the righteous rewarded at last. What does that mean for us?"

"Chaos and criminals, sir!"

"And what is the only way to deal with chaos and criminals?"

"Guns and gas, sir!"

"That's right. Now get on the ground and round up those godless bastards. I want the cells packed by the end of the day! You hear me?"

"Yes, sir!"

Fifty-odd officers file out of the room to fetch the guns and gas to help them win the war against anarchy. Vee rolls her eyes behind her colleagues' backs and wishes she were in bed.

"Vee."

She turns around, flustered. "Sir?"

Dube's expression is grim. "Your arrest rate hasn't improved since that debacle last year. Your kill rate is even worse."

Vee feels sweat drip down her back. "I'm sorry, sir."

"If you embarrass me today, you're out." He pushes past her.

It's because he's so small. He's overcompensating,

Vee thinks, before giving herself a mental kick for insubordination. This is exactly why her career hangs in the balance. She has a bad attitude. She's a doubter, which is almost as bad as being a godless criminal.

When she reaches the safe where all the gas canisters are kept, she grabs what's left and follows her colleagues out to the yard, where the transport is waiting. Vee reaches under her hat to wipe sweat from her forehead with her sleeve.

It's a short drive to Protectorate Plaza, and as soon as they arrive, the officers move out to their assigned positions, covering the five main sections. Vee is on Plaza Junction duty for the first time, where Carnage will be the most intense. Not that she minds. She's not afraid of pangas and screaming. But she likes covering the edges, where there's room to move around, and she can give chase without dodging civilians.

There are tanks set up around the Plaza this year. This seems excessive, but Vee keeps her opinions to herself. Her only job is to boost her arrest rate, drop a couple of rioters and then go celebrate the end of End of Days with sizzling steaks and beer.

"*Bagaetsho*, peaceful greetings on this holy day." The President's voice comes from giant speakers overhead, loud enough to be heard across the parking bay. "As we celebrate with our loved ones, let us remember the scripture: 'For those who love the Maker are blessed with treasures. Mighty are the bearers of these precious gems and sanctified are all their deeds!' Amen!"

A chorus of "Amen" fills the Plaza.

"There are ten routes leading directly to the Diamond Tabernacle to make your pilgrimage as smooth as possible. Please take a moment to pray for all those nations under the yoke of economic hardship. *Pula*!"

The Plaza is already bustling with activity, though it's just after 7 a.m. Vee pauses to help a frazzled woman find her son and earns P20 for her trouble. She pockets the money surreptitiously. Although tipping is encouraged, anything less than P50 on holy days is frowned upon. But Vee is in no position to be picky – or pious, for that matter.

She shifts her pack to the other shoulder and checks the canisters and gun at her hip as she takes her position at the main entrance to Plaza Junction. This is the eye of the storm, where the five sections meet, and the foot traffic is heaviest.

"I can't believe I finally have a chance to serve on Black Friday. I've been waiting for this my whole life! I'm going for a ten-fifteen minimum."

The relentless, peppy voice belongs to Sebele, Vee's new partner, who couldn't pull a five-twelve on his best day.

She glances at him. "I hope you get it."

"What about you?"

Vee sighs. Small talk with freshers is one of the worst parts of End of Days. "I just want an improvement on last year."

"What was your rate last year?"

She hesitates. Well, he'll find out sooner or later. "One-five."

One kill, five arrests. The lowest rate in decades and the reason Dube has been shadowing her all year, waiting for an excuse to cut her loose.

Sebele looks away, embarrassed for her. "Sorry."

"I'll do better this time." She has to. Her daughter wants to go to the same school as her friends and Vee could buy three houses with the money those people charge in fees.

"That's the spirit!" Sebele says. "The Maker is on our side! Amen!"

Vee's not so sure about that, but she mutters, "Amen," anyway.

Every year, the rioters are rounded up and crammed into holding cells until they're covered in their own filth. The stink fills the station, but no one complains. The footage alone is worth a fortune. When they've been there a week or two, a few rioters are processed and transferred to prisons. The rest are tagged and released on grace.

The single kill Vee made last End of Days was a juvenile, a year or so older than her daughter. She was aiming for the guy behind him, and the child moved. It wasn't her fault, and the boy would probably have ended up dead or jailed at some point, so what difference does it make? Maybe she saved him another year of misery. At least that's what Vee tells herself because she has to tell herself something.

She checks the tracking screen on her wrist. "They're coming."

Sebele lets out a whoop and pulls out both his guns.

"Holster those weapons before you hurt yourself. They haven't even reached the gates."

Sebele obeys, looking sheepish. "I want to be prepared."

"You're prepared. They have pangas; we have guns."

"And gas."

"Yes. And gas."

* * *

Don't get caught.

Sese's blood is pounding as the rioters approach the Plaza, waving placards and yelling slogans.

Don't get caught.

Many of the other young rioters are tagged. The tags change them, make them moody and weird and easy to catch, which makes them useless. But seven (and a half) crusades and Sese has never been caught. She's slippery and clever; even Boss says so. And then he says, don't get caught.

Maybe he's worried about her because she's so slippery and clever, and he has big plans to give her a leadership role one of these days, if she proves herself. Maybe that's all it is. But he says it every time. Every single time.

Her slingshot is tucked into her jeans, and stones weigh down the pouch around her waist. She spots the automated tank at the Plaza gate and laughs. Ah, Bo-skwata are something else. A whole big tank like this, the size of a house, for what? Are they going to fire that clumsy thing into a crowd of rioters? So stupid.

Sese can't wait to put a dent in one of their heads. Boss doesn't like rioters to hurt Bo-skwata except in self-defence because We Are Not Mindless Savages, but Sese sees nothing wrong with hurting the people who ruined the world.

Rioters pour through the open gates. Bo-skwata are in position, but they don't do anything, not yet. They always play this game, like they don't want to hurt anybody, but

Sese knows their trigger fingers are itching. She doesn't know why they wait for Carnage to start before they attack.

The protesting part lasts about an hour. Sese drifts from one section to the other to kill the boredom, waving her placard and shouting about Imperialist Greed. OK, she also does this so she can window shop. She's planning so that when justice is done, she won't have to waste precious time trying to decide what she wants. She can use her time to do important things like… Well, she's not sure. Once the fighting is over and the battle is won, what happens next?

She watches Bo-skwata shout over the rioters and try to push them away from shop entrances. Wretched Righteous kids are laughing and pointing and taking photos. They always do this during the protest, when things are still a bit quiet. Just now, they'll be screaming their heads off, and Sese will aim her slingshot and bust those stupid phones.

The chanting grows louder and faster. Sese grins and starts to head towards Plaza Junction. It's almost time for her favourite thing: the destruction of the Idol, the slaying of the Beast. Rioters will flood the Plaza and go for the Diamond Tabernacle, the Temple of Greed, and throw everything they have at it.

Sese lives for Carnage. It's the whole reason she became a rioter. OK, not the whole reason. She believes in the cause, but belief is only ideas in your head. Breaking things, evil, diamond-funded things; that's real.

She tosses her placard aside, takes out her slingshot and opens her pouch.

* * *

The screaming begins. This time, Sebele waits for Vee's cue before whipping out his weapons, grinning so much it makes her face hurt to look at him.

"At last!" He chuckles. "At long last!"

Vee frowns. "Gas first, remember."

"Of course. Atmosphere counts for forty per cent of the overall result, and the lower the visibility, the higher the payday. I read the study two weeks back."

She gives him an appraising look and signals him to follow her lead. She waits for the first wave of shoppers to spill out of the sections, then rolls two canisters towards them. Their screaming intensifies as the gas fills the air.

Vee didn't see the polls this morning, but she can tell that more people have paid for the full experience than last year. She doesn't understand why they're allowed to bring children. She knows that it heightens the experience, and thanks to intensive training, there has never been a civilian casualty, but she'd never let her daughter out on Black Friday.

"Keep left!" she calls out. "Everybody, please keep left and shield your faces!"

Right on cue, the rioters come in, smashing as they go. Vee dodges fleeing shoppers and flying shards of glass. Her contact lenses adjust quickly, allowing her to see through the reddish haze. Sebele is herding shoppers to the left with one hand and firing at rioters with the other. She sees one rioter go down, then another. Maybe he'll get his ten-fifteen, after all.

Vee pushes a shopper aside so she can fire at a rioter demolishing an ice-cream machine with a metal beam. He jerks and the beam drops from his hand. Vee rushes at him, pulls a cuff from her pack and slaps it around his ankle. He drops to his knees, the cuff binding him to the floor. One.

In the glass of a nearby shop window, Vee sees a panga swing towards her. She spins on her heels and cuffs her assailant. Two. A window explodes somewhere on her right. Vee ducks and then runs after the culprit. It's a girl, tall and thin, with a slingshot. Vee watches her take out another window and an ATM. The kid's aim is flawless.

Cocking her gun, Vee fires a warning shot. The girl's next stone finds its mark. Vee watches in amazement as an officer crumples to the ground. Then she sees it: a way to salvage her career and make enough money so she won't have to play this twisted game for the rest of her life. Anyone who can use a slingshot like that, anyone with the guts to drop an officer, is Rebel Fanatic material. And every Rebel Fanatic needs a Jaded Enforcer.

Maybe this is the role Vee was born to play. Maybe everything – killing the juvenile, losing her faith – was leading her to this. With grim determination, Vee fires again, aiming carefully. The girl trips, falls. Screaming people run past, trampling her in their curated panic. Heart pounding, Vee rushes to claim the girl before another officer jumps in. She reaches for a cuff.

"Please," the girl gasps. "I'm not supposed to get caught. Just kill me. It's better if you kill me."

"I can't. You're going to solve all my problems." Vee looks into the girl's wide, fearful eyes, cuffs her and plunges back into the action.

* * *

Sese feels small and fragile. Bo-skwata have moved all the arrested rioters, and now she's sitting on the floor of a huge room with a high ceiling, empty of furniture,

29

with a sullen man on her right and a bug-eyed woman on her left. Sese's bleeding a bit, but she knows the bullet only grazed her, which is too bad because they're going to tag her, and she'll become useless like those other ones, and all the work she's done will be for nothing.

"What now?" she asks the man next to her.

He gives her a pitying look, which just makes her angry. She's not useless yet!

"Now we get paid," the woman says.

Sese doesn't understand what that means. Maybe it's another thing she would know if she'd stayed in lessons and read all the struggle books.

"Don't you get it, first-timer?" The woman laughs. "The truth isn't sinking in yet?"

"Let her enjoy her innocence," the man grumbles. "She'll find out soon enough when they explain the terms."

"What terms?"

Nobody answers. Sese is left wondering what the hell is going on and how anyone can call her innocent after seven (and a half) crusades.

Bo-skwata file into the room. Sese watches them, one after the other, walking up to another Skwata in a yellow traffic jacket, logging how many arrests they made and collecting tokens before going to round up their rioters. Then comes the female Skwata who shot her.

"Officer Vee Phiri," the traffic Skwata says, and the woman nods. "Well done. Seven-twelve." He hands her a token.

Unlike the others, she doesn't smile when she takes it. She just puts it in her pocket and comes towards Sese and the other rioters she arrested.

"On your feet."

Nobody argues. Where's the rioter spirit? Sese is scared to make trouble because she's pretty sure none of the others will support her, so she stands up as well. That's when she sees Boss.

Her heart screams, and blood pounds in her head. If Boss has been caught, then it's over, it's all over, and there will never be Justice for anyone.

But Boss isn't cuffed like the other rioters. He's standing in line with Bo-skwata and talking to them. Not the "You are my enemy, and I want you to change your wicked ways" kind of talking, but the "Ah, it's too hot" kind. Friendly. Smiling. As Skwata Phiri shoves her towards the exit, Sese sees Boss reach the front of the line and receive not just one token but a whole glass jar full of them.

"Now you know," says the bug-eyed woman rioter.

But Sese knows nothing, and now they're outside and Boss is out of sight.

"I don't understand," Sese says. "Why is Boss getting paid?"

The woman sighs. "Wake up, child! We're all getting paid. How do you think Boss feeds us? Clothes us? Where do you think all the things in the Black Market come from? How do you think anyone can afford to make them or buy them?"

Sese can't wrap her head around this. "But… Honest Enterprise."

"There are ten times more Wretched than rioters. There can't be any enterprise unless they're part of it."

"But…"

Sese thinks of the Wretched kids taking photos and Boskwata hanging back until the gas hits. She thinks of the rioters who get caught and how strange and quiet they are when they come back. She has always wondered why Boskwata release so many rioters and keep so few in prison. She thinks about the hole in her shoes and the running, screaming Wretched who keep returning to the Plaza, Black Friday after Black Friday, even though they know Carnage is coming. She thinks of the Skwata she killed with her slingshot.

It's a lie. A performance, a job. But the Skwata is really dead, and her clothes are really torn, and the world is really wrong. Her hunger pangs are not a lie. Her parents, both killed during Carnage, are not a lie. How can it be a performance if some of the actors don't know that they're acting?

Phiri looks at her. "You killed an officer with a slingshot! One shot, too. Who trained you?"

Sese is too stricken to answer. She just stands there in the sun, mouth hanging open, brain short-circuiting.

"You'll play a more prominent role next Black Friday," Phiri continues. "We must start working on a backstory. I can coach you; take you through some of the basics of how to play to the audience. It works best if we're in sync."

Sese stares at her. What?

"Look, I know you're in shock, but this is the kind of opportunity juveniles rarely get. You can make good money playing a type. Build a house for your family in a proper neighbourhood; get out of those filthy camps."

Sese imagines digging her parents out of their graves and propping their bones up on fancy furniture in a fancy house. Is that what Boss did? Build a house? No, because his grandmother still lives in the camps, and what kind of person would make an old lady live like that if there was a proper house available?

"We'll explain the terms of the agreement to all the first-timers once we get to the station." Phiri's words gouge holes in Sese's worldview. "The contract is good; you'll see. When I tell Boss how well you did, he'll be proud. He can start mentoring you. You might even replace him someday. I think he's only got a few years left on his contract."

Sese is still trying to put the pieces together. She thought Boss was mentoring her already, but he's as much a lie as the rest of it. She doesn't know how to feel. Angry? Hurt? Afraid? She feels all of it and none of it. More than anything, she's confused.

"What about your scriptures? Don't you believe in them?" She doesn't know why she cares about this, but it suddenly seems very important. The scriptures are wrong, and it's bad to believe them, but not nearly as bad as only pretending to believe.

The woman rioter laughs. "Phiri's a backslider."

Phiri shushes her and looks around in case someone's listening. "A job is a job. I have a family to look after, just like you people."

"And the rioters you killed?" It occurs to Sese, in a flash of desperate hope, that there might be some good in all of this. "Are they really dead? Or did you hide them somewhere?" She tries to call up her parents' faces, but it's been so—

"Don't be stupid," the female rioter mutters. "Of course they're dead. Only leaders and stars are allowed to fake it."

The hope dies without ceremony.

"Their families are cared for," Phiri says. "It's part of the agreement."

Oh, the agreement. Well, that's fine, then. Something rises inside Sese, like she wants to vomit but doesn't dare, in case her soul comes up, too.

"Some rioters don't know about your agreement," she says. "Some of them die believing. *I* could have died believing."

"It's better that way." The sullen male rioter shrugs. "Better to die for something. Even a fake something."

When rioters fall, sometimes their families leave the Protectorate. Boss always said that when people have suffered too much, they go away to heal, but Sese can't think of any grieving families that have returned. Where did they go? Are they all fat cats now? Maybe one day, after all the Black Fridays and killing and families leaving and Bosses cashing in, there will be no more rioters. Only fat cats, Wretched Righteous all the way. The thought makes Sese's stomach turn even more. She swallows down the nausea.

"This is how it works," Phiri says. "You'll adjust."

Sese stares at the ground, not sure she wants to adjust.

"Why didn't you tell us about this one?" Phiri's voice is raised, calling out to someone. "She could be a star."

Sese lifts her head and sees Boss coming, carrying his pay under his arm, grinning like the Wretched he condemns. When he spots her, the smile slides right off his face. It would be funny, except nothing will ever be funny again.

He sighs. "Ah, Sese. I told you not to get caught."

* * *

They sit side by side in the truck on the way to the station.

"I never wanted you to find out like this," Boss says. "I was going to tell you when you got older."

Sese says nothing. It's like her insides have been scooped out.

"This is the way the world works." He spreads his hands in a gesture of surrender. "You'll adjust. I did."

Sese wants to tell him that she will never adjust, but how can she know for sure? Clearly, she knows nothing.

He holds out a token. "This will feed you for a month."

She looks at it, numb.

The transport comes to a stop. All the prisoners are taken to a small room in the station. Sese isn't the only first-timer, but she's the youngest by far. Phiri makes a long speech about mutual benefits and enduring partnership, but Sese's head is pounding. She sees her emotions mirrored on the faces of the other first-timers. They're shell-shocked, like they're not quite sure this is real.

Her stomach picks that moment to rumble, reminding her that she hasn't eaten today.

Phiri glances her way. "Don't worry. You get fed before we put you in the cells." To Boss, she says, "Prep the girl for a camera test. I want to see that rioter fire."

Boss takes Sese by the shoulders, and mutters something about playing her part. Phiri moves around the room, shoving a tablet in the rioters' faces. When Phiri reaches her, Sese looks at the blinking dotted line on the screen.

"Listen," Boss says, "a star rioter makes a lot of money. We can feed more people, and take better care of them. You can retire in twenty years as a hero. That's a good thing."

There are no good things, not anymore. "What will happen when *you* retire?"

He avoids her gaze. "I'll get arrested. We'll say I died in custody."

"Resisting to the very end." Phiri taps the tablet. "Sign the agreement, girl, or you'll die in custody for real. And it will be slow and painful."

37

There is no David, no Goliath. No Justice. No Maker. No Black, pure and precious.

"You're strong, Sese," Boss says. "You're going to make me proud. All you have to do is sign."

The tablet stares at her, that dotted line a smirk on a Skwata's face. Her parents didn't retire. They weren't leaders or star rioters eligible for options. Did they die believing, or did they sign agreements, too?

Sese doesn't want to know. She writes her name with her index finger. The screen flashes a smiley face at her. CONGRATULATIONS! YOU ARE NOW AN EMPLOYEE OF THE PROTECTORATE.

Boss beams, a proud teacher. "Your life is just beginning."

No, it's not. Sese's life is running down her back in rivulets of sweat, leaving a vacant shell. Everything that used to matter goes, goes, goes, until all that remains is: blkbbbbbbllllkkkkkkaaaaaaaaahhhhh.

Which means exactly nothing.

Clickbait

RULE NUMBER one in the new-new South Africa: knowledge is money.

One secret after another flashes before my eyes via my headset, all waiting to populate the Filter Free database. I don't have to sift. I have two researchers, and one of them is pretty good. But I like getting up to my elbows in the muck. Lying on the couch in my office, curtains drawn, lights off.

"Save. Skip. Skip. Ooh, good one! Save."

Sure, I make a living selling dirt to the highest bidder, but I'm not the bad guy. Well, I'm not the *worst* guy. A sense of questionable and wrong is the only gift my parents left me, apart from the house and surveillance tech I altered to fit my purposes. Their corporate security company went to hell when they embezzled millions and fled, forgetting to take their daughter along.

Rule number two: what doesn't kill you makes you bitter. And bitter people get shit done.

I sigh at a selfie taken beside a corpse. Humans are such predictable scum. "Save."

I put little stock in profiles, but the imaginary good qualities that users trade on provide a baseline for my daily bread – confiles, consisting entirely of users' less favourable qualities (i.e., the truth). When clients approach me with a confile request, I do my due diligence. If the client is cleaner than the subject, or at least upfront about how dirty they are, they get the confile. If not, they get the boot after paying me for review and consultation.

If you think about it, I'm sort of a hero.

A face pops up in my feed – a call from one of my researchers. Gao, the one who isn't pretty good.

"What?"

"Sorry, Yoli, but I think I found a unicorn."

I'm on my feet and in front of my screen in seconds, transferring everything from my headset, including Gao's excited face. I'm ninety-nine per cent certain he's wrong, but when I see the photo, something inside me shifts.

The user is a young woman of eighteen, cute, but not in the usual camera-ready way. Her username is SunshineGrl12. She's – I rack my brain for an appropriate old-fashioned word – wholesome. Cherubic cheeks bunched over a grin of sheer delight. There's nothing on this godforsaken planet to be that happy about.

TZ, my other researcher, pops up next to Gao in the top left corner of my screen. "High?" she guesses.

Gao shakes his head. "Doesn't even drink coffee."

"RL-shy." Even as I say it, it seems unlikely. The user doesn't have the dazed look of those who spend so much time in the virtual world that they can no longer handle the real one.

TZ lets out a low whistle. "She's on three platforms. *Three*. Proper Stone Age, yoh."

The longer I stare at the profile, the more obvious it seems. "False file. Probably a privacy nut pulling a swap to kick us off the scent. Dig deeper."

"I already ran a two-level trawl," Gao says.

"Why would you do that on a regular sift?"

"She came up and I thought it was a prank, you know? Was gonna dismiss, but then I thought, if she's For Real and I let her slip, I'm out of a job."

"True."

"So, I let the two-level run on background while I kept sifting."

I regard Gao with a modicum of respect. I might have to stop mocking him. "I'm still calling false file."

"I think she's FR, Yoli." Gao shifts in his chair. "Put her photo through the stripper, and it comes up exactly the same."

I give him a look. Assuming For Real is a rookie mistake.

"Well, she *seems* FR," he corrects himself. "Three platforms? My gogo's on twelve and she's seventy, so ja. And the trawl came up clean. Like clean, clean."

I fold my arms and risk another glance at the unicorn's baffling grin. "Run another two-level. If she managed to bypass it the first time, it'll get her on the second round."

"No need." TZ's voice holds a note of panic or excitement. Maybe both. "I just did a one-level. She's clean."

A prickle starts at the back of my neck. "One-level deep?" Impossible. No one is clean one-level deep. We are all liars, cheats and degenerates, to varying degrees.

"Yep. I went all the way in, while we were talking." TZ licks her lips and stares at me in wonder. "She really is a unicorn."

Only a brilliant hacker can dupe my two-level trawl. My one-level? Impenetrable. No one outside this office even knows a trawl that deep exists. Either Sunshine is smarter than me or she's the real deal, someone who made it to the age of majority without incident in a world where incident is oxygen. Frankly, both possibilities terrify me.

42

My screen pings as the trawl results show up in my feed. I don't need to read very far to see that TZ is right. Sunshine has come up clean enough to lick.

"Prep her."

"Sure thing." TZ starts tapping away at her keyboard.

"I meant Gao."

They both stare at me in horror.

"He's never prepped a real confile," TZ reminds me. "Besides, *I'm* the one who went one-level to confirm!"

"She's right." Gao swallows hard. "I haven't done a prep since training."

"Gotta start somewhere." I shrug. "You know the rules, guys. Gao found her; Gao preps her."

TZ purses her lips. "Sure thing, boss." A second later her camera is off, and she's muted. Probably calling curses down on my head.

* * *

Within five minutes of putting Sunshine's confile up on our catalogue, it attracts three hundred and forty-two requests.

"Is this a record?" TZ asks, now back on camera. "It feels like a record."

43

"It's a record," I assure her, watching the numbers go up. The higher the demand, the more we can charge for a consultation.

"Should we help you vet the requests?" Gao asks eagerly.

TZ scoffs. "One prep doesn't make you a master."

"Just forward all of them, Gao."

I've had a few big hauls, mostly gang leaders and politicians trying to one-up each other, but a clean user brings the scum to the surface, desperate to absolve themselves in the pool of her virtue. All the other confiles are pushed to the side as I pick out the most desperate requests for consultations.

ThaDctrIzIn says he loves extreme sports and has three dogs. I know he lost his medical licence for drinking on the job and would probably go into cardiac arrest if he engaged in anything more than moderate physical activity. He does have three dogs, though.

GuidingLight22 is a drug dealer posing as a youth mentor. My mouth waters at the prospect of bleeding her dry. 2ndChances has a murky past, including a regrettable incident with a goat. None of these contenders are worthy of the unicorn, but they don't need to be. At this point, they're only paying for the opportunity to find out whether she's too good to be true.

I dial up 2ndChances. My consultation notification attracts an instant payment, and then his line rings.

"Hello?"

"Yoliswa here, from Filter Free. This is your preliminary consultation."

"Yes! Ah, great, excellent! What do you need? I guess you already have my info, so…"

"We do. This initial consultation is just to verify a few things."

"Sure, sure. Anything you need."

Poor, randy soul. "Can you justify your request? Based on your own confile, I'm not sure you qualify."

"Oh. Right." He clears his throat. "I've done some stupid things."

I grin, scrolling through his confile. "Would you care to elaborate?"

"Petty theft. Some drug stuff. Armed robbery. I was only the driver, but still…"

At least he's semi-honest. "You have been speaking to the user for the past two weeks?"

"Just DMs, but we have a genuine connection."

I roll my eyes. Yes, I'm sure true love is blossoming. "May I ask what you're hoping to gain from this connection?"

He pauses. "Usually I'm after a good time, maybe

something that leads to work. But with Sunshine, I think we could build something more. If she's legit."

It doesn't hurt to dream, I guess. "Thank you for your co-operation. We'll be in touch."

"I can pay extra to get to the front of the line," he says.

"We'll take that into consideration."

I hang up, and then repeat the process with several other users.

"I wasn't drunk in the ER," the former doctor insists. "I don't get drunk, that's the point. I shouldn't be punished for my ability to hold my liquor!"

The drug dealer is no better. She begins the review by asking me to contribute to her campaign for at-risk youth.

"Ka-ching," TZ announces when I ask for a report of the day's profits. "We've made more today than in the past three months! I feel like we should call Sunshine and thank her."

"Yoli, have you decided who gets the confile?" Gao asks.

I scroll through the options. Anyone can do their own research, but a Filter Free confile is the guaranteed truth, a rare commodity in the new-new South Africa. Sunshine will soon be the most desirable person in the country – the cure for all ills, poked, prodded, and targeted for ritual sacrifice. What kind of person would I be if I allowed any harm to come to her?

I catch myself quickly, relieved I didn't say that out loud. I don't know where it came from. What I meant to say was, what kind of person would I be if I let any harm come to her before milking this situation dry?

"No one yet," I decide. "We'll stall as long as possible and see how much we can get."

Gao looks nervous.

TZ shrugs. "Sure thing, boss."

* * *

For the next two days, we work like fiends, watching our balance climb. We run several more checks on Sunshine. They all come up spotless. I start to think that maybe it's possible for someone to remain untainted. Maybe life isn't a giant cesspit, after all. I find myself staring at her profile pic for ages, falling into those innocent eyes.

And then…

"Consumer Care called," TZ says, as soon as I clock in on the third day.

My stomach drops. There's not much in the way of authority anymore; law enforcement is wholly corrupt and the government is nothing more than a playground for whatever cartel is trending. Consumer Care, however, is serious business. Without any checks and balances, the parastatal has amassed the kind of power that could shut us down in minutes.

"We haven't reneged on our Ts and Cs," I say.

TZ clears her throat. "They've had user complaints."

"So?"

"One thousand and fifty-seven complaints."

Ah. "What do they want us to do?"

"They say we must sell the confile, else we're violating the terms of our trade licence. If a product is for sale and there are buyers, we can't hold onto it."

"People aren't paying for the product, they're paying for the privilege of being considered as buyers," I point out, but I know I'm skating on a technicality. "With this level of traffic, it would be reckless to send the confile to the first person who asks. We're doing our jobs."

"That's what I told them, but they said we're dragging our feet so we can cash in."

Nothing's more annoying than perceptive people. I kiss my teeth. "How long before they shut us down?"

"Twenty-four hours." TZ frowns into the camera, sweat beading on her forehead. "Maybe we should just pick a buyer. We've already made a fortune."

I don't answer. I'm thinking. And then Gao chimes in.

"Guys, I think we're being hacked."

* * *

It's not a hack. It's an *attempted* hack, perpetrated by several different users at once. That's how desperate they are to get Sunshine's confile. They'll never get near the data, but I admire their audacity.

"What's the plan?" asks TZ. "Cite and report? Reverse hack?"

"I'm already blocking them," says Gao. "But they'll get more aggressive."

I don't answer. I'm thinking.

"Let's just pick a user and hand over the confile." TZ's impatience is showing. "We don't have time to fend off this shit on top of worrying about Consumer Care."

"Ja, I'm with TZ. This is getting wild."

Thinking. Thinking…

Maybe she's not real. But what if she is? If she is, then she's a kid. Just starting her life, trying to make friends and give quaint cooking tips to her followers. And maybe I'm getting soft in my old age or something, but I don't think I can sell out a kid, especially if she's a genuinely *good* kid. I don't trust any of those bastards out there with her info.

So, I guess I get to be a hero. FR, this time.

"Scrub the site."

TZ freezes.

Gao adjusts his headset. "Eh? Did you say *scrub*?"

"Do it. Now."

Nobody moves.

TZ clears her throat. "We'll lose every confile made in the last twenty-four hours. That's—" she does a quick check "—thirty-four files. Not to mention how long it will take to put the site back up. We're looking at no revenue for about two weeks."

"Good thing we just made a fortune, then. Scrub it and call Consumer Care to report the hack. Tell them we lost everything and have to shut down. Solves all our problems." And buys Sunshine two weeks.

There's a long silence.

"She better be worth it," says TZ.

A few minutes later, I watch the Filter Free user interface crash. TZ is right. Two weeks without sales is going to hurt, and there's only one way to know whether I made the right call.

With a long sigh, I reach out to Sunshine. She replies my message in seconds. She's stoked AF to hear from me! Of course she'll meet me IRL! OMG! Emoji, emoji, emoji, emoji.

She sends her location. Just like that, without confirming that I am who I claim to be. Jesus, this kid is lucky I stepped in when I did.

"Heading out," I tell my team. "Gotta run an errand."

"Now?" Gao is flabbergasted. "In the middle of—"

"It's cool," TZ interjects. "We've got this. See you later."

Gao opens his mouth like he's going to protest, but doesn't. I put my workstation to sleep, hunt down some clean clothes and leave my house for the first time in weeks.

* * *

Sunshine lives in Braamfontein – or what's left of it. The streets are mostly empty, save a few trollies – kids the gangs recruit to patrol the area. They look alive when they spot me, making a big show of being busy, adjusting headsets, standing tall. It would be easier to monitor the streets from behind a screen, but the gangs like to make a statement.

"Wat sé, Yoli?"

"Niks, laities. Just getting fresh air."

"Shoot me a con, Yoli, just the one, hey? Goodwill."

They always ask, knowing I'll never agree. If I went around handing out confiles for charity, Filter Free would be out of business in a month. Besides, any handout I give them will only support whatever nasty habit they've picked up this year.

I offer them nothing more than a sly grin. "Tell your boss I'm updating his confile. He can bid on it in a couple of weeks." Gang leaders pay well to keep their secrets out of the hands of their rivals.

Skirting past the trollies, I swerve into an alley. The streets aren't safe, but everyone knows Filter Free caters to the gangs. No one will touch me. It takes a good twenty minutes to find Sunshine's building. It was one of the nicer ones, back in the day, now a little the worse for wear.

I climb five flights of stairs to reach her flat. If I get there and she's not what she claimed to be… If so much as a dimple is off… Well, I don't know what I'll do. But it won't be pretty.

I find the door. Knock. Wait a few seconds, knock again. There's the sound of a key turning. A padlock coming off. Another key turning. A bolt rolling back. Another. And then another key turning. No wonder she's pure, living behind so many locks.

My heart races like I'm about to meet my first big crush. Please, please, let her be worth it.

The door opens. It's her. Barefoot, wearing blue tracksuit pants and a white tank top with Hello Kitty on it –

of course. Toenails painted pink. Hair in long braids. Eyes so clear I can see myself in them. She smiles and it feels like Christmas. I can't help smiling back. My chest is full of fire, but in a good way, like I'm about to vomit rainbows.

She's real. She's sweet and good and *real*. Tears – I can't even believe it – sting my eyes. I can't remember the last time I met someone older than twelve who didn't have a jaded, haunted look about them. Not even rich kids are fresh like this anymore, cheeks plump with health. They're all hollowed out from the horrors of life, or riddled with the drugs they use to quiet their inherited remorse.

"Yoliswa!" says Sunshine, her voice melodic. "You're here!"

"Ja. Er… Hi."

"Mama was right!" She beckons me inside. "She said you wouldn't be able to resist."

Mama? Oh, right. Parents. Of course a girl like this would have them. Good ones, too. Obviously – how else would she have lasted this long? Parents who must have checked me out and guessed that I'd come looking for the unicorn. *Their* unicorn.

I follow her into the flat, though I wasn't really prepared for a lot of socialising. She's real and I made the right choice and it was worth it, and now I have to figure out how to protect her forever. Maybe I'll just say I sold her confile to her. Sorry, guys, she paid the most. The end. But that won't deter the vultures. I'll tell her parents to take her away. Someplace quiet.

"It was the only way," says Sunshine, leading me past a room full of servers and monitors, into a living room. "To get your attention, to see you safely."

Sure, whatever. I nod, barely listening, grinning like a fool.

"Mama, Yoliswa's here," Sunshine announces.

I glance at her, seeking any trace of guile, but her face is a heartwarming family movie, all earnestness and cheesy lighting. And then, just like a movie, she ends. Disappears with a flicker into nothingness, like she was never here.

Shit. Shit! How could I be so stupid?

There's someone else standing in front of me, holding the device that turned Sunshine off. The unicorn's words make sense at last. *It was the only way.*

"I'm sorry for the deception, Yoliswa. I had to see you."

It's a woman, over fifty. Thick glasses hiding sharp, all-seeing eyes. The only person in the world who could fool my one-level trawl, not to mention my eyes, because she taught me everything I know. She's supposed to be missing. A fugitive. And all this time, my mother has been hiding right here in Braamfontein.

She smiles, like I'm supposed to be glad to see her.

The funny thing is, it doesn't even matter that she's alive and well and looking for absolution. The only thing that matters is the empty space where Sunshine stood and the hole in my chest that I thought she had filled. Serves me right, risking my whole enterprise on something as antiquated as hope.

Stupid, stupid. Everyone knows there's no such thing as a unicorn.

"Yoli? Your father and I never meant… Let me explain. Will you sit down, at least?"

I don't answer. I'm thinking.

"Yoli, please."

She's nervous now, worried that I might not forgive and forget. She should be worried. Who forgives anymore? Well, maybe Sunshine would, but she's a lie, so tough luck. I stare at my mother, trying to figure out what I'm meant to feel. I know what she wants, but what do I want? To run into her arms, sobbing with relief? To ask where my father is?

No. What I want right now, more than anything, is to be back in my house. The house they left me. The house they left me in, alone. I want to be at my desk, in front of my screen, elbow deep in the muck. Alone.

I turn around and head for the door.

"Yoliswa! Wait! Please, you can't just leave!"

Yes, I can. So, I do. Not much of a parent, my mother, but she did teach me some valuable lessons before ducking out. I remind myself of them as I hurry down the stairs.

Knowledge is money.

Trust no one.

What doesn't kill you makes you… Numb.

The Way of Baa'gh

A Sauútiverse Story

RED IS a sign of decay.

A new patch of red has bloomed on my fourth left leg, until now the only leg that was still blue. Beneath every hot patch on my shell, the flesh itches. It's Tor-Tor calling, reminding me that I cheated it. I've heard Baa'gh say as much when I pass them in Kuu'uum: *Ss'ku would be long dead if not for The Maadiregi.*

Easing sideways into a cove, I sink below the sea, pincers opening wide as the cold water soothes my pain. I can't go back to the safety of Kuu'uum. Not when I'm the only Og'beh left in the colony who hunts true Nududu.

A ripple moves through the water as a zje'lili fish passes me. Designated Nududu thirty generations ago for their ability to glow in the dark, the soft, billowing creatures have shown no growth since. I turn my gaze to the plants that rise up from the water, seeking more promising prey. Their bright leaves and long stalks mock me. Same as last juzu. Same as ten juzu past. Everything the same, generation after generation.

Only Baa'gh change.

"How many times must we tell you to stay out of the suns, Ss'ku?" Kirikiri's familiar call grates behind me, croaks deep and sonorous. "Leave the hunt to us. Rest in the cold before you lose all your blue."

"Is there blue left to lose?" Baa'ka mutters. The others click their amusement.

The four Og'beh scuttle to the water's edge, pincers waving. Only Kirikiri and Mmoh have begun to form patches, but red will come for them all as we get closer to Tor-Tor.

I have told them that starting the Nududu cycle again, from plant life or insect life, perhaps even from our tiny cousins in the sea, will yield the best results. We'll find new traits to harvest. We must. But they're so fixated on po-li-tic-al evolution that they don't hear me. Power is the new Nududu, they claim, Empire is the new goal. How does one eat power? I asked them. And they said, "...*thinking is a kind of eating*." Keh! It almost aches my joints to be near them.

Og'beh rarely roam the wilderness now that they hunt knowledge like humanoids. As though patrolling those monstrous colonies alongside Empire guards requires any kind of skill. As though it reaps any reward. All they bring home is more mind-stain to pollute the way of Baa'gh.

"You're not at the High Place." My tone is polite. I will honour the class of Og'beh, even if they won't. "Is something wrong?"

"The weaning is close," says Mmoh. "We must go."

I look to the sky, surprised to see how much it has darkened. I lost track of time. Rising from the water and moving out of the cove, I wince at the sensation of warm air on my back.

Baa'ka clicks at my discomfort. "Will you even make it to Tor-Tor? Kiri, look at this shell! Red-red-red, like waterweeds!"

"A miracle you've lasted this long," Tetete hums in sympathy.

"All thanks to The Maadiregi." Kirikiri's eyes swivel on their stalks. "Without its efforts, we would have lost Ss'ku."

"All thanks to The Maadiregi," the others chorus with reverence. Reverence for the enemy. For my tormentor.

I keep the anger under my shell because tonight is sacred, but it breaks me that mind-stain has gripped Baa'gh, our minds and bodies twisted by forbidden ways and mediocre meat. Only true Nududu can cure us, but I have searched all the wilderness and failed to find any.

Is this how we will end? Red and shell-less, selling the way of Baa'gh for a place among the stars? Trading growing for knowing and believing the lie that they are the same?

No. Not if I can help it.

* * *

The beach is crisp when we arrive, the light fading fast. Wind sweeps the coastline, strong enough to disturb the sand but not the remains of the last Baa'gh generation or the young feeding on them.

Indeed, the weaning is close. Only small pieces of shell litter the beach now, each young Baa'gh working hard to consume every last scrap of their parent. The young have spent the first thirty bés of their lives here, eating their way through their parents' corpses. They are now fully matured, bigger even than Kirikiri, shells glowing blue in the gathering darkness.

Our old tales say that Nakoko, a beast from beyond the stars, starved of time and ravenous, rode the solar flare that shook the world countless juzu ago. Nakoko took a bite out of time before being snatched back into the sky. This is why we grow so fast; why each Baa'gh generation lasts only one juzu.

Baa'gh are the only species on Mahwé that maintain steady numbers. Five hundred per colony, give or take. Each mate fertilises the other, and both lay eggs, one egg for each Baa'gh. Then, they cover the eggs with their bodies and die, providing both protection and food so the vulnerable hatchlings don't have to stray from the beach until they are strong enough to hunt.

We approach slowly, wary of disturbing them before they wean, and also to give ourselves time to observe any deviations from the previous generation. Their size already alarms me – so much body to sustain, and on what? Their shells protrude, forming a hump, as their parents' did, to protect the larger brains we got from eating humanoids. Larger brains with larger flaws.

The spikes that form a ridge down the shells of Kirikiri's generation have remained, though they appear shorter now. Thick, ugly hair covers the young's undersides – a side effect of their parents feasting on rodents in the High Place. I told them those creatures would foul our bodies, but no one listens anymore. I see no other discernible differences. All eight legs are accounted for, strong and gleaming blue. Four eyes are perched on sturdy stalks.

We sit in the sand, waiting. The young don't acknowledge us, still in a feeding frenzy, unable to focus on anything else. When, at last, they have devoured those who bore them, they raise their pincers and bellow. One after the other, long, low sounds that rumble through my body. I look up at the sky, dark now, Pinaa shining above. Kirikiri takes up the call, and we all join in, shells glowing. As our sound rises within, it lifts us slightly off the ground.

"Make way, make way!" we call out, pincers clicking furiously.

"They birthed us, they sheltered us, they fed us," the young ones drone. Their shells grow brighter as their sound wakes.

That's when I hear the Og'beh among them. Their sound is different, higher-pitched. The four of them rise off the beach slowly until they hover above the others. Our replacements. Every fifth generation, four Og'beh are born. There are only four Og'beh at a time, always. Except now, because of me. Because of…The Maadiregi.

Before my eyes, tiny patches of red blossom on Kirikiri's back, then Mmoh's, then Baa'ka's, then Tetete's. If my entire body wasn't already aflame, I'm sure I would feel another patch coming as well.

Our calls grow louder. "Make way, make way!"

"They are gone, and we are here," the Baa'gh respond. "They were Baa'gh before, and we are Baa'gh now."

"The way is made!" Kirikiri cries. "Baa'gh, we are Og'beh. Welcome."

"Og'beh, we are Baa'gh," the Baa'gh chorus. "Lead, and we will follow. What is the way?"

If only I had an alternative answer. But I don't.

"The way is power," says Kirikiri. I refrain from clicking a mocking remark. "The way is in-for-ma-tion."

"In-for-ma-tion," the Baa'gh repeat.

A foolish, humanoid concept without meaning, a concept for things perceived, as if all things are not perceived. How I loathe the word. How I loathe the fact that we even know it.

I glance at the emerging Og'beh. I see now that there are stripes of green on their legs, differentiating them from the others. They are also slightly bigger.

Kirikiri launches into the greeting song, and we follow suit, Og'beh and Baa'gh. We will sing until we are worn out, and tomorrow, the Baa'gh will hunt for the first time.

But instead of setting out into the wilderness and the sea, instead of relying on speed and wits and the brutal power of their pincers to catch slippery prey, they will learn to play humanoid games in the High Place. They will learn to say what they don't mean. They will learn mi-li-ta-ry stra-te-gy and other obscene things, the names of colonies and starships, and humanoid tales of a Mo-ther-god, as if Baa'gh is not enough. They will learn to be useless, relying on weak rodents and simple fruit to sustain their bodies, all their energy spent on evolving (polluting) their minds.

I'm not expected to participate in imparting this in-for-ma-tion because apparently, I don't know it.

"Ss'ku is old," Kirikiri told the last generation on the first bés of the hunt. "Ss'ku can't even understand humanoid language."

The young looked at me with pity, and I let them. I let them believe I was ignorant of all things humanoid. With all my might, I wish it were true.

* * *

I don't recall the details of the bés it happened. I know I was hunting, separated from my peer Og'beh. I don't recall the sound that caught me, drawing me away from the trusted routes, too close to the High Place.

We know to listen for humanoid traps. Humanoids birth metal-young in numbers, creatures of metal, stone and lightning formed into varied shapes to serve their wicked purposes. The clicks of metal-young are dull and warm compared to ours and lacking in substance. We know the subtle whir of metal-young hearts and the rasp of humanoid breath behind a shield.

All those sounds must have been present that bés, and yet, somehow, I missed them.

I was scuttling among plants, and then I was caught and held aloft in a metal prison with a clear part I could see through. It whirred and clicked and spoke to me in lightning. When I shrieked, it struck me silent. It carried me into the humanoid colony, a seething horror of towering caves and strange light that gave off no warmth. Lines, lines, so many lines, curving and snaking like entangled waterweeds. Metal-young walking and rolling about, some treated as beasts of burden with humanoids in their bellies. And everywhere, those tall, monstrous structures like hungry hills dotted with many-many-many eyes, swallowing and vomiting humanoids.

Fear sent sound bursting through my legs. Scuttling, scraping, running to nowhere, and then rising into the air. My shell struck the top of the metal prison hard enough to daze me. The prison clicked and whirred and flashed lightning into my thoughts. A soothing image of the sea, waves licking the sand.

Mind-stain. The humanoid weapon of choice, meant to confuse and corrupt, to plant their wickedness deep in the minds of other creatures and coax pliant thoughts to grow. I struggled, pincers clicking in panic. Not a single hum came from the chords in my sides, not a croak from the depths under my shell, as though my body was not my own.

The prison clicked and whirred again. The same number of clicks as before, the same pace, the same decibel. It occurred to me then that the sounds were meant to have meaning. The prison spoke once more. It was trying to speak Baa'gh. It couldn't, of course – no other species could match the nuanced flow of our language, the layered sounds and gestures accumulated over many juzu of evolution. What arrogance to even try. And yet, I was curious about what the metal-young wanted to communicate. Lies, of course, but what sorts of lies?

So I listened. Stripped of blue, the sounds were weak and naked. Negation. Negation again; an emphasis. And then…Tor-Tor – no, humanoids couldn't know that name. Dying… No. Danger? Fear! The prison was telling me not to be afraid. I would not be harmed.

A lie I would never have believed, even if it hadn't carried me into the tallest, hungriest, ugliest structure of all. The one visible from the hilltop where Baa'gh made our home.

The one surrounded by walls, which metal-young birds were flying in and out of. The one that expelled black smoke and shuddering, sparkling thunder and blades of light so long they touched Pinaa. The one we called the High Place.

There were so many humanoids inside the High Place. Without shields, they were even more hideous. Naked faces, sinister, white-ringed eyes, bodies covered in strange layers of plant fibre that offered scant protection, babbling in their narrow little tongue. And mind-stain everywhere, tainting their voices, rippling through the air. They swam in it, these horrors, and their metal-young, too.

The prison took me into another prison, one that flew straight up-up-up and then stopped. My vision swam, sound swirling, unsettled, inside me. A humanoid was waiting inside a too-bright cave. It bared straight, harmless teeth at me through the clear part of the prison, then called out to its kind. One of them tapped against the prison with soft, fleshy claws. Even their appearance was a lie. Everything so soft and fragile: no shells, no pincers, no talons, no venom. As though they resembled the gentle, furry beasts they kept as pets. As though they could be trusted.

As the humanoids continued to garble among themselves, I heard something else. The whisper of sound stirring inside them, coiled and waiting to do their bidding. Sound power didn't come naturally to all humanoids, the way it did to Baa'gh. Only some of them could wield it. These ones all could. Then, the others moved away, leaving only the first humanoid. It bared its teeth again, the corners of its mouth lifting, but I refused to be cowed.

The prison had bound my body somehow, preventing me from releasing sounds beyond the clicking of my pincers, but I was still half as tall as the humanoid. Big enough to put up a fight. If not for the prison, I would already have torn the humanoid to shreds.

It uttered a long stream of nonsense. The prison clicked and whirred, trying to translate. It told me the humanoid was a particular type of sound bearer. Maa-di-re-gi. The Maadiregi wouldn't harm me. It only wanted in-for-ma-tion.

I couldn't reply. I watched the humanoid, analysing its head for clues, seeking weaknesses. We knew every species on Mahwé, everything that crawled and swam and flew and grew from the soil. But we knew little of humanoids beyond what we absorbed from our prey. We knew that they took things at will. They returned them addled, if they returned them at all. They walked the world as though they owned it, although they were the last of us to call it home.

The humanoid tapped the side of the prison, sending vague vibrations through me, and a croak of relief escaped. I could speak once more.

The prison repeated its message. The Maadiregi wouldn't harm me. It only wanted in-for-ma-tion. It wanted to understand my kind. Fool. It could study us for a thousand juzu and never understand.

"Release me or I will devour you," I said.

The prison translated my message, poorly: Freedom. Food. The Maadiregi went away and returned with a small, live rodent, the sort of thing Baa'gh might have consumed when we were still lowly, mindless sea-life, before the solar flare. To even present such a creature as a meal now was an insult.

"Your ignorance is repulsive," I told the humanoid.

And the prison translated: No knowledge. Bad. The Maadiregi bared its teeth and bobbed its head. I studied its delicate neck and thought of a hundred ways to break it.

* * *

The alliance with the humanoids was Kirikiri's idea – the next step in our po-li-ti-cal evolution. The humanoids agreed so quickly, that I wondered whether they had forgotten how we'd hunted their kin, or whether they had sacrificed them to draw us in. Maybe they knew how sweet their flesh was, how it inflamed the senses. Anything was possible with them.

I still see only trouble when I look at humanoids. And so when the new Baa'gh prepare to follow Kirikiri and the others to the High Place the evening after weaning, I decide to remain in Kuu'uum.

A massive cave filled with countless tunnels and hollows, Kuu'uum has been home to our colony since we left the coast after the solar flare. The larger we grew, the deeper inland we moved, seeking more suitable shelter. In the hollows of Kuu'uum, we were safe from predators long enough to become predators in their stead. But the call of the sea persists, no matter how much we evolve, so we go down to the coast to mate, and lay eggs, and die.

"Ss'ku, are you sure you'll stay?" The question comes from the freshly named Kuu'kor, one of the new Og'beh. Already, I hear a commanding note in Kuu'kor's calls, pincers clicking faster and louder than anyone else. Kuu'kor will be the next Kirikiri. The way Kiri's spikes bristle shows that Kiri knows it, too.

"I must tend to my patches for a bés," I reply.

There's no argument. They don't want me in the High

Place anyway, embarrassing them with my, "What is it saying? Kiri, translate for me; that metal-young sounds like a dying fuúzimwazii." It is a mark of how much I loathe the High Place that I resort to comparing innocent shelled amphibians to monstrous metal-young.

It strains me. The pretence, keeping my reactions under the shell so no one knows how much I understand of humanoid ways, and how their mind-stain has affected me, too. Baa'gh and Og'beh alike would celebrate my corruption; they would congratulate me, singing praises to The Maadiregi. How could I bear such sacrilege? I couldn't, not even for a moment. So I let them go, and after Kuu'uum is empty, I wait a bit to make sure they're long gone, then return to the wilderness to keep seeking true Nududu.

I scan trees and shrubs. I watch insects and birds. Same. Same, same, everything unchanged. We have eaten birds before, seeking flight. The part of me that is Ss'ku doesn't remember, but the part of me that is my predecessor does. Eating feathered creatures is why Og'beh can hover, yet flight never really took with us. We could try again. Why not? It might work better now.

Heat spreads across my back, itching with a fury. At this rate, I will soon be begging for Tor-Tor. I'm the oldest Og'beh in our history. If there was no Tor-Tor, would I live forever? What will happen if the red consumes me whole before Tor-Tor comes? Questions that would have haunted me if I didn't have more pressing concerns.

As I'm debating whether to raid a nearby nest of eggs or be more ambitious and try to catch the parent, I hear loud, ardent clicks. The Og'beh are coming back. Why so soon? I flee to Kuu'uum by way of the river so I can arrive long before they do. When they enter, I emerge from my hollow.

"Back already?"

Their excitement is palpable. They click over each other, a cacophony of sound. What excites them will only frighten me, I'm sure.

"Did something happen in the High Place?" I ask. And then, with fervent hope, "Are the humanoids in danger?"

How I wish some tragedy would befall them! A great illness that sweeps through their ranks, some new sound power that renders them infertile, a swarm of tiny, biting tso'tso that creep in and devour their colonies, reducing them to dust and rubble. In the name of Baa'gh, any sort of trouble will do. I'm not picky.

Mmoh's clicking laughter is shrill enough to crack an egg. "Danger? Humanoids, who think of everything?"

"They are unsurpassed," Tetete gushes. "The things they can do, Ss'ku!"

"Yes, I know, they have put colonies on Pinaa." Humanoid ambition is a mystery to me. Such complex thoughts, such pointless pursuits.

"No, that's nothing!" Mmoh declares. "They have bigger plans! So daring, so clever! The things they will try – no fear!"

"What plans?" I ask, the itch under my shell getting fiercer. "Tell me of these clever-clever plans."

Kirikiri steps forward, eye stalks waving wildly. "They will change time."

The others dissolve into ecstatic clicking and humming like Baa'gh enticed by the mating song. I long to strike the mind-stain from their stupid shells.

"What does that mean?" I ask. "What is there to change?"

"To go forward. Or go back." Kiri's eyes shine in the glow of our shells. "One bés, one juzu – even more. They have been working on it for a long time, they said. They're close."

The idea confuses me. "They want to be like Nakoko?"

"No! Not devouring time. No. Kssss!" Kirikiri is losing patience with me. "You're so old, Ss'ku! I mean *moving* in time. Going back two juzu and then coming back to now. Or going forward two juzu and then coming back to now. Just to see. Not to undo anything. Just to travel."

A prickle of panic starts in my joints. "What for?"

"To learn, Ss'ku! To *know*."

"The humanoids talk nonsense." I hope I'm right. Please, let me be right. "No one can do that."

"*They* can." Kirikiri taps my shell in excitement. "And they can take us with them!"

Oh, the fear! It burns even deeper than the red patches, beyond my flesh, into the very way of Baa'gh within. Take us with them? *Take* us?

"No," I tell Kirikiri. It's a protest and a plea.

"They have found a way to save us from stagnation, Ss'ku." Kiri's eyes shine so blue, they look like pond pebbles. "They have metal-young, too small to see, that they carry inside their bodies."

"Na-no," says Baa'ka. "Na-no-ma-chins? Na-no-ma-shine? Anyway, they call them na-no-something."

Kirikiri's pincers wave, demanding silence. "They said they will make some na-no for us. To grow us. To help us evolve so we can do what they do. Combined with our sound, they will make us unstoppable!"

I stumble to the right, tripping over my own legs. "No, Kiri!"

"We have decided. We will designate these na-no the next Nududu. It's not too late for the new Baa'gh to learn another way. We will eat na-no and evolve more than we ever have before!"

74

"You're mad," I say. "Your nonsense about eating knowledge was bad enough, but this? Metal-young in our bodies? No! I will never allow it!"

The cave falls silent. They all look at me, their excitement gone, replaced by steady, scary stillness.

"We need consensus," says Kirikiri. "Concede, Ss'ku."

"No! Baa'gh is Baa'gh! Humanoid is humanoid! You can't mix them!" The mere thought of it makes me shudder. "Mind-stain will never be Nududu. This your na-no... No. In the name of Baa'gh—"

Kirikiri moves towards me. "It's decided. Concede."

"No."

"We will say we have consensus."

My sides hum in consternation. "But it isn't so!"

"We will say it is so." Kiri's eyes swivel towards the others. None of them speak.

I falter. They wouldn't. "No, Kiri."

"Poor Ss'ku. You forget." Kiri comes closer still. "Letting you join us was a mercy. You were lost and missed your own Tor-Tor. Poor, lonely Ss'ku, out of place, already reddening. We did you a kindness. You are not true Og'beh."

I feel it rise from them like a buzzing host of bloodthirsty ntum'tum. Heat. Red rot. Not a rotting of the shell this time, but of the Baa'gh way, the effect of more mind-stain than I could ever hope to heal. The only sound in the cave comes from the spikes on their backs rubbing against each other. A scratchy, scraping sound. A threat.

They *will* do it. They will lie, discredit me, to gain this so-called na-no power. To play with time like their humanoid friends. And I will become less than nothing among my own.

I look at Kirikiri. My peer. My...enemy? "We have consensus."

Kirikiri's spikes go still. "Good. We will tell the Baa'gh at dawn."

I don't want Kiri to mistake my acceptance for weakness, and so I say, "Tor-Tor is coming for all of us. Remember that. None can escape it."

"Ss'ku." Kiri clicks two legs and one pincer as though I've said something shameful, as though *I'm* the problem. "What sort of Og'beh wants to escape Tor-Tor?"

* * *

I don't know how long I was trapped in the High Place. The Maadiregi doused me with lightning, current flowing through me, sounds pouring out. I shrieked and groaned, and The Maadiregi collected each sound with care and then sent mind-stain to confuse me, sounds of the gentle tide and the rain falling outside Kuu'uum and old-old Baa'gh calls, stolen from my ancestors.

All the while, the prison brokered a faulty dialogue. I made increasingly violent threats as pain and fear took over. The Maadiregi assured me I wouldn't be harmed and then proceeded to harm me. After some time, I realised that I found it easier to understand the prison's patois, though it still failed to understand me. It threw question after question at me, each one punctuated with a burst of lightning.

What do you hear?

And now?

How does this feel?

And now?

What do you call humanoids?

Why do you avoid us?

We think that your kind changed after the solar flare. Is that true?

Did the solar flare give you the ability to incorporate genes from other species?

Can you hear this?

And this?

Long ago, maadiregi believed that your kind could make food from sunlight, like plants. Could you? Can you still?

How do you know which genes to take and which ones to ignore?

How do you select your prey?

How do you select your prey?

How do you select your prey?

As though I would give up Baa'gh secrets.

We had been small and stupid once, vast in number, prey for anything with a jaw strong enough to break our shells. After the solar flare, we became hunters. We realised that food was no longer just food. It changed us. Expanded us. It became Nududu, sacred prey, a step in our progress. We could no longer eat whatever was available. We had to choose with precision and claim genetic traits that would make us stronger. Og'beh emerged, distinct from the other Baa'gh, longer-lived and infertile, for the sole purpose of searching the world for Nududu and teaching Baa'gh to hunt it.

The first generation I served as Og'beh, we ate only a'bata, the small, winged creature chosen for its sonar and night sight. We spent a juzu creeping along cave walls, the cold turning our shells blue-black. The a'bata traits lingered, giving us an advantage when hunting in the dark. Next generation, we consumed only a'pim, the beast of a thousand spikes. We would tell stories of our hunts for

generations to come. Oh, those spikes! Even after a'pim was
no longer Nududu, when we saw them in the wilderness,
we bowed.

But these were things the humanoids would never learn
from me.

One bés, after a time that seemed interminable, The
Maadiregi stopped feeding me lightning. The High
Place grew quieter as some of the humanoids left it. The
Maadiregi remained. Whatever it had hoped to gain from
me, it had failed. It paced the ground, its face marred
with grooves that I now knew indicated displeasure.
It garbled.

The prison clicked, translating: The Maadiregi was
desperate. It had to try something different. Something new.

The Maadiregi took me, in my prison, outside. There
was a place at the back of the High Place, something
almost like true wilderness. Almost, except for the snaking
paths and small metal-young flying through the air. The
Maadiregi garbled some words, and the front of the prison
fell away. The Maadiregi bared its teeth and beckoned. A
trap, I thought.

Yet when my eyes swivelled around the space, they saw
no sign of trouble. We were alone, my captor and I, none
of its soft, fleshy friends nearby.

I struck quickly, knowing that the metal-young would soon come to aid their parent. I had the element of surprise. With a single blow from one pincer, I broke through The Maadiregi's shield and cracked open its skull, then took it in both pincers and ripped it in two. I was ravenous, having refused to eat anything offered to me during my captivity. I shouldn't have done it, but I was too hungry to resist that spongy brain. Just enough meat to hold me until I reached Kuu'uum.

A whirring noise sounded behind me, cutting my meal short. Covered in blood and flecks of humanoid flesh, I scurried down a path, scaled the boundary wall and disappeared into the wilderness. The metal-young, preoccupied with their dead parent, didn't follow.

I reached home by dawn, to find that the fellow Og'beh I had left behind had already passed through Tor-Tor. Their replacements greeted me in disbelief. They were Kirikiri, Mmoh, Tetete and Baa'ka.

"We were told you were lost, Ss'ku," they said.

They welcomed me to their ranks and we became the first Og'beh of five. I quickly learned that Baa'gh were in crisis. Recent searches for Nududu had yielded nothing. Baa'gh were still consuming the small kalabash, selected two generations earlier for its unique, sonorous sound, which enhanced ours. We had to find new Nududu or risk stagnation.

In my absence, the new Og'beh had begun to speak of a different kind of evolution. They claimed that the lack of organic Nududu was a sign that it was time to look beyond, to seek another way to progress. Still reeling from my abduction and torture, I ignored their raving and focused on recovery.

It was several bés before I was well enough to recount what had happened to me. I must have failed to accurately relay the brutality of it because when I was done Kirikiri said, pincers clicking with passion:

"Ss'ku, you have saved us! You have found our next Nududu! Humanoids have built an Empire. They fly through the stars. Why shouldn't we take our place among the stars, too? We must hunt them. Hunt them, claim their knowledge, their skill, and advance."

I thought, at first, that Kirikiri was joking. But several bés later, the Baa'gh brought down two humanoid sentries and feasted on them, brains first. It was done.

The consequences came faster than we could have anticipated. Humanoid flesh made us aggressive and quarrelsome. The next generation exhibited strange traits. Some would go off by themselves and pick fights with other creatures; some would throw themselves from great heights and seem surprised when they were injured. We began to name things that had never needed names before, like the world we called home.

To my enormous relief, we returned to eating kalabash, supplemented with cave wasps. But the taste for humanoids remained, and Baa'gh sometimes resorted to digging up humanoid graves, against direct guidance from Og'beh.

Even I felt the changes creeping in. The desire to resist, to question. I had consumed very little humanoid flesh, secretly reverting to kalabash long before it was decreed Nududu again. That fact was itself cause for concern. Og'beh breaking tradition, consuming something other than Nududu? Sacrilege.

And yet the humanoid parts in me revelled in that rebellion, even as the Baa'gh in me despaired.

* * *

The Baa'gh way is to hunt from dusk to dawn and then feed until mid-bés. When the suns are highest in the sky, we sleep. We must give Nududu time to settle inside us, and so all of Kuu'uum goes quiet. Little things come out of their burrows and down from their treetops, knowing they can creep past our pincers without fear.

Humanoid colonies don't sleep, not completely. They keep time, but there seems to be no place in their way for total silence. There are always sounds. Always movement. Always metal-young, clicking and whirring.

I have been to the High Place several times since my captivity – first to support Kirikiri's misguided alliance, and then to learn to take in the in-for-ma-tion that now serves as Nududu. I hoped I would never have cause to come to the High Place again, but here I am. No one saw me leave Kuu'uum and scuttle through the bush, the broad plane of my shell burning all the way. I had to swim part of the distance to ease the sting.

As I approach the colony, I debate the best way to enter. Thanks to the alliance, I can go in openly, but the humanoids are familiar with our habits and will find it strange that I've come during rest time, alone.

I'm forced to relive my escape, scaling the same wall to get inside that I once used to get out. Little has changed in the false wilderness surrounding the High Place. I see the same snaking paths, the same flying metal-young in the air.

I head for the side of the structure and start to climb. The rough surface is a combination of stone and metal, covered in ridges and grooves. I pause every so often, listening for the place where The Maadiregi do their wicked work. Metal-young, now accustomed to the sight of Baa'gh, ignore me. I'm close to the top of the towering monstrosity when I find what I seek.

The vibrations here are different. Stronger – I feel them throb deep under my shell – but also more nuanced. Layer upon layer, each one on a slightly different frequency. A song, rather than a series of random sounds. A purpose. This is the place.

Moving to the right, I peer through one of the structure's large, clear eyes. Beyond the eye is a place similar to the one where I was held. Big, dark, with only faint light coming from something out of view. That something is what gives off the vibrations I'm sensing. Powerful sound. I can feel my shell start to glow in response to it.

My first instinct is to shatter the eye to get inside, but that will draw attention. I recall watching the humanoids open and shut the cave's eyes, but only from inside. Then I see that the eye to my right is open. Moving towards it, I pry it open further and launch myself through the gap and into the space beyond. It's one of the meeting places the humanoids put us in during the early bés of the alliance, when we discussed terms. Empty now, apart from all the funny wooden things the humanoids like to perch on. I push past them towards the wooden slab that blocks the entrance. Door; that's the name. I still don't understand why anyone would create an entrance, only to seal it again. Typical humanoid idiocy.

I tear the door away and quickly move down the tunnel, following the vibrations to the next door. I see no humanoids, but I can hear them nearby. I must hurry. I tear this door away as well, though it takes more effort than the other, and then I'm in the place with the vibrations. A metal prison stands to one side, twice as tall as a humanoid and five times as wide as a Baa'gh. A light blinks on the prison's face, on and off, on and off.

Inside. That's where the sound is, the treacherous song that can change time. It will take too long to try to tear the prison apart, and I don't know what manner of evil I might find inside. It could kill me.

I came here without a plan. I knew only that I had to do something to stop this time-change from taking hold. If it fails, maybe the Baa'gh will finally cease to admire the humanoids and we can be free of them. Now, as I hear the call of the mind-stain horror in front of me, I realise there is only one way to stop it.

Sound for sound, power for power. The thing inside this prison sings a song so cruel it wrings groaning complaints from my shell. I must sing, too. A song for a song.

I stand before the prison, the vibrations rolling through my flesh like a storm, and sing the only song I know that is strong enough to break something. The song the Baa'gh sing while their Og'beh go through Tor-Tor. A song for endings. A song to die to.

Clicking to call up the memories of my predecessors. Humming to calm the time-change sound and lull it to sleep. Croaking to summon my own sound. My legs leave the ground as sound lifts me into the air. The red glow of my shell fills the room, at war with the blinking white light.

Krrr'iiii'sssss'kkkk'aaa.

Mmnnn'uh'mmmnnn'uh'mmm.

G'booh. G'booh. G'booh.

The metal prison shakes. It reminds me of the one that held me, juzu ago.

What do you hear? I hear The Maadiregi's ceaseless garbling as it pumps lightning into my body. *And now?* I taste its blood when I break its skull open. Hot and red, the sign of decay.

I don't know whether this is mind-stain. Maybe the metal prison in front of me is trying to distract me from my duty. Or these could be memories, dredged up by the sight of the prison, the strange, unnatural light in this space, and the horrible way the vibrations tug at my insides like an anxious tide.

I sing louder.

Krrr'iiii'sssss'kkkk'aaa.

Mmnnn'uh'mmmnnn'uh'mmm.

G'booh. G'booh. G'booh.

I hear it before I see it – a crack in the air above me. No, it's in the space beside me, or in the ground… A crack, somewhere, for time and life to leak through. Someone is coming. Who is it? Is it the Baa'gh of times past, come to aid me? Is it Nakoko the time-eater, come to take a bés or two? I shiver. No. I have too little time as it is. But *someone* is coming to pry the crack open, slip through, hungry and sly, and—

Heat blasts through me, then darkness.

* * *

I wake to the first strains of the call to Tor-Tor. On my back on the beach, legs curled up tight, I am red all over, ripe with hot, searing pain. I look to the left and see Tetete and Mmoh. I look to the right and see Kirikiri and Baa'ka. All of us on our backs, in full submission. Our time over at last.

Kuu'kor is the one sounding the call, the other three new Og'beh answering it. How did we get here so quickly? I was in the High Place. Wasn't I?

"We are Baa'gh," says Kuu'kor. "Show us the way."

"We are the way," says Kirikiri. "Feed on us and remember."

"First, Og'beh, give your account."

I think back to the last thing I remember. My plan worked. I sang well. I saw a crack, a sign that something had shifted, that I had destroyed the time-change. Didn't I?

"I have served Baa'gh all my life," says Kiri. "I have worked for Baa'gh advancement. The way of Baa'gh is to grow."

"The way of Baa'gh is to know," the new Og'beh reply.

That's wrong. They're supposed to repeat Kirikiri's words exactly. "No," I say, but no one pays any attention. They have changed, but this is fine because they will change back. When the humanoids fail at their time-change, when it becomes clear that they are not the allies the Baa'gh need, everything will be as it should.

When it's my turn to give an account, I begin the same way as the others. "I have served Baa'gh all my—"

"Liar!" Kuu'kor cries out. "Humanoids dragged your body from the High Place after you attempted to sabotage the time-change! We were summoned to come for you. Kirikiri had to beg the humanoids' forgiveness. You shamed us all! Tell the truth, Ss'ku!"

Kuu'kor is so big, possibly the biggest Baa'gh ever. I look at those green-striped legs and that bright blue shell. The shell of a born leader. "It is the truth," I say. "All I've done has been for Baa'gh. Always."

"What did you do to the time-change, Ss'ku?"

"I performed the song of Tor-Tor. The song of endings." The song the Baa'gh will soon sing for us. For me.

Tetete's legs quiver beside me. The new Og'beh click their pincers furiously.

"It was the only way to save Baa'gh. To cure us of mind-stain."

"You failed," says Kuu'kor. "The time-change will be performed tonight."

"It won't work," I counter. And we will be redeemed.

"No one can properly perform the song of Tor-Tor alone. You failed, Ss'ku!"

But I saw the crack. I remember. A crack in a face, red and spilling. Broken bone. A crack big enough to crawl through. So much blood, everywhere. Wasteful. Typical humanoid idiocy.

I know I succeeded. I know it. So I tell Kuu'kor, "We will see."

* * *

There is always a lot of screaming during Tor-Tor. The Baa'gh who have gathered to commemorate the ceremony do their best to drown it out with clicks and singing, but there's no way around it. The new Og'beh eat the old ones alive. I remember eating my predecessor, trying not to hear the screams, filling my thoughts with Baa'gh, Baa'gh, Baa'gh, reminding myself that it was my duty.

Baa'gh flesh is soft but flavourless, or maybe that's what we tell ourselves to make it easier. So we don't take pleasure in what must be done. I remember cracking shell and ripping limbs. We are not allowed to cheat by striking a killing blow. The longer the predecessor lives, the more of them becomes part of us. The more we remember of our past.

I don't know if I'm screaming. Someone is. All of us, probably. I don't know which pain is the red heat claiming my body and which is the young Baa'gh tearing into me. I hear screaming and clicking and singing, and then I hear something else. Something sweet.

It's bigger than Baa'gh. I didn't know anything could be, but it is. It's stars and dust and a thousand tides. It's all the deaths and births of all the creatures that ever lived. And I think I understand what the humanoids mean when they speak of Mo-ther-god. I think I'm close to hearing it, the sound from which all other sounds emerged...

And then I hear something else. Coming closer and closer, a storm that is not a storm.

Nakoko, is that you? Coming to devour time?

Yes, it is I. Go to sleep, Ss'ku.

Predecessors, are you there? Coming to embrace me?

Yes, we are here. Go to sleep, Ss'ku.

Ah! What a relief, to know that my efforts weren't in vain. I am only sound now, rising out of the broken pieces of my body. I listen down to hear the Og'beh finishing their meal and beginning their reign. Let me give them my blessing.

I'm greeted by... Silence. Dust. So much dust. Something is wrong. I smell...age and bones. Shell fragments. Old, old, everything is old and dead and the world is a ruin. A thousand juzu, gone in an instant.

I hear...

Go to sleep, Ss'ku. You are no more.

And then I hear only silence.

Lady Abra's Butterflies

GREETINGS, TRAVELLER! Can you spare a coin for an older woman down on her luck? Ah! Bless you, bless you. Safe travels, my dear.

Oh… Oh, no, I wouldn't go that way if I were you. That road leads to Zanetor. Nobody goes there. You see, in the village of Zanetor, there are no people. There are only butterflies. Yes, it's true!

To be fair, they are quite beautiful. Come rains or Harmattan, hundreds of thousands of them fill the skies. Some plants are so thick with butterflies that one might be forgiven for mistaking them for leaves, flowers, or fruit! They dance among the abandoned houses and alight on the empty streets. They flit along the banks of the silent, lonely river.

The only place they don't go is the house on the hill, a crumbling relic of a mansion. It is said that there is no room for them there – the house already overflows with butterflies. Not living ones, but jewellery fashioned into butterfly shapes. They can be found in every room, on every surface, each one unique.

Many have ventured beyond the dilapidated gates, hoping to plunder the place. None have returned. Indeed, it's all quite mysterious. Once, long ago, the mansion was called Hawthorne House, and it was the pride of Zanetor... Forgive me, I get carried away. Please, continue with your journey.

Unless... Well, if you have time, dear traveller, I can tell you the story. Would you indulge an old woman? Yes? Bless you. Now, where to begin?

* * *

Ah, the house on the hill... Lady Abra Hawthorne had lived there as long as anyone could remember. Since the death of her husband, the philanthropist had opened her home to the orphans of the village, raising them as her own. There were so many of them over the years that the villagers nicknamed them the Hawthorne Hundred.

Lady Abra became famous for her wards, who grew up to be doctors, engineers and ministers; her farm, which she turned over to the community; her Montessori

School, over which she presided as headmistress; and her open-invitation Christmas parties.

Most of all, Lady Abra was known for her butterflies: a collection of butterfly-shaped trinkets fashioned from copper and silver and gold filigree, pendants, bracelets, and ornaments studded with precious and semi-precious stones alike, most of them gifts from the late Lord Hawthorne.

As the woman herself never had the collection valued, it was left to the villagers to speculate on its worth. No consensus was ever reached, but the speculation was a favoured pastime all the same, year after year. The butterflies, beautifully crafted, were displayed in polished glass cabinets in Hawthorne House. Lady Abra hosted an exclusive dinner party every New Year's Eve, culminating in an exhibition of the collection at dawn on 1 January.

Mind you, dear traveller, the butterflies were not stagnant masterpieces, frozen forever in the artists' chosen medium. Each New Year's Day, the collection underwent a metamorphosis – a deviation in the design of an earring, an engraving on a bracelet that had previously been bare. Every so often, new pieces appeared out of nowhere.

It was impossible to determine the cause of these changes. For despite their best efforts, all of Lady Abra's guests fell into a deep sleep at midnight on New Year's Eve and didn't wake until dawn. Attempts to capture the events of the evening proved futile. Recording devices stopped working. Footage was mysteriously erased.

The villagers were delighted rather than alarmed; after all, the mystery was part of the fun. As a beloved pillar of the community, Lady Abra was entitled to her secrets. Everyone indulged her, dismissing the butterfly business as harmless trickery that attracted tourists and kept wonder alive.

Everyone, that is, except a young woman named Cressey.

* * *

Oh! How strange! We seem to be approaching Zanetor... I don't recall leaving the main road, do you? Ah, well. Such a lovely day; we might as well keep walking. Now, where was I?

Ah, yes... One New Year's Eve, Cressey returned home after eight years away. Stepping out of a rundown taxi which had stammered and wheezed its way to the hill, she looked up at the open iron gates of Hawthorne House. A paved driveway beckoned, stretching on an incline to the front steps of the mansion. Several cars were parked there already, all of them shiny and expensive.

Cressey paid the taxi driver, including a generous tip. "Please, try to fix your car before the engine falls out."

He just laughed, wiping sweat from his face with a towel as he drove off. Hoisting her overnight bag onto her shoulder, Cressey started up the steep driveway, somewhat nervous. She had come home with a mission – to uncover the mystery of the butterfly collection once and for all.

You see, Cressey had never fit in in Zanetor and nor had her father, as evidenced by his decision to name his only child after the author of his favourite book. With a name like Rodney-Cressey Edortomi Agbenyo (a mouthful quickly shortened to Cressey Agbenyo), the child's friendless fate was sealed. As soon as she was old enough, she left to study in Accra. Apart from her father's funeral, this was the first time she'd been home since.

A tall young man stood at the door of the Hawthorne mansion, welcoming guests. Cressey recognised those shoulders, hunched as if he were trying to fold himself in three. Afarens, one of the Hawthorne Hundred. As Cressey approached, his smile faded.

"Happy New Year, Afa," she said. "Long time."

"Cressey." He didn't seem pleased to see her. "Welcome home."

"Thank you. Can I come in?"

"Enh, the thing is…" Afarens cleared his throat. "You know the rules. Christmas is for everyone. New Year is only for donors."

She smiled and said, "I bought my ticket a month ago."

His eyes widened, then dropped to the clipboard in his slender hands. "No. No, I have all the names on my list."

Cressey had anticipated that. "I bought it under the name C. Rodney." What fun would it be to warn them when she could show up unexpected?

"Oh." Afarens' face fell.

"What's wrong? Am I still banned after all this time?"

Afarens had the decency to look embarrassed. "Of course not." He managed to paste a polite smile on his face. "Please, go down the corridor and through the first door on the left. Sefirell will show you to your room."

Thanking him, Cressey sauntered down the corridor. Sefirell, another of the Hawthorne Hundred, stood in a small, neat office, attending to an elderly couple who exchanged whispers in French. Cressey entered the office and sat down, waiting her turn.

Sefirell handed the Francophone couple a key, and they left the office. She turned her reserved-for-wealthy-donors smile on Cressey, giving it a special edge. "So. You're back."

"Finally managed to get some time off."

"Mm. What is it you do again?" Sefirell blinked, eyes wide with feigned ignorance.

Cressey knew very well that the villagers gathered in her mother's chop bar to discuss the articles she wrote for the *Weekly Graphic*. If Sefirell wanted to be petty, that was her problem.

"I'm a journalist," she replied politely. "I hear you're waiting to be called to the bar. Well done."

"Thanks." Sefirell picked a key from the box on the desk and held it out. "If you're planning to write about the exhibition, I wouldn't bother. It's been covered so many times."

"You never know." Cressey rose and took the key. "I might find a new angle."

"I doubt it. Room 12."

"That's the same room I had last time."

"Is that a problem?"

"Not at all." Cressey smiled. "I look forward to the party."

* * *

You see, dear traveller when Cressey was a teenager, her parents had given in to her begging and saved up to buy two tickets to the New Year party. Her mother, who hated wasting money on frivolities, refused to attend on principle ("If I want to see butterflies, I can go outside"), and so Cressey went with her father. She had been hawking goods in the market for years to help her mother set up her chop bar, and the small commission she had received for her efforts was enough to pay a tailor to make her a new dress.

Cressey wasn't interested in Lady Abra's collection of butterflies but rather her collection of guests. Anyone who could afford to spend a small fortune to admire someone else's jewellery could help Cressey make her way in the world. She arrived at the party on her father's arm, giddy with excitement.

Mr. Agbenyo injected himself into every conversation, greasing the wheels before springing the trap: "Oh, here comes my brilliant daughter. Did I tell you she wants to be a journalist?"

Cressey enjoyed herself immensely. In addition to the fancy folks she met, there was more food than she had ever seen outside of a wedding or funeral. As the evening wore on, the topic of discussion shifted to the butterflies. Wine and soft drinks were replaced with coffee, guests guzzling caffeine in the hope of staying awake past the witching hour.

Cressey drained a mug of coffee and joined the rest of the guests as they went through the usual inspection of the display room. The room, on the third and topmost floor, was only accessible through one door. The windows were covered with burglar bars. The butterflies lay in their display cases, sparkling with innocence. The cases were locked, the keys on a keyring Lady Abra wore around her neck.

The inspection continued throughout the house. Under beds, inside cupboards, tapping on walls and floors, moving furniture. Nothing seemed amiss. Satisfied, the guests returned to the display room to wait for midnight. By now, it was 11:30 p.m., and no one seemed the least bit in danger of suddenly falling asleep.

"Do you think she puts something in the food?" Cressey asked her father. "Maybe a slow-acting sleeping drug?"

"Maybe. But there are those who abstain from all food and drink provided here, just in case." He nodded at village elder Fo Nusetor, who managed to find a benefactor to fund his ticket every year.

Cressey rolled her eyes. "Fo Nusetor thinks Lady Abra is immortal! Not a reliable source."

"Mrs. Frimpong also abstained. See? She's drinking from a flask she brought with her. That German gentleman abstained as well."

Cressey pondered for a moment. "An odourless gas?"

"Possible, but we searched the house and found nothing suspicious."

"Well, it's a trick. It must be. We're missing something."

"Some say it's all the work of the late Lord Hawthorne, reminding Lady Abra of their love so that she never remarries."

"Nonsense," Cressey scoffed, making her father laugh. "I don't believe in ghosts." She still didn't feel the slightest desire to sleep, and it was 11:45. "I'm staying awake."

"Enh? You alone, in this room full of people, some of whom have been coming here year after year?"

"Yes." Cressey folded her arms, jaw set. "I'll fight the effects of the gas or whatever she uses."

She glanced at the hostess, who was having an animated discussion with the French-speaking couple. It was said that Lady Abra and all her children fell asleep as well, but Cressey didn't see how that was possible. Someone had to stay awake to perform the trick. Her gaze slid towards the corner of the room where Lady Abra's older wards sat. The younger children had set up mattresses in the corridor.

She turned to her father. "Lady Abra must take something to help her resist the effects of the sleeping gas, and then she just pretends she was asleep."

Her father grinned. "You're sure of this your sleeping gas, enh?"

"It's the only thing that makes sense. If it's not the food and drink, it's the air."

"OK. Let's say she is pretending." Her father tapped his chin thoughtfully. "How does she change the butterflies?"

"She makes a switch while we're asleep."

"You mean to tell me she has a whole new set made every year, just to trick us? Can you imagine how much that would cost?"

"Maybe she just alters the originals."

"*Those* originals?" Her father pointed at the display cases. "She alters them in a few hours? While we're sleeping? Does she have the fastest jeweller in the world hidden under her skirt?"

Cressey chewed her lip. There was an answer. There had to be. She just wasn't seeing it. She was missing some obvious clues. If only she could—

Cressey blinked, consciousness dragging her up from the abyss. It was daylight.

"Ah," her father murmured, rising from his slumped position in the chair. "Sorry."

"No." Cressey looked around her. She couldn't even remember falling asleep, yet everyone around her was waking, getting up, and making their way to the display cases. "No! How?"

Leaping to her feet, she peered into the nearest case. Sure enough, the pieces inside had changed. The large butterfly pendant now had two amethysts in each wing, whereas before it had had only one. The gold bangle had three butterflies carved into it instead of four.

Cressey wasn't sure what came over her. A combination of shock, frustration, disappointment, and anger, perhaps. She screamed and started pounding on the glass display case. "It's a trick! It's a trick!"

When Lady Abra approached, trying to calm her down, Cressey turned on her.

"You're a liar and a fraud!" she cried, lunging at the woman.

Her father held her back in time to prevent a tragedy, but the damage was done. Afarens escorted the Agbenyos from the premises and asked them not to return.

Cressey's father, humiliated, barely spoke to her for two whole days, while the village could talk of little else. Her mother forced her to write a formal letter of apology to Lady Abra. When Cressey reached out to the guests who had given her their details at the party, they made excuses not to see her.

* * *

Now, years later, her father was gone, and the past was past – for some, at any rate. When Cressey arrived in the dining room for dinner, Lady Abra came to greet her. The old woman looked just as Cressey remembered, her eyes still shining with cunning.

"My dear, my dear," she cooed, taking both of Cressey's hands and squeezing them. "How wonderful to see you! Did you come with your mother?"

"Unfortunately, she couldn't leave the chop bar." Cressey had practised her smile in the mirror. Sweet, respectful. The smile of a mature young woman who had learned from her mistakes.

The evening proceeded as expected. She participated in the inspection with the rest, though she now understood that it was a futile exercise, and when the party settled in the display room to await midnight, she went to bid her hostess good night.

The old woman's eyes widened in shock. "You're not going to stay and wait for the exhibition?"

"I've set my alarm to wake me in time," Cressey said. "But it was a long trip, and I'm quite tired, so I think I should turn in. Please, enjoy the rest of the evening."

A murmur swept through the room as she made her way to the door. No one had ever refused to wait for midnight. Cressey had checked. Over the last few years, she had read everything written about Lord and Lady Hawthorne and the butterfly collection. She had even tried to get in touch with Fo Nusetor, only to learn that he had passed away.

Cressey went to take a bath and returned to Room 12 to find Sefirell waiting at the door.

"What are you doing?" Sefirell asked.

"Going to bed."

"Why?" Sefirell's eyes narrowed in suspicion. "You're up to something. What is it?"

Cressey sighed. "I'm tired. I just want to go to sleep."

"So, sleep upstairs with the rest of us."

"Why would I sleep in a chair when I paid for a bed?" Cressey kissed her teeth, pushing the door open. "If you want to come inside and police me the whole night, feel free."

Sefirell lingered for a moment as though debating what to do, then turned on her heel and left. With a smug smile, Cressey closed the door, swapped her bathrobe for her nightdress, and took a bottle out of her bag. She had prepared the herbal mixture before coming to Zanetor so it would have time to steep.

After placing her alarm clock, set for half an hour after midnight, on the bedside table, she sat down on the bed, opened the bottle, and drank half the contents. The alarm was a contingency, one Cressey didn't think she would need.

She believed the key to the mystery was in the deep sleep that came over everyone. Once 11 p.m. struck, all the guests could think about was staying awake. But what would happen to those who were already asleep? Cressey's research had provided no concrete answers, so she developed her own theory. What if the strange force that put people to sleep would have the opposite effect on those who already slumbered?

The herbs had begun to take effect. She had consumed just enough to knock her out for a couple of hours, and it was 9:53 p.m. She lay back on the bed, eyelids drooping, and was asleep in seconds.

When she jerked awake and glanced at the clock, it was eleven minutes after midnight. Elated, Cressey got out of bed, turned off her alarm, and went to the door. She opened it a crack and peered outside. There was no one there, but the sound of music wafted down from the display room upstairs. Cressey followed the music, heart racing at the thought of what she might find. There were no little Hawthorne children now, and no mattresses in the corridor. She might be the only one in the whole house who was awake – apart from Lady Abra herself.

The door to the display room was open. Cressey crept towards it on silent, bare feet and then froze in wonder at the sight before her.

All over the room, guests and Hawthorne wards were fast asleep in their chairs. On the floor in the middle of it all was a crumpled thing, a dress with something else added to it, something brown and wrinkled and topped with a tuft of grey. With a jolt of horror, Cressey recognised it as Lady Abra's form, sloughed like old snakeskin.

High above, along the domed ceiling, fluttered the biggest butterfly she had ever seen, its wings a wild mosaic of colour and light. Smaller butterflies flew around it.

A voice burst inside Cressey's head, the voice of her fifteen-year-old self, drunk on vindication. "Look, Daddy! I solved it! I knew I would! Aren't you proud?" There was no answer, and she had expected none. Despite the bizarre sight before her, Cressey still didn't believe in ghosts.

"Come in, my dear!" Lady Abra's voice came from the giant butterfly rather than the crumpled-up thing on the floor.

Cressey recoiled as the butterfly alighted on top of a display case. "You're not a fraud," she murmured. "You're a witch!"

"In the old days," Lady Abra replied, "they called me a god."

For a long time, Cressey could only stare at the creature, curiosity and fear at war within her. At last, curiosity won out, and she found her words. "I don't understand. If you can pretend to be human, why not stay human? Why risk exposure? Why change the butterfly jewellery? Why court attention?"

Lady Abra's wings folded up like some heavenly napkin. "I'm a god, my dear. I *like* attention."

Cressey moved a little closer, studying the creature, trying to find the familiar old woman in those massive, black, compound eyes. "Did your husband know?"

"Before the end, yes." Lady Abra looked up. "Along with many of my children."

Cold, sticky dread seeped into Cressey's bones as she raised her gaze to the butterflies dancing on the ceiling. "Those... those are people?"

Lady Abra didn't reply, which was answer enough. Cressey knew all the Hawthorne Hundred, not just the ones she had grown up with. Many of them had moved abroad and never returned...

She swallowed her disgust. "None of your children ever went abroad, did they?"

"Depends how you define abroad." Lady Abra chuckled. "I think Valikem is my favourite. Such a lovely boy. Look! He made the most stunning Citrus Swallowtail. His pattern is the most fun to play with."

Cressey looked up, spotting the black butterfly with white patches. It was exquisite to behold, but it wasn't a butterfly. Not really. The wrongness of it sat in the back of her throat like bile. "You're a monster."

"Not at all. They're perfect now, forever. If they could have thanked me for changing them, they would have. I plan to bestow this gift on all my people, one at a time."

Although she couldn't see any movement in the creature's long proboscis, Cressey felt that Lady Abra was smiling.

"You can't do that!" Cressey cried in dismay. "You can't transform a whole village. People will know!"

"You'd be surprised at what people are capable of ignoring," the creature said. "Now, what would you like to be, my dear? A Calypso Caper White?"

Cressey ran. A foolish thing to do, perhaps, as no one could outrun a butterfly god, but we can forgive her for trying.

The end came down on her in a blunt blow down the middle of her back. She heard her spine break before she felt it, a sickening crack that wrenched a gasp from her lips. And then cold light ran through her like sparkling wine in her veins, chilled to perfection, spilling out of her pores in glowing drops.

She knew who she was for one blinding, precious moment, and then that knowledge became a crumbling memory or perhaps a dream. The world was air and light and too much colour, and held her aloft on invisible fingers.

She was flying. It seemed Lady Abra had been right, for if Butterfly Cressey could have spoken, she would indeed have thanked her. She could fly forever, wanting nothing more.

But all too soon, it ended. She fell, her body weighted and stiff, everything but her perception frozen. She didn't understand. Where was she? What had happened?

"Welcome to the collection," said Lady Abra.

* * *

Come morning, the guests woke to find that the butterflies had changed again. Rubbing sleep from their eyes, they gathered to admire the collection. Lady Abra stood in the centre of it all, back in her human skin, eyes gleaming with pride.

"Oh, look!" said Sefirell, clapping her hands with delight.

In the display case closest to the window lay a new butterfly piece, a bold obsidian ring formed from the curving wings of the insect, clustered with sapphires and a smattering of diamonds. The guests oohed and aahed.

"There's something familiar about it," Afarens murmured.

"Yes," Sefirell agreed.

They exchanged glances, then looked around them, both experiencing the nagging sense of having forgotten something.

"We get this type in the garden all the time," Lady Abra said. "Karsch's Sapphire."

Ah, yes. That must be it.

When Sefirell checked Cressey's room and found it abandoned, bed made, she felt that odd sensation again. However, Cressey was temperamental – it was just like her to leave without saying goodbye. Within days, Sefirell and Afarens would have forgotten that she had even come to Hawthorne House.

Cressey's mother would soon be telling people that her daughter had found a job abroad. No one would ask where, precisely – the people of Zanetor suffered from an astounding lack of curiosity – and just as well, because the poor woman couldn't have answered. She only knew that her daughter was abroad, where people were safe and happy.

As for the notes Cressey had entrusted to her editor, the editor would search the entire office and fail to find them. It would occur to him that Cressey wouldn't need them, anyway, now that she had gone 'abroad'.

But for now, no one thought of Cressey at all. Certainly not at Hawthorne House, where any feelings of foreboding had faded in the glow of celebration

* * *

Pardon? Oh, my goodness, you're right! We've reached the house on the hill. Hawthorne House, once a gem, now a ruin. Remarkable! I barely recall the journey. And yet here we are, walking up the steps – apologies for all the dust, there's no one to sweep, after all – and in we go! Don't worry about the doors locking behind us. Perfectly normal.

Ah! Alone at last. Now, my dear, what would you like to be? I think you'll make a gorgeous Ashanti Forester…

Armour

I'VE DECIDED.

I stand at the door that leads outside, hand raised to push it open. The Dress keeps me upright; its wires moulded to my shoulder blades, the base of my spine, my ribs. As though I might collapse without it, as if I were an earthworm, wriggling and fragile in the unforgiving light of day. But I'm tired of wriggling. I know what must be done.

Life before the Dress, before him, is darkness. There are stories, logs, records and detailed accounts of the fighting. Days of desolation, we're told. There are pictures too, in blistering colour. Towering killing machines that waged their wars in the distance, where they could do us no harm. Metal exploding and cables sparking. All very dramatic.

The Dresses came soon after the Armistice, once we'd been purged of the poison. I don't remember the purging; none of us do. Better that way, I guess. I don't even remember being fitted. It's as if the Dress has always been there, cradling me. The Dresses are for our own protection, we're told. To make sure we remain pure and amenable, to keep the poison out.

Sometimes, I wonder why we were the only ones touched by the poison, why it left him and his kind alone. I asked him once. He pushed a button and the Dress sang pain into my bones. I never asked again.

Now that I know what I must do, there's no time to waste. I walk through the garden, across the brick walkway, down the deserted path. The castle's quiet at night. He says night is for sleep, but deep in the dark, I often hear the sound of music. He holds parties down in the cellar, where none of us are allowed to go. For our own good, we're told. Because revelry wakes our demons.

My shoes are almost silent on the ground. I look over my shoulder, just in case. Nothing. Only jade-hued creepers snaking up the walls and flowers pretending to be asleep, secretly watching me from behind their petals.

Everything's tainted by the night, eerie and menacing. I walk faster. When I reach the end of the garden path, I almost trip. I pause to regain my balance, and then I start to run up the steps, through the front door, into the main wing of the castle.

The Dress cuts into my flesh. The skirt rustles as I hurry across the floor. I hug the walls, fingers running across the cold, rough cement, aware of the thin fragments of skin I'm leaving behind. Evidence.

We who wear the Dresses aren't meant to run. We walk sedately, sweeping the floor. We glide like phantoms. Our pulses never race. We never break a sweat. We're impassive painted portraits, gilded statues in our stylish black cages. But I *can* run. And if I can, why shouldn't I?

It's thoughts like this that torment me when I'm supposed to be getting my beauty sleep. On the outside, I follow the rules because that's the sort of thing queens do. Be dignified and responsible. Set a good example. But on the inside, my mind is a riot, alive with treachery, biting and kicking and *wanting*. Now the rebellion has spilt over, out of my mouth and nose and ears, coating my feet.

That's why I went into the cabinet yesterday and stole the key. I thought the Dress would punish me, but it couldn't. Sometimes, I forget that it only sees with his eyes, and he wasn't looking. He was asleep, so I went in and went out, and the Dress did nothing but sweep the floor behind me, wiping away my footsteps.

Every step I'm taking now – down the dim hallway, around the corner, through the passage, up the stairs – is an act of treason. He'll find me, of course. He'll come home without warning and know that I'm gone. The thought fills me with euphoria. Let him come. I've decided.

Reaching the top of the staircase, I find myself at the foot of the tower. For the first time, I hesitate. The next staircase is long and steep. Dust has collected on the wooden railing, thick as face powder. I reach out and wrap my shaking hand around it. I feel the grit beneath my skin – ages and ages of dust. When I pull my hand away, the dust comes with it, leaving a clear print on the railing. More evidence. Now, fear sets in, holding my legs together, pulling my feet to the ground.

The Dress seems to devour me, wires closing in as though it knows what I've been plotting. It can't see without his eyes and he's blind outside the castle, but it can sense the change in me. My heart is pounding, my feet move faster than they should, and the Dress doesn't like change any more than he does. But I can't stop. My chance might never come again.

"I'm not doing anything," I whisper, running my hand down the front of the Dress, willing it to calm down. "I'm only going for a walk."

My pulse slows, and the Dress's grip eases. With a deep breath, I start up the steps. This isn't like the times I practised in my head, standing in front of the mirror, picturing my escape. I'm doing it for real, and I can't go back.

Soon, I'm moving as fast as the Dress will allow me, stumbling twice and carrying on until I reach the door. And what a door! Older than anything else in the castle. No bolts, no bars, no clever gadgets. Just wood and hinges and a rusty keyhole.

I reach into my pocket for the key, a heavy thing made of brass. My hands shake as I put it into the keyhole and turn it slowly. It stops, and I turn it the other way until I hear the click. Then I reach for the handle and turn it.

The door creaks open. The room is silent, the air thick with filth and rot and dust. My breathing grows uneven, nostrils twitching against the stench. Few people have been up here since the Armistice, I think. Since the creature was imprisoned.

My eyes grasp in the darkness as I step inside, trying to find their way to the cage. I hear it before I see it: the sound of something hitting metal. I can just make out the bars, filthy with grime, and around one of them is something that looks like a hand. Thin, with leathery skin and long, dirty nails.

Now, my curiosity outweighs my fear. Closer, closer, the hem of the Dress gathering dust. There's a faint glow coming from inside the cage. I scan the bars for something resembling a keyhole or a lever. The hand releases the bar and points at the wall, and my eyes follow. There it is, a rectangle of buttons and flashing lights encased in dusty glass. I remove my shoe and break the glass with the heel. As I slip the shoe back on, I try to determine which button does what. There's a red one, the writing long faded, the light beneath it blinking yellow. I push it. Nothing.

I glance back at the shape curled up in the shadows. The hand has been withdrawn, offering no further guidance. I frown at the control panel. I can't remember how it works. That knowledge was purged along with the poison.

The bells begin to chime outside. In twenty minutes, the guards will do their rounds and find my bedroom empty. What do I do? My mind screams, fingers flying over the control panel, trying everything until finally I hear a groan, and the bars begin to shift. They slide to the left, sluggish, creaking so loudly I think I might as well die now and save myself the torture. The creature remains in the cage.

"You're free," I tell it, growing impatient. "Come on. You're free!"

It moves. It's only then that I think to fear for myself, to run and hide. I step back towards the door, preparing to throw myself down the staircase if I have to. But when the creature emerges from the cage, the fear melts. It's not a monster at all.

Eyes sunk deep into their sockets. Hair long and matted, twisting into ragged clothes. She might have been beautiful once. The only remarkable thing about her now is her skin, illuminated by that terrible power of hers.

I run to her, grab her hand and pull her to the door. "We have to leave. Come!"

We hurry down the stairs, the bells still pealing. One of my maids stands at the foot of the staircase, staring up at me in confusion.

"Madam, what are you doing here? Didn't you hear the bell?"

I hurry past her, dragging the feeble excuse for a monster behind me. "What are *you* doing here?" I ask the girl.

"They sent me to find you. When they came to adjust your Dress for sleep, you weren't there. They got worried." She's breathing hard, trying to keep up. "Who is your guest? Why were you in the tower?"

I ignore her questions. The bells stop, and all is quiet as we rush towards my room; the guards haven't stirred yet. And then the pain strikes, a jolt through my chest. The Dress closes in, and I'm forced to slow my pace. He's back. He knows.

"Madam, you must go and confess!" the maid whispers. "He won't be too harsh. You're only a few minutes late."

I turn the corner. My quarters are up ahead. Another jolt goes through me, bending me almost double. The Dress is so tight now that I can barely breathe.

"Madam!" The girl's small hands take hold of my free arm.

I'm still holding onto the creature. She hasn't said a word. She has been docile and compliant, one of us already. We reach my room as the pain hits again. The door closes behind me, and at last, the pain subsides. I release the creature and sink to the floor, gasping, clutching my chest.

"Take it off." The creature's voice is hoarse from lack of use, but commanding, the voice of someone used to obedience. Her hand rises to point at me. "The dress."

The maid gasps at this blasphemy. I look at the creature. In the few minutes since her release, she seems to have grown. She stands upright now, head high, eyes blazing. Her skin is thick and supple. Strong.

"The Dresses came after your time," I recall. "You've never seen them before, have you? You wouldn't know. We can't take them off. If we try, we die." I stand up and lean forward to show her how the rods and wires are attached to me, an exoskeleton of metal and fabric.

She smiles, and the filth seems to vanish from her skin. "That's what he tells you." She walks around me, examining the Dress. "And like a fool, you believe."

A trumpet sounds, summoning me to be disciplined.

"You don't answer to him." There's a note of finality in her voice, and I remember that there's something in this castle more dangerous than him.

Maybe I made a mistake. Maybe, in my anger and frustration, my eagerness to hurt him, I've only hurt myself. She seems like one of us, but at least some of the stories must be true. I don't remember. I only know that he locked her in that tower because he feared her, and maybe I should fear her, too.

"You must take off the dress," the creature says again. "All of you eventually, but you first."

The maid is frightened now. "Madam, who is this traitor?"

"She's the creature," I tell her. "I set her free."

The girl backs away, but I think she only half believes me. The creature's hands snake around my waist, and I feel a sharp jab in my spine as her nails break through the Dress.

"Don't!" I gasp. "I set you free so you could help us escape!"

My words seem to amuse her. She pulls. I scream as the Dress is peeled away from my back, taking the skin with it.

"Madam!" The maid is sobbing now, but she doesn't dare come closer.

I steel myself against the pain and cry out as the creature pulls harder, lifting the Dress from my sides, my chest, my arms. Agony all over, stinging and burning and blood. My own horror reflected in the maid's stricken face. And then stillness. Silence. The Dress lies broken on the floor.

"Let's go," says the creature.

Go. Go? As though it's a matter of opening the door and walking out, as though there won't be consequences. What was I thinking? I freed her to save myself, and she's going to kill us all. I drop to my knees, weak from my wounds.

"If you stay, you'll die."

I'm already dying. What does she mean?

"She's mad," the maid whispers. "Madam, let me get help."

The creature moves to block the door. "Take off your cage and come with me while you still can."

"I'm not going anywhere!" the maid cries out.

Their voices fade. I see stars and wonder how long it takes to bleed to death.

"Do you want to be free or not?"

I think she's talking to me. I whimper, and then I nod. After all, I've decided. My gaze strays to the Dress, and I reach for it. The creature opens the door and returns to grab me around the waist. Before she carries me out, my fingers close over the Dress's familiar folds. I can't walk the world without my skin.

We run. Well, she runs, and I stumble along, reeling. Corridors. Stairs. Left – no, right – and down, then up. Tiles. Stone. Grass. And then, suddenly, sand. My mind returns from the brink just in time to see that we've left the castle and are moving towards the beach. The cold air is merciless against my wounds.

"Please," I beg her, "I'm dying!"

"You're not. You're fine."

"But it hurts!"

"It doesn't. You just think it does." She stops at the edge of the moat. "Look at yourself."

I shake my head.

"Don't be afraid. Look."

Well, I've come this far. Why be a coward now? I look down at my chest, where the rods and wires stripped away my flesh, and my head pounds with shock. There are no wounds. Marks, yes, deep and bruised purple. Scratches. But no blood. I'm covered in beautiful, living, glowing skin.

"I'm like you," I whisper in amazement. "Underneath, I'm like you!"

"You were always like me."

"But what are you? Not a girl."

She laughs. "No. A woman."

I repeat the word, enjoying its taste on my tongue. "Then he lied. He said you caused the fighting. He said you were a monster, that you filled us with poison, and only he could save us."

"He had to say something to make you agree to be purged."

Looking back at the castle, I think of the other girls.

"You can't save them," she tells me. "They must leave willingly, and they won't. Not tonight."

"Will they die?"

"Maybe. Maybe not. By tomorrow, one of them will be the new queen." I stare at her, confused, and her smile turns sympathetic. "My dear, did you think you were the first?" She shakes her head. "It's time to go. There's a whole world on the other shore."

I watch her walk into the water without fear, stripping off her rags. I follow slowly, and then I hear the sharp report of guns and follow faster. She swims as though she hasn't spent an eternity locked in a cell. I swim as though I'm carrying a mountain instead of a Dress. It soaks up water, weighing me down.

The creature looks back. "What are you doing? Drop it, or you'll drown!"

"But…" But it's mine. In the small world I come from, it's the only thing that's mine.

"Leave it, you fool!"

This isn't what I practised in front of the mirror. Liberation is not what I imagined. It's not as simple as a key, a tower, a grand escape. It's labour and loss and panic. It's cold things clawing at me from beneath frothing waves, bullets raining overhead, water, water, water as far as the eye can see, cold and uncertainty that make terror dance in my chest and spin in my head. And yet…

Though I can't see the shore, I know it's there. I know there is a world waiting for me. So liberation is also hope, I guess. It's knowing that whatever happens next is up to me. I, strong-willed and glowing from within, chose this.

I was a girl in a Dress she could never take off, and now I'm naked and woman and wise. Knowing this, treading water, I have to ask myself whether I still want to be free. The castle is warm. Safe. And the Dress…well, the Dress kept the water off and the cold at bay. That's the thing about cages. They keep you in, but they also keep things out, like coffins nailed shut against ravening dogs. Like fortress walls. Like armour.

Maybe I will be naked forever, vulnerable, barefoot. Maybe I'll slip in the sand and break. But still, I want that freedom. Desperately, unequivocally, more than I've ever wanted anything.

So I relax my arms and let go. Of the Dress, the rules, the illusion. The skirt catches on a rock. Wind fills it, and it billows out, blustering and angry, flapping its fabric at me one last time. But I don't back down. I don't reach for it. After a moment, it comes loose, deflates and is swept away. It's only a dress, after all.

"Well?" the woman calls out. "Are you coming?"

I nod, teeth chattering, and paddle towards her. I've decided.

Sikami

I AM not afraid.

"That's your problem," my father used to say. "You don't know when to be afraid and when not to be. Something… is…broken…right…here!" He would dive into my stomach, tickling me without mercy, and I would scream-laugh until my mother came running to see what terrible misfortune had befallen me.

He was right. I'm afraid of silly things, like the sight of too many ants all at once, or grasshoppers the same shade of green as maize stalks. But I'm not afraid of the raucous noise of crows landing on the iron roof or perching on the windowsill to watch us while we sleep. I'm not afraid of the cup in my hand or the thick liquid inside it, black as coal, its scent sweet enough to make you drunk.

"You don't have to do this."

I glance at my mother, sitting cross-legged on the floor beside me. Both her hands are in my father's tight grip to keep her from doing something we will all regret.

"She made a vow," Papa reminds her.

"She didn't know what she was saying!"

"Mama." I shake my head, then turn my attention back to Kofi, the mage. "I'm ready. Tell me how this works."

He's a scrawny man, smaller than me, though a good decade older. The lines in his face are so deep that, at first glance, one might mistake them for tribal scars. He smiles, revealing gaps between all his teeth. "Very simple. You just drink it all. Leave nothing behind. Then lie back and wait. It won't take time."

"Will it hurt?"

Kofi frowns. "Ah, that one I can't be sure of. I wanted to test it on myself first, but if something went wrong, I wouldn't be able to fix it, so…" His narrow shoulders lift and drop. "Let's be optimistic, enh?" He beams at me as if that should ease all my worries.

He's lucky I'm not afraid. Mama starts to keen like someone in mourning. Papa swears under his breath. I meet his gaze, and we exchange knowing looks. Mama can be so dramatic.

"It's not like I'm going to die. Right?" I look to the mage for reassurance.

To his credit, his grin falters only a little. "Oh, probably not!"

The windows are covered. The door is closed. Crow eyes are everywhere. We keep our voices low because where there are eyes, there are ears.

"After she turns, what are we to do?" Papa asks. "Can we touch her? Move her?"

"Yes, yes. You can even cut her up and make chips!" Kofi laughs. No one else does. His laughter dies. "Enh, yes, you can touch her. Just stay with her, watch her. The important thing is that she must be convincing. She must turn all the way and then, in some hours, turn back. That is all. Very simple!"

There's the sound of a throat being cleared from the shadowy corner of the hut. I almost forgot that our chief, Tobge Mawutor, was here.

"Edem, what you are about to do could save us all." His voice is soft and calm. "Few among us were willing to take the risk, and so we honour you. We celebrate you."

"Thank you, Tobge." I bow my head, the heady sweetness of the brew in my cup filling my nostrils. "The honour is mine. If there is any chance of freeing us, I am happy to take the risk."

He nods his gratitude. "But your mother is right. Even though you made a vow, these are special circumstances. If you change your mind, no one will fault you. So I must ask once more: are you sure?"

I pause, even though the decision has long been made, and I have no intention of changing it. I pause to look into the cup and let the smell wash over me, to tell myself it's like honey and overripe mango doused with charcoal, and the worst it can do is give me a stomach ache. I pause to dig inside myself, seeking the fear the same way the boars dig in the earth for sikaroot.

But there is no fear, only resolve and a glimmer of excitement. What we have is a half-life. There is nothing to lose. And if this works, if I can turn for long enough, everything will change.

"I'm sure," I say at last and drain the cup.

The brew is so sweet it makes my head pound and my heart run. I feel…cramped and constricted, as though I'm being squeezed into a small box. The world begins to fade. The last thought in my mind is how funny it is, how absurd, that in a few seconds I will be a yam.

* * *

Five months ago, hope was still a fantasy; every day the same as the one before.

We woke before daybreak. We took the piglets out to the sikaroot fields and led them through furrows of earth, their little snouts pressed to the ground, sniffing for ripe root. At the edge of the fields, a line of hogs waited with riders on their backs. We worked in fours. One piglet with one handler, one hog with one rider. As soon as a piglet gave the signal – a long, unbroken squeal – its partner hog would trot into the field and start turning the earth with its massive tusks, its rider guiding it with soft commands and a gentle nudge.

We took turns. Rider today, handler tomorrow, to keep all our skills honed. And once one field was full of hogs and the piglets had been taken into the next field, piles of sikaroot would accumulate, their hard orange shells peeking through the dirt that coated them.

Crows circled above. The eyes of the Occupation. Some would settle on power lines or perch in trees while others kept circling for hours as if to show off their stamina. I would look up at their black bodies and white collars and picture what they saw.

An army of grey hogs, bristly hairs slick with sweat, legs covered in soil. A crowd of Boar Caste labourers in our uniform of red shirts and trousers and black rubber boots, hands sheathed in black gloves, black masks covering our mouths and noses. Even at this stage of production, long before we were ready to press the sikaroot into sikami, the most expensive oil in the world, we wore masks. Our Crow Caste colonisers kept us sheathed like deadly blades, terrified that one drop of sikami on our tongues or fingers might be enough to slice through their power.

Did we look like people to the beaked sentries above? Did they consider us living beings, same as them, same as their masters? Or did they see us as nothing more than objects, pieces of machinery moving in tandem? It was impossible to tell. The crows spoke to no one but each other and their masters, unlike other totem animals, which communicated with all.

I was on handler duty the day hope came. Nene, my charge, had been put to work for the first time that week and was still a little excitable. She kept running along the furrows, sticking her precious nose into clumps of basil, goat droppings and anthills, inhaling all the world with relish. I yanked on her leash, struggling to shorten it. The metal clasp was jammed.

"Nene! No! Root, Nene! Root only!" My scolding was half-hearted; it was difficult to begrudge her – or myself –

these small joys. But joy was for private moments. Not for the fields.

I grabbed her round the middle a moment before she threw herself into an old burrow that likely housed trouble. Nene let out a loud grunt to inform me what she thought of my disciplinary efforts, then wriggled out of my grip and shot off down the furrow, yanking the leash from my hand and forcing me to chase her. Disapproving shouts trailed us.

"Look at this fool now, bested by a piglet!"

"Edem, catch her quick! Eyes!"

As though I could forget our feathered watchers, looking for any infraction they could hold against us. If Nene went out of bounds, we would both be whipped. I caught up to her before she crossed the boundary, at the point where the field dipped into a small valley peppered with subsistence crops for Boar labourers – chillies, cassava, okra. Nene's nose was buried in a mound of okra in a basket on the ground. A distraught farmer tried to chase her away by waving a dirty handkerchief at her.

"I'm sorry," I gasped, grabbing the piglet around the middle once more and lifting her, squealing, into the air. "She's still in training. I hope she didn't destroy the harvest."

"It's fine, it's fine," the farmer said, now shooing me away with the same dirty hanky.

I backed away, but not before I saw the pile of okra flicker. It was the strangest thing, as though, for a moment, it was not a pile of okra but a pile of something else entirely: little bags of cotton tied with string.

I blinked. "What was that?"

"Come!" the farmer called out, ignoring me.

Two boys came scampering out of the nearest house, scooped up the basket of okra and fled. But I had already seen the okra change, this time permanently, from plump green fingers to round little cotton packages. Drugs, perhaps, or some other illicit substance.

"Are you mad?" I clutched Nene's wriggling form close to my chest, staring at the farmer. "Smuggling so close to the fields? They'll catch you!"

He shrugged, not the least bit ashamed. "You found your piglet. Go back to work."

"How did you do that? I've never seen that kind of magic."

"Enh, new type. From over the border." He sighed. "Go back to work, my sister, before you bring eyes down on my house."

I went, but I couldn't stop thinking about what I had seen. After we were released from work that night, I returned to the room I shared with my parents and recounted the incident over a supper of smoked fish and kontomire.

"The mages from the north are full of tricks," Mama said. "It must be their doing. Stay away from that place, Edem."

Stay away? Oh, no. Not when my mind was alive with ideas. "If people can turn things into other things to hide them, we could—"

"No," Papa said, shaking his head in the darkness. "You think we haven't tried to smuggle sikaroot before? We always get caught."

"Have we tried magic, Papa?"

"Just eat your food," Mama said, and that was the end of the discussion.

But I wasn't the only one who had ideas. As gossip of the new magic spread through Boar territory, more and more of us started to wonder about the possibilities. It was not long before Togbe Mawutor, our chief in name only since the start of the Occupation, gave permission for people to explore the options.

The Crows – both the people and their totem birds – made no effort to learn about other castes. Certain that nothing of note could take place beyond their borders, they paid little attention to the foreigners who frequented our village, apart from checking their possessions at the border to ensure they hadn't stolen any sikami. They also lost interest in the Boar people once we crossed into neighbouring lands. Their arrogance was a blessing.

We asked the hogs to take one sikaroot into their mouths while they dug. Just one per hog. When they were taken off the fields, they would wait until they reached their pens, then bury the roots in their troughs. When we came to clean the pens, we collected the roots along with the waste. We were all searched upon leaving the fields for our nearby village, but no one searched the buckets of waste we took home to make into fertiliser, which we traded with our Mosquito and Grasscutter neighbours.

Once we connected with the northern mages behind the new transformation magic, our foreign friends would return home with fertiliser and okra, or beans, or cassava – sikaroot in disguise. It was impossible to smuggle pressed sikami, the oil under guard at all hours of the day, so we sent a few labourers across the border to press the sikaroot and pack the oil. Our Mosquito friends stored it for us, safe from Crow eyes. Within a few weeks, we had smuggled about one hundred and fifty kilos of raw sikaroot across the border.

It was good. It was more than we had dared to hope for. And yet, we knew we could do more. Hope blossomed into motivation, which exploded into determination. One day, we were all gathered in the community compound after the burial of one of our elders. Kofi the mage, now considered an honorary Boar, was there, surrounded by curious children who bothered him with ceaseless questions.

I'm not sure which child asked: "Can you use this your magic on a person?"

Kofi laughed so loudly that we all turned to look at him, and then he stopped laughing as if struck silent. He set his bowl down on the ground and said, "You know... You know... I think so."

And hope became a fire in our souls.

* * *

I was born into the Occupation. By the time I was old enough to work the fields, I had heard all the stories of our illustrious history. I knew that sikami's value lay not in its rich flavour, but in the visions the oil evoked. Only the Boar Caste could summon the visions and decipher them. Others who tried would succumb to meaningless, sometimes dangerous hallucinations, yet they continued to try, nonetheless.

I knew that one bottle of pure sikami, small enough to fit in my palm, sold for the same amount as a second-hand motorbike. Sikami was the reason the Crow Caste had occupied our lands, believing it their duty to claim it for the Crow gods that had made them. I knew that they were wrong. The Mosquito gods had buried sikami on the Boar gods' land precisely to keep the Crow gods from reaching it, and when it had formed sikaroot and the Boar gods had dug it up, the Mosquito gods had told them to treasure it, and fled.

I knew all the facts. All the stories. And yet the world my elders spoke of, in which sikami belonged to the people of the Boar, in which it was bartered with caution and reverence but never, ever sold, was unimaginable to me.

"But it's so valuable," I'd said when my mother first told me the stories. "Why wouldn't we sell it for profit?"

"Only a fool would sell what is priceless," she had replied.

"I still dream of the taste of it," my father had whispered.

"Me too." He and my mother had exchanged glances that hinted at a longing too deep and painful to express.

"How does it taste?" I had asked them.

"You will know it when you taste it," my father had said. "There's no taste like it in the world."

"But *how* does it taste?" I'd persisted, desperate to be part of their old and sacred knowing. "How, exactly?"

My mother had sighed. "Like riches, my daughter. Like freedom."

"Yes." The word a wistful, lonely breath on my father's lips.

Dissatisfaction had settled then, heavy in my belly like old meat, as I had realised that I didn't understand. I couldn't understand. No one would ever say it, yet I knew it all the same – I was Boar Caste, but I wasn't truly Boar.

All of us born under Crow rule were something different from those who had gone before. We were shackled and yet untethered, bound and yet drifting. Our birthright, a god-given gift, was nothing more to us than a product we made for our masters, a luxury beyond our reach. A mystery.

I tried not to think about what my life would have been like if I had been born a few years earlier. Born into magic, into wisdom, rather than servitude. It would do no good to be bitter. Bitterness seeped into the root, the elders said, and ruined the oil. And if the crop was bad, all of us would pay in blood.

* * *

I never planned to be a hero or the subject of a magical experiment. But our gods have their own plans and rarely share them with us in advance.

I open my eyes to find my parents staring at me. A blanket covers me, and I quickly realise that I am naked beneath it. That makes sense, all things considered. Yams are not in the habit of wearing clothes. My body aches, my head throbs and my vision swims. But I am alive and human.

Someone squeals in delight. I turn my head towards the noise and see Kofi the mage dancing in a circle, pumping his fist in the air.

"I take it the experiment was a success," I mutter, my voice hoarse.

"How do you feel?" Mama's fingers are already prodding, checking my pulse, my temperature, feeling me for lumps as though I were freshly pounded fufu.

"Sore." I flinch at her touch. "Every part of me is painful."

"The pain will pass," says Kofi. "Ah, do you see? Do you see what we have achieved?"

"How long was I...?" I can't bring myself to say it. Part of me still thinks it is a hoax Kofi is playing, in which my family and Togbe Mawutor have agreed to participate.

"Almost five hours," Papa tells me, bringing me a cup of water.

I gulp the lukewarm liquid gratefully. Five hours. I was a yam for five hours. The world cannot possibly get any stranger.

"What do you remember?" Togbe Mawutor pulls his stool closer.

Pulling myself into a seated position, careful to drag the blanket with me to protect my modesty, I try to send my mind back. "I remember drinking the medicine. And feeling...small. Squashed. As if I was trying to squeeze myself through a narrow pipe."

"That was the start of it," says Kofi, with a sage mod. "And what else? After? Do you remember anything after?"

I frown, straining, but my mind is blank. I shake my head. "It's as if I stopped existing between then and now."

"You did, you did!" Kofi cackles. "You were a yam, and yams don't have thoughts and memories. Ayeeee! It works! Didn't I tell you?"

He does his little dance again, and though the expressions on the faces of the others are more serious, more restrained, I feel the excitement in the air. We have proven the efficacy of this magic beyond a doubt. Now, it is time to graduate from smuggling small amounts of sikaroot to something far more ambitious.

"One person is not the same as one thousand," Mama whispers. "There are so many ways it can go wrong. What if it doesn't affect them the way it affects us?"

"They are human," Togbe Mawutor replies. "It will work.

The gods have given us this chance, and we must take it."
He smiles at me. "Edem, you have saved us all."

"Not yet," says Mama, and even though I catch Papa
rolling his eyes, I have to agree with her.

One person is not the same as one thousand. The real
test is yet to come.

* * *

We use the funeral of one of the Mosquito chiefs to hatch a
plot. The funeral takes place across the border, and we all
beg leave to attend, as our culture demands when an ally
falls. Our Crow masters grumble, annoyed at the prospect
of losing a day's labour, but they know we will grow
tiresome if we are made to miss a major cultural event, and
so they relent.

Gathered in the courtyard of the Mosquito chief, we hash
out the details of our plan with our Mosquito Caste friends.

"The Crows hold a monthly party in honour of their king,"
Togbe Mawutor tells our neighbours. "He has never set
foot on Boar soil – he wouldn't deign to leave his mountain
kingdom to mingle with us on the ground – and most of
the Crow Caste occupiers have never even seen him in the
flesh. But they honour him all the same, with a big feast,

compulsory for all their people, in the commander's yard. Everyone comes for the food and drink, but they mainly come for the sikami."

We all shake our heads and wrinkle our noses in disapproval. The commander insists on having the oil hand-pressed fresh for the gathering, as it would be an affront to their 'great' king to use factory-made sikami that has sat on a shelf for weeks. Several precious bowls of sikami are shared among the occupiers. They dance and dream. Not the way we used to, when sikami was ours. They dance and dream like the drunk, slurring their words and missing steps, for no one can make sikami work the way the Boar Caste can.

"The next Crow party is our chance to put Kofi's magic to work," says Togbe Mawutor. "We will dose the Crows with his medicine and turn them all into yams. The task must fall to the Boar labourers who prepare the food for the feast, for it is they who must spike the delicacies with Kofi's pungent medicine and ensure that the Crows suspect nothing."

"We should put it in the drinks," someone proposes.

Kofi shakes his head. "The medicine is strong. If we only put it in the drinks, they will taste it."

"In the soup, then," someone else suggests. "They take it with plenty of fish and pepper."

Kofi shakes his head. "I told you, the medicine is strong. If we only put it in the soup, they will taste it."

"Then it must be mixed into all the food in small proportions," says Togbe Mawutor. "It must be mashed and stirred and spooned into every sip, every morsel, to ensure each person is dosed with enough."

"Those who eat and drink first will turn first," Papa points out. "And that will alarm the rest. How can we ensure that they all turn together?"

A murmur ripples through the crowd, for there is no way to ensure such precision. Panic flares inside me. Have we come so close, only to fail? There must be a way.

"The sikami." It is the widow of the Mosquito chief who speaks. "They must take the sikami first."

"They never take it first," Togbe Mawutor replies. "They take it at the end of the evening."

"You must *make* them take it first," says the widow, leaning forward on her stool. She pulls her shawl tighter around her shoulders against the Harmattan chill. "The oil brings on hallucinations. Nothing they see after taking it will trouble them – they will believe they are having visions. Someone turns into a yam and they will laugh, convinced that at last they have unlocked the secret of sikami, that the Crow gods have blessed them with the Sight. Make them take the oil first, and you can do as you please for the rest of the night."

Her words are both a balm and a stimulant, renewing our hope. But how do we alter the Crow routine? How do we force them to begin with the sikami and only feast after the oil has taken effect?

Kofi lets out a peal of laughter. "I have it! I have it! The food will be late!"

"They will never allow us to be late on their sacred day," says Togbe Mawutor.

"They will have no choice because there will be no Boars available to cook until evening!" Kofi slaps his knees, cackling at his own cleverness. "You will all be occupied with a grave matter, the only matter the Crows respect. A funeral. And the Crows will be so pleased by this death that they will be only too happy to rearrange their festivities to accommodate it!"

"Who are we to say has died?" I ask.

Kofi beams. "Togbe Mawutor, of course."

* * *

On the day of the party, we all rise early as usual. We start our work as usual. I am on duty in the fields again and assigned to Nene once more. The piglet has grown somewhat more disciplined, and I don't have to pay too much attention to her as she sniffs her way through the furrows. This allows me plenty of time to fret over our plan. If even one thing goes wrong and we are caught, we will never have another chance.

As Nene and I prepare to hand over to the hogs, the alarm goes up. A plaintive wail carries from the village, spreading until it reaches the fields. We all know what it means, and take up the wail. Our leader is dead. As one, we collapse on the ground, sobbing and moaning our grief.

Above us, the crows circle, discomfited, and then fly off as one to alert their masters to this anomaly. Soon, the field is full of guards, dragging us to our feet.

"Our chief is dead!" we cry out. "Oh, our chief is dead! We must go and pay our respects! We must wash his body and pray to our gods! Our chief, our chief is dead!"

The commander himself leads the party of guards that escort the labourers back into the village. He pushes past the crowd of mourners, right to the centre of Togbe Mawutor's compound, where our ruler lies on a gold pagoda, his face ashen, his arms crossed over his chest, his body draped in our finest kente. He is not breathing. Kofi has done his part, using his supernatural wiles to give the impression of death.

"What a sad day for your people," the commander intones, his voice full of false sympathy even as his eyes glow with triumph.

Togbe Mawutor's son, Kosi, steps forward. He will become the next chief. Or would, were his father truly dead. "Please, Commander, we cannot return to work until we have completed the First Rites. All our people must attend."

The commander frowns. "Our festivities begin at sundown. You all know this. We begin with the feast – your people must be there to prepare the food."

"We will finish with the Rites by late afternoon, and then the labourers can go and prepare the food for the feast," Kosi says. "Perhaps, in your generosity, you can proceed with the rest of your programme and end with the feast? We would be in your debt."

The commander likes the sound of that. He announces, as though the idea were his in the first place, "This is what I will do. In honour of this tragedy, I will give you the morning and afternoon to grieve, even though it is a sacred day for my own people. You will return to work promptly at five p.m. We will begin our festivities at sundown, with the prayers and speeches and sharing of sikami, and as soon as the food is ready, you will bring it out so the feast may begin."

"You are most generous, Commander." Kofi bows low.

Satisfied, the commander leaves, taking his guards with him, and we continue to wail and tear at our clothes in feigned grief. Crows fly overhead, watching us, and so we go through the motions, performing all the Rites as custom demands for our 'dead' ruler.

Come late afternoon, Tobge Mawutor is laid in state inside his home, where he will soon wake, and we return to work. We have only two hours before sundown, so we work the fields as quickly as we can, while our people in the kitchen do their part. There are no guards in the kitchen, for the Crows don't care if we swipe a few shallots or a basket of fish. Food holds no real value for them beyond basic sustenance and ceremonial purposes.

When dusk falls, I lead Nene back to her pen with the other piglets and hogs and then help clean and refill the troughs for the evening. As we march back into the village, we hear music and laughter wafting from the commander's yard. The festivities have begun. The crows fly over the yard, diving to the ground every so often to snatch up a piece of food.

Mama, Papa and I, as well as many others, take our evening meal outside. The crows aren't watching us tonight, preoccupied with hovering around their masters and partaking in their revelry. We are the ones watching and listening from the valley, our eyes focused on the lights and sounds coming from the commander's yard on the hill.

"What if it doesn't work?" Mama whispers.

"It will," Papa whispers back.

A few minutes later, a pair of crows fly overhead, coming from the commander's yard. Their movements are jerky and erratic, their wings fluttering madly. One drops into the fields. The other makes it closer to the village before dropping to the ground near the boundary. We are on our feet in seconds, running to see.

A small girl reaches the fallen crow first. She emerges from the bushes, holding something high above her head, face flushed with glee. It is a large yam covered in black feathers. Before our eyes the feathers disappear, and there is no crow left. Only a yam, thick and brown and hardy.

Is that what I looked like during my transformation, I wonder? Half person, half yam? I shudder at the thought.

"It is time," says Kofi, the mage.

We make our way to the commander's yard. The path is littered with yams; some shattered to pieces upon impact when they fell from the sky. When we reach the yard, we find more yams. Small ones, large ones, of varying shapes. Some have many knobbly bits, some smooth and shapely. Yams on the floor, yams in chairs, yams under the table. Yams in puddles of wine, yams among bits of shattered glass and fragments of clay bowls. Yams upon yams upon yams.

We stare at them for a moment. I can scarcely believe it. These are people. *Were* people. *Are*…people? If it is as Kofi said, they are not people anymore. They are yams, and yams don't have thoughts. Yams don't feel. Yams are starchy dead things, good for boiling and roasting and frying. But if we linger, they will become people again, and it might not be so easy to do what must be done.

So I bend down to pick up one, and then another. Slowly, we all remember the task at hand and gather up the occupiers, as many as we can carry. We take them down to the river, where our fisherfolk have set aside a boat, and we pile them up inside. Every last one. Because we can't afford to miss anyone, we take every yam from the commander's compound, including the ones stacked in the kitchen. We don't know which is truly a yam and which might be a human guard or a crow sentry. We search all the houses and take any yams we find there, as well. We take the yams that dropped onto roofs and landed in the middle of the roads. Any yam that seems out of place. Just in case. Just in case.

And when the boat is full at last, we light a fire atop the pile of yams, and set the boat adrift on the water.

They are not people. They are yams. Only yams. I tell myself this over and over, but somehow, the smell of burning flesh still assails my nostrils, and when the boat sinks below the water's surface, something in me sighs.

Mama takes my hand. "This is the price of freedom," she says.

I look up into the starry sky. "The Crow gods are watching, Mama."

"Good," she says. "Let them watch. Maybe now they will teach their children not to take what doesn't belong to them."

When the last trace of the boat is gone, we return to our village. Togbe Mawutor is stirring, and we must deliver the good news. Boar Country is no longer occupied. Our people are free.

* * *

We were born under the Occupation. We have never known the taste of sikami. But now we will discover our birthright.

We are gathered in Togbe Mawutor's compound, sitting in a circle around a giant pot of sikami. My mouth is already watering. The elders, the old women of the caste who carry the old ways with them, and who were already old when sikami was stolen, have taken charge of today's ceremony. The first tasting in decades.

They told us to fast for two days. My stomach is rancid with hunger, spots dancing before my eyes as they call me forth to be the first to taste.

"Because your courage is the reason we are free," the eldest of the matriarchs tells me, patting the stool in front of the pot. She squats beside it, one hand on the handle of the ladle inside the pot.

"Are you ready?"

"Yes, Grandmother." I am not. How could I be? I don't even know what to expect.

She dips the ladle into the oil and scoops up a small portion. It runs golden-red down the side of the ladle, dripping into the pot. "Take some. Not too much. Just enough to coat the fingertip."

I recall my parents' words: *You'll know it when you taste it. There is no taste like it in the world.* I dip my forefinger into the ladle and look at the scarlet liquid gleaming on my fingertip. I have never seen anything so vibrant, so beautiful.

"Open your mouth, close your eyes, and put it on the tip of your tongue."

I close my eyes, heart racing, and raise my finger. The scent alone is enough to make my thoughts spin in circles. A wave of dizziness sweeps over me, making my breath come in short bursts.

"Slowly, Edem. That's it. Slowly. Brace yourself. The first taste can be overpowering."

But how will it taste? How exactly?

My finger touches my tongue and the world explodes with light and colour, shapes dancing before my closed eyes, taking one form and then another. The shapes don't just dance. They sing, like human voices, like early morning birdsong, like the squeal of piglets at play.

"What do you see?" the matriarch asks me.

I see…a beach of pale, wet sand, boars playing on it. A mountain of sikaroot, hard and shiny in the sun. A group of children with sikami-stained lips and teeth, fingers dripping. In the distance, rows and rows of fishing boats in the water. And then I lift my gaze to the sky. Blue. Boundless. Nothing but sky and more sky and a whisper of clouds. No birds. No danger. Not a single Crow to be seen.

I start to laugh as tears spill from my eyes. "I see the future!"

"And how does it look? How exactly?" Her fingers close over my arm. I can hear the tears in her voice. I open my eyes, letting the vision fade without regret because I know I will soon see it again.

The matriarch takes my hand and presses it to her damp cheek. I brush her tears with my fingers, grateful and honoured to be able to give her the message she has longed to receive.

"Like riches, Grandmother. Like freedom."

Empathy

THEY FOUND another one in the night. Young, even younger than Aten. They say she hung herself with trapwire, too tight, and it sliced her throat.

I lie awake in the dark and try not to think of her body hanging from the rafters, of her terrified soul trying to untether itself from her body, of the loved ones she left behind.

That makes twelve deaths now. Twelve suicides.

"Ma?"

I turn to my son. "You're supposed to be sleeping."

"Are you thinking about her?"

I hold my breath, willing time to stop. If only it could be night forever. If only I could keep us in this moment, stillness and frayed reed fibres scratching my skin. My resolve wanes. I take in air, and time moves on.

"Go to sleep, Aten."

"I don't want you to worry." His voice is soft, sweet.

Even at sixteen, he sounds like a child. "She's free now. She's safe."

"I know. Go to sleep."

He turns over on the mat.

It frightens me when he talks like that. I worry that someone is listening despite the lining on the cottage walls, and they are collecting and sorting data streams, picking Aten's voice out of the chaos. I worry that one day the People will decide to care that twelve Servicers are dead, that they will come to the village. Knocking. Seeking. And there will be nowhere to hide.

* * *

Days pass without incident. No one comes for us. No one else dies. There are the usual glances when Aten and I walk through the village, the usual murmuring, but apart from respectful greetings, no one speaks to us. No one ever does.

The few Servicers who can afford it wear partial armour. Sleek metal gloves that reach the elbows, silver masks with flashing blue eyes and sculpted chest plates. Most Servicers are unarmoured, dressed in ragged hand-me-downs, but they have dusted their skin with silver, faces highlighted and contoured to give the illusion of flawless metal planes.

I try not to judge, but their longing to be like the People galls me.

"Stay close," I tell Aten.

"Yes, Ma."

My list of errands is short. Cash in my pension chips, pick up some food, pass by the club to get Aten's medicine. The price will have gone up, but I'm prepared to negotiate. The bag slung over my shoulder contains the last of the treasures I brought from the nursery. I clutch the bag close, wary of pickpockets.

"We have to go through the market, or I won't make it to the club in time. Take my hand, Aten. You know how those crowds can be." I stretch my hand out, waiting to feel my son's fingers close around mine. Nothing. "Aten?"

I turn around. There's no one behind me.

* * *

The club is rank with sweat and a faint rusty scent. Music pulses from the lower floors, a mindless, repetitive beat designed to disguise the data traffic. A hologram of a feminine Person stands beside the dark staircase. Tall, lithe, everything about her smooth and practical. Beautiful, but no match for the real thing.

"Be like the People," she says. "Experience true sentience."

She flickers and then repeats the words. I look away as a patron enters, an older Servicer in a battered chest plate. He shoves money at the guard, spares a longing glance for the hologram and disappears down the staircase to experience true sentience.

The guard directs me to a seat in a dark corner. I look down at the grimy stool and remain standing. A moment later, a side door opens, and Zeinab steps out. She's in full armour beneath her white tunic, chrome gleaming. I've never seen armour so well-crafted, so effective. It can't be legal.

"Do you like it?" She does a little spin, and her chrome lips curl in a smug smile. "Brand new technology that mimics the real thing." She makes a face, showing off the way the metal moves over her cheeks as though it's part of her rather than an obscenely expensive costume. "Off-planet, of course."

"Of course. I hope you have somewhere to hide it when the raids come."

She laughs. "Are you worried about me, Old Mother?"

I wince. No one calls me that anymore. "I'm worried about my order. Do you have it?"

Zeinab reaches into her pocket and takes out a small bottle. "Seventy."

"That's twice what I paid before."

Her shoulders lift in a delicate shrug. "Cost of living, I'm afraid. Where's the boy, anyway?"

Ignoring the question, I open my bag. "This is worth at least seventy, maybe seventy-five." I hand her the trinket, a flower on a chain.

She gasps. "Is this from your old life?"

"Will you take it or not?"

She pockets it with haste. "You can't protect him forever. They'll find him."

"Are you saying your medicine doesn't work?"

"I'm saying it can only hide so much. Your boy is growing. The thing inside him grows, too." She cocks her head to one side, studying me. I'm unnerved by the uncanny accuracy of her false face. "There is only one fate for him. You know it. If you don't have the stomach, there are options. Better you than them."

I know all about the *options*: cloaked figures, sleight of hand, my boy bleeding in the middle of the market. Fire surges inside me. I swallow it before it leaks into my fingers and wraps them around that slender silver neck.

I snatch the bottle and leave, Zeinab's words working a hole in my thoughts. The world outside is bright, and it takes me a moment to adjust. I hoped Aten would have come to meet me by now, but there's no sign of him.

Fear forms knots inside me. One day, Aten will grow beyond his medicine, but for now, he is safe, as long as he doesn't stray too far.

I walk for a bit, hoping to spot him, then return to the cottage to wait.

* * *

He comes home after dark. Calm, happy. Like the other times. My heart sinks.

"Where did you go, Aten?"

"Don't worry."

"Don't tell me not to worry! Where did you go?"

He doesn't answer. He kisses my cheek and eats his supper like a good boy, then rubs my aching feet for me before going to the well to fetch water. He falls asleep with a smile, and I lie awake, knowing that I will hear the news in the morning. Another suicide.

I was pregnant when I left the nursery. It was too early for the tests to catch, but I knew, even as I signed the retirement forms, as I ate cake during the grand farewell, as I walked among the cots to see my children for the last time. Fifty babies I'd birthed in my time there. Fifty perfect hybrids, flesh and blood and circuitry. Bridgers, they called them. I was Old Mother all those years, the first of the surrogates. The People were so pleased with my work. So proud. They sent me off in glory with a pension no other Servicer could ever hope to earn, and I was Old Mother no more.

Coming home to the village, I had my son in solitude, far from their eyes and ears. I gave him a father, a Servicer who would say anything for a pocket full of chips and a gallon of beer. Aten was born, fully Servicer. Fully mine. Or so I told everyone because I knew how far Servicers would go to win favour with the People.

But I'm not sure they believed me. We are treated as guests here, respected but not befriended. Maybe I was wrong to bring Bridgers into the world, one more being we can't compete with. On days like this, when my boy comes home late, smiling that smile, I wonder. He feels too much. It will be his undoing.

Sleep eludes me. Zeinab's words come back to me in the lean hours of darkness. There is only one fate for him. I crawl to the mat in the corner and shake Aten awake.

"What's wrong, Ma?" Sleep slurs his words.

"Tell me."

"What?"

"Tell me what happens when you wander. Where you go, who you see. What you do." I sit back on my haunches, afraid, yet needing to know. "Tell me everything."

Aten hesitates. "I don't want you to worry."

"I will never stop worrying."

His eyes are bright in the dark. He seems fine, red blood in his veins, circuits silenced by the drug. The lights that used to dance along his temple have faded. Dormant, for now.

"They talk to me," he whispers.

"Who? Those who…hurt?"

He shakes his head. "The colours in their heads. All kinds of colours, Ma. Those who hurt have more colours than everyone else. Too many. They spill."

Fear starts an ache in my chest. "What do you mean?"

Aten sits up. "Like a cup with too much water. I'm the only one who sees them, so I go to help. To empty them. So there's space, you see?"

I swallow. "So, you go to those who have too many colours and you…talk to them?"

"Yes."

"What do you say?"

He looks at me. "I don't think I should tell you."

And I know then. I have always known, underneath. He is mine, after all. I know every line on his palm, every hidden wire. Tears come to my eyes. I blink them back. "Tell me."

He shakes his head. "You're not going to like it. You'll send me away."

I pull him against me. "Silly child. I would never do that. It will be fine, I promise."

A lie. As I hold him close, the fear spreads. Fear of what Zeinab calls the thing inside the child I stole from the People. Fear of the part of him that is me and the part that is them, and the mysterious ways in which the two intersect.

"I talk to the colours, not the ones who hurt," he says into my shoulder. "The ones who hurt sit and listen, but they don't understand. The colours do. When I talk, they stop spilling. They go back inside. I think they must go deep because it takes a while, and then there is space inside the ones who hurt. A big emptiness. And then they go away and I come home."

"That's all?" It doesn't seem so bad. Mad and strange, but not bad.

"When the colours go down, they move things around inside the ones who hurt," says Aten. "To make the big emptiness. And the ones who hurt, sometimes they hurt more. So, I tell them how to make it stop."

I'm frozen in place now, my arms still wrapped around him.

He sighs. "Don't be angry, Ma. It's for their own good. If you could see the colours, you would understand. It would be cruel to leave them like that."

"How do they make it stop?"

The silence lasts so long that I think he means not to answer. And then he says, as if it's the simplest thing in the world, "They die."

I squeeze my eyes shut. They die. They die. I open my eyes again and hold him at arm's length. "Did another die tonight?"

He nods. My boy. My special boy, the killer. The thought makes my body shudder.

"You must stop this. Do you hear me? Next time the colours talk, you must ignore them."

"But—"

"Aten! You must stop."

He is silent. Listening. Mine were small words, ordinary, far too small for the circumstances, but what else can I say? What can I do? How can I explain to him that telling others how to die is not compassion? How do I know I'm right?

"It was different today," he says, lying down once more. "Fewer colours, mostly silver and gold. A pretty gold, like the sun."

The fear returns with claws. "Who was it? A child? Someone from the village?"

"No," he replies, already half asleep. "It was one of the People."

* * *

I pack the little we have in my bag, shoving things in, terror making my movements jerky and haphazard.

"But this is home," Aten protests.

"They will come for you. Don't you understand? Put your shoes on. Quickly!"

"They don't see me. You said."

"That was before you killed one of them."

"I didn't kill him. He killed himself."

"Shoes, Aten!"

"I didn't do anything wrong. I was helping. He was broken and I fixed him."

"The People don't break like Servicers. Remove an arm and they make another. They're nothing like us."

"If they were nothing like us, they wouldn't have colours."

166

He's still sitting on the mat, barefoot. His features are stony, resolute. I don't have the time to coax him. My only thought is to get him out of here before they find us.

I take a deep breath. "If you don't get up, they will find you and throw you on the pyre. You're no longer one of their precious hybrid young. You've been tainted by the stench of Servicers. You are just meat to them, meat they will burn until nothing is left but ashes."

He rises, eyes wide with fear, and puts on his shoes. When I take his hand, it's trembling.

* * *

We make it as far as the edge of the village before their hovercraft finds us, loudspeaker blaring threats. There's no point in running, so we stop. I have one thing left to bargain with. I push back my headscarf so they can see my face in the headlights. The engine goes quiet. The craft opens, ejecting four officers.

"Forgive us, Former Old Mother, we didn't recognise you," one of the officers says. His voice is muffled by a black mask. "I'm afraid the boy is a murderer. I'm sure he told you some tale to convince you to help him, but his words are false. Please step aside so we may take him in."

I place myself between the officers and Aten. "He's just a child. Let me plead his case. If the People want blood, they can have mine."

"The People don't want your blood. You are an honoured servant. Please step aside."

All four officers wear masks as if to protect them from the rampant disease in the village. But the People are immune to illness.

"You didn't introduce yourself," I remind the officer.

"Apologies. I am Captain R67, leader of the First Regiment."

"Are you of the People?"

"My entire regiment consists of Bridgers."

My stomach clenches.

"It will make you proud to know that all of your brood survived," he goes on. "We are strong, loyal soldiers."

My children have come hunting their brother, asking me to step aside so they can kill him. Proud, indeed. "Take me instead," I tell them. "Leave the boy."

But Aten, who always wanders when I tell him not to, has already slipped away. By the time I turn around, he stands beside the hovercraft, one of the Bridgers slapping cuffs on his wrists.

"No! Aten!"

He looks at me. Smiles. "My colours are starting to spill, Ma."

I step forward. "No!"

Powerful arms pull me back. Yes, my babies have grown strong. And loyal. Who could forget *loyal*?

"No! Don't touch my boy! I said don't touch him!"

My shouting has no effect. The Bridgers know I'm their mother, but it means nothing. They're not like Aten. He's mine. He's mine, and they're taking him, and I can't let them. I scream and claw at the officers as they carry him into the hovercraft. They push me aside, once, twice, harder, until I topple over in the dust and watch them speed away. I run after the craft, even when all I see of the vehicle is a light in the distance. I run until I reach the city gates, then collapse on the ground and bang against the iron doors, calling for my boy.

I don't know how long I'm there. Someone comes for me, lifts me up, takes me away. Darkness closes over me.

When I open my eyes, I'm back in the village, in a chair in the courtyard behind the club. It's daylight, and when I glance toward the city I see a column of thick black smoke curling into the sky. The pyre. I struggle to get up, then realise I've been bound to the chair.

"For your own good," a languid voice says.

I turn to see Zeinab standing behind me. Only partial armour this time, a sleek exoskeleton that exposes her angular face and jutting collarbone. I shout something incoherent, my tongue refusing to co-operate. I need to find my boy. I need to…

"He's gone," she says. "They put him on the pyre at dawn. It's been hours now. I had to give you something to calm you. He's gone." She looks at me with eyes full of pity. "I told you, Old Mother. Better you than them. You should have listened."

I stare at the smoke, too broken to do anything other than sob. Was she right? Would it have been better? A quiet injection in his sleep, painless, swift, rather than the torment of the pyre? I don't know whether I could have done it, even to spare him.

The smoke begins to clear and as I watch, I can almost see the colours Aten spoke of. Gold and silver, but blue and red and violet, too. Colours for all the parts of him, the parts I let flourish and the parts that had to be hidden. They are free now, those hybrid lights, to blink and glow at will.

I can almost hear him whisper.

"Do you see the colours, Ma?"

I see them, Aten. Blurry through my tears, but I see them.

"Aren't they beautiful?"

Yes. Yes, they are.

"I don't want you to worry, Ma."

I will always worry.

"I'm free now. I'm safe."

I know. Go to sleep.

I almost see him turn over on his mat, breathing slow and steady.

Easing In

SITTING ON the organorug with her 1Device in her lap, Fafa frowned at the notification on the screen. She longed to click IGNORE, but her daughter Estelle was watching.

"Mummy, it's a free medical upgrade. Why the hesitation, now?"

Well, because the notification opened with the words: "Ghana Wellbeing Bureau wants you to live forever". The thought made Fafa's skin crawl. What was the quest for immortality, if not a kind of madness?

The implant injected into her body along with the usual battery of childhood vaccines, plus the medical facilities that had become accessible when she had moved into Asante City, ensured that she would live a long, healthy life, barring some unforeseen anomaly.

Oh, wait – there would be no unforeseen anomaly. The implant would catch any issues and nip them in the bud. It had already informed her of the potential impact of excess sugar intake, extrapolated from the single piece of chocolate she'd had last week. It was a party, for goodness' sake. What was the point of going if one couldn't indulge?

But Fafa could feel her daughter's eyes boring into her, so she accepted the invitation to her next scheduled update. Her stomach started to twist into a knot.

"Healthcare is supposed to be a right, not a compulsion," she muttered.

"That attitude is exactly why you need to stay in group therapy," her daughter told her. Curled up in an armchair in the tiny flat, Estelle peered at her mother over the rim of her mug and kissed her teeth.

Fafa's bare feet kneaded the organorug, toes plunging deep into the spongy fibres. The rug grew right out of the mycelium floor at a rate of two centimetres a month and it had been ages since the last trim.

"They're trying to make us more malleable." Fafa heaved a weary sigh. "They'll never admit it, but that's exactly what they're doing."

"Conspiracy theories! OK. Well, all I'm trying to do is protect your health. Forgive me for being a good daughter, eh?"

There was no point in arguing with Estelle. If Fafa wasn't careful, her daughter would start harping on about all the sacrifices she had made to move to Asante City with her. Fafa would have preferred to live on her own, but Estelle was not the type of person you said no to.

"You know, I think you forget what I went through, joining you in this place."

Dear God. Fafa lay back on the organorug, letting its earthy scent wash over her.

"You can't imagine what it was like. I tossed and turned every night…"

Tossed and turned, indeed! She had her every need catered for.

Fafa had always been able to support her daughter on her own until Estelle turned seven and realised that she had that mysterious quality people referred to as 'star power'. She had demanded to be allowed to explore her talents as a performer. Once it became clear that her only true talent was attracting stares, she had given up the performing arts to become an influencer.

Fafa had no say in the matter. Estelle was less a child than an epidemic, sweeping through the world and taking no prisoners. She was not charming nor personable, but she possessed a remarkable ability to command attention, like a terrible accident people couldn't look away from. She amassed victims – sorry, followers – like a fiend. Fafa found herself facing a level of scrutiny she couldn't fathom, let alone manage. Fortunately, Estelle managed it well enough for both of them.

"…but I knew that coming to Asante City was what you needed, you see, because Papa came to me in a dream and said…"

Fafa rolled her eyes. She should have gone for a walk after work as usual, but she'd been feeling a little drained. She worked from home, designing historically accurate African costumes for computer games, movies and VR nerds. It was a great job; she hardly had to talk to anyone. Except Estelle, of course.

As a student, the girl was often home. What she studied, exactly, was unclear. A month ago, it had been Metasphere Dynamics Theory. A year ago, Community Psychology. A week ago, Estelle had set up "spore collection pockets" all over the house, claiming to be starting a course in mycelial production. Fafa had stopped asking.

If only Estelle would stop talking.

"…and if you would only take my advice, you would realise…"

Another notification chimed, telling Fafa it was time to leave for her meeting. She got to her feet, almost grateful for the excuse to leave.

* * *

The Easing In Gently Support Group met once a week in the community centre on the fifty-second floor, between the church and the mosque. Like everything else in Asante City, the support group was the collective brainchild of the City's residents, formed by consensus. The consensus of the well-meaning and well-adjusted, of course. The maladjusted, like Fafa, had voted against the group's formation.

Fafa opposed forcing people to pretend to be something they were not. She was also opposed to the informal policy of serving pineapple juice and atsoomo hard enough to crack a tooth at *every single meeting*.

Nevertheless, she made her way from her Level 4 flat to Level 52, trying to arrange her resting bitch face into some semblance of neighbourliness as she ignored the other passengers in the lift. She experienced a pang of longing when the clear lift doors slid past the stadium, and then the park, and then the promenade. All places she would much rather have been going to.

Asante City was the first vertical city in Ghana, a single building constructed as a sustainable living pilot project, entirely powered by solar and mycelial energy. It was the biggest and most expensive partnership in Ghana's history, driven by civil society and funded by the government. The knowledge that its failure would be catastrophic had been incentive enough for all 500,000 residents to develop and then comply with the strict regulations governing their stay. Thanks to unprecedented levels of community collaboration, the project had succeeded so far, apart from a few teething problems in the early years.

There were seventy-two levels, including the two underground floors that housed the Mycelium Management Department and the train station. Residents were not permitted to own cars – there was little reason to leave, anyway, when all their needs were catered for within the building – and shared the train system with the rest of the region. Each unit was the collective property of the residents rather than the tenant, as were the gardens that fed them and the materials used to make their clothes. There was no need for money, as all residents were allocated supplies and services according to their needs, so work was done for the greater good and personal fulfilment rather than compensation. Scrupulous records were kept and audited by the entire City to prevent mismanagement or favouritism.

The skyscraper had been rooted into the mycelial network of the area. It was as much a giant tree as a giant building, a feat of bio-architecture modelled on the eco-high-rises of Singapore and the Treehouse Project in South Africa. The maintenance team included botanists, microbiologists, engineers and sociologists.

Fafa and Estelle had moved in when Estelle turned seventeen – to escape the media glare, Estelle liked to tell people, though her novelty had long worn off by then. If anything, Fafa suspected that her daughter had joined Asante City to escape the *lack* of media glare, which hurt her pride more than she'd ever admit. There was enough buzz around the Asante project to tide Estelle over for a while.

Every time the lift doors opened to let people out, Fafa felt a stab of envy. *There go seven people who don't have to attend a stupid support group*, she thought bitterly. *There go thirty or so people who don't have to attend a stupid support group. There goes one person – why is only one person getting off on this level? So weird. Anyway, there go fifteen people…*

The passengers were happy, or at least they seemed to be. They chatted and smiled and laughed, their wellbeing stirring up an envious fury inside her. By the time the lift reached Level 52, Fafa had worked herself into a foul mood. Arriving at the community centre just in time to watch Nana-Yaa, the refreshment supervisor, set out a tray of atsoomo, didn't help at all.

Everyone was present. No one ever missed a meeting – apart from the fact that attendance was strongly encouraged, most of the members actually seemed to enjoy it. Appiah was a supposedly reformed terrorist; Salima and Sayid, general misanthropes and Nana-Yaa, the proverbial doormat. Shanaz had a habit of planting herbs on her windowsill, tending to them with painstaking devotion and then digging them up so she could watch them die. Several fines and a brief stint in a reform facility had helped, but Appiah and Shanaz still seemed to struggle with Asante City's strict 'do least harm' policy, which applied to all life forms.

"How is everyone doing this evening?" Quarshie, the support group guide, looked around the room. Short and heavyset, they had a penchant for oversized kente smocks worn over skinny jeans.

"I had a hard week," Sayid spoke up.

A groan went up. Every week was 'hard' for Sayid. He and Estelle would get along famously, swapping embellished sob stories over a glass of wine.

"Are you sure?" Quarshie asked, in their typical no-nonsense fashion. "Have you been taking time to think about how fortunate we all are, like we discussed at our last session?"

"Yes, but my wife changed all the settings on our 1Device again." Sayid looked distraught.

Quarshie sighed. "Did you hear about the child who fell from a balcony on Level 12 and almost died?"

Sayid blinked. "I would have been able to hear about it if my wife hadn't changed all the settings."

Quarshie was silent for a moment, debating the best way to respond. Sayid had once been misdiagnosed as a sociopath. Fafa had found that fact fascinating for about five minutes – a brief conversation with the man was enough to tell her that real-life almost-sociopaths weren't nearly as interesting as the ones in popular literature.

She sympathised with Quarshie. After all, things in Ghana were better than they had ever been. The last round of devastating floods had inspired vociferous activism and drastic policy changes; the economy was stable for the first time in generations; Ghana Wellbeing Bureau's health drive had provided medical implants to the whole population; and Asante City was proof that a sustainable way of life could be achieved long-term.

The City provided safe accommodation, healthcare, education, food, and recreation. All that was required in exchange was full participation in the community – in the form of regular voting on issues of communal concern and a few hours of weekly work in the farms, community centres, shops, waste reclamation services, schools or clinics. It was a sort of paradise, really. Residents were allowed to take on old-form work if they chose to, provided it didn't interfere with their Asante duties; however, the work-for-money model was slowly being phased out across the country in favour of a work-for-barter system.

Despite these changes, here was a group of six people who seemed allergic to happiness. Their existence hadn't bothered anyone for years – frankly, everyone else was too busy to mind them – but a recent Ghana Wellbeing Bureau report on citizen satisfaction had implied that Asante City could not truly be called a success if even the smallest minority of residents were unhappy.

And so, the community voted on the best way to help the maladjusted integrate fully into the Asante City community. The support group was formed and Quarshie assigned to lead it. As far as Fafa was concerned, the sort of integration GWB was after was impossible, but one had to admire the guide's perseverance.

Giving up on Sayid, Quarshie smiled at the rest of the group. "Everyone else? Appiah? Any more intrusive thoughts?"

Appiah shifted in his chair. He wore his dreadlocks so long he was practically sitting on them. He had a perpetual look of panic in his eyes, like a cornered grasscutter.

"I had one just now, in the lift," he said. "There was a woman there with a long neck. Graceful, kind of. And fragile. And while I was looking at it, I saw myself putting my hands around it and squeezing—" He grimaced. "I did the breathing thing, like you taught us. And I said sorry to her when I was getting out."

Quarshie leaned forward, nodding. "Hmm. OK. Appiah, remember what we talked about before, eh? We don't want to go telling people about these thoughts. I don't think that poor lady needs to know that you imagined strangling her."

Quarshie glanced around the room once more until their gaze came to rest on Fafa. "Fafa? Anything new?"

Fafa shrugged.

"Are you in a better mood today?"

Fafa shrugged.

"Have you done any of the introspective exercises we talked about?"

Fafa hesitated for a moment, then shrugged. It was her go-to response, a sort of amalgamation of yes, no and everything in between. It seemed the simplest way to express her discomfort at being spoken to at all.

Quarshie looked at her, clearly struggling to maintain their composure. The support group members had a bet going about how long their beleaguered guide could last. It had been three months since their first meeting. Fafa had Quarshie cracking after a year. No one could put up with this lot longer than that.

"You know what?" Quarshie plastered a smile on their face. "Maybe we should start with refreshments today."

Everyone except Fafa was pleased with that arrangement, and they made their way to the refreshments table. Nana-Yaa, a chronic people-pleaser, kept asking whether the food was fine. The group, wary of evoking a panic attack, assured her that it was, even as they were forced to suck on the atsoomo to soften them before daring to sink their teeth into the biscuit-like treats.

"OK," Quarshie said, dusting crumbs off their fingers, "let's get back to—"

The centre was plunged into sudden, disconcerting darkness, followed by the unmistakable sound of the community centre's main doors locking. For a moment, the group was too stunned to respond. Power cuts and load shedding were as foreign to Asante City as highways and landfills. The light was provided by bioluminescent fungi in the ceiling – there couldn't be a power cut, not in the typical sense. As for the locking of the doors, well, that was another matter altogether.

Someone whimpered, opening the floodgates for raised, panicked voices to fill the space.

"How is this possible?"

"Well, the ceiling's alive, so maybe it's sick."

"I'm more worried about being locked in!"

"God help us! Did you say *sick*?"

"Or someone poisoned it..."

"Someone like who?"

"If this ceiling is sick, the whole building will be sick within hours!"

"Hello? Didn't anyone hear me say *locked in*?"

"Everyone, remain calm!" said Quarshie, in a tone that was not calm at all.

"I knew this would happen," a voice muttered near Fafa. It was Appiah.

* * *

Appiah wasn't a monster. While he had done monstrous things in the distant, colourful past, he had also done his penance (seven years in reform – twice as long as his criminal career). He was now a respectable and productive member of society, with an honest job growing giant mushrooms in a lab on Sub-level B.

He was old. Not old-old, at only 63, but old like petrol and Netflix, like MSG and plastic bottles. He wasn't quite sold on this fair, new world. He still believed, in a quiet place he'd never tell anyone about, that life could only be difficult, messy, and inconvenient. For every other species, survival was a daily struggle. Predators on all sides, starvation never too far behind, babies that must toughen up fast or never make it to adulthood. Why should it be different for humans? Because they were self-aware? Ah, but that very self-awareness was the problem, the Achilles heel of the species! It was bad enough that death was inevitable. Knowing it was inevitable could only drive you mad.

This fair new world, all kind and shiny, relied on humans to be sane and sensible. But Appiah knew that human beings were insane and self-destructive. Putting a dog in a sweater and a pretty kennel did not change its bite. He had joined Asante City because his family had insisted on it, hoping it would calm him down. He had agreed out of sheer curiosity, certain that a place like this could never work. In Finland, maybe, or Narnia, but not in Ghana. Asante City was doomed to fall apart.

It would begin, apparently, with power cuts.

"There's no need to panic," said Quarshie. After a few seconds of fumbling, a beam of light appeared. Quarshie held up their 1Device, torch on, bathing the room in garish fluorescence. "There! See? Nothing to worry about." They set the device down on the table beside the now abandoned refreshments. "I'm sure it's a minor issue that will soon be fixed."

Appiah let out a sceptical scoff. All eyes turned to him.

"Oh my God," said Shanaz. "He knows it won't be fixed...because he's the one that caused it!"

Quarshie sighed. "I don't think it's helpful to start—"

"Isn't he a terrorist?"

"*Reformed* terrorist."

"Allegedly."

"How very convenient."

"A reformed terrorist who just happens to work for Mycelium Management."

"Which means he has access to the entire mycelial network..."

"Oh my *God*!"

Appiah would have been offended if he'd had the slightest interest in the opinions of these people. He only attended the meetings because Asante City's populace strongly recommended it (a polite way of saying he could be voted out of the residence if he refused). The truth was that, if he'd wanted to, he could have crippled Asante City's water or poisoned the air. But ending the world wasn't his job anymore. Fate would take care of that, so he just folded his arms and looked around.

The only person who had made no comment was Fafa. She was dressed strangely, as usual. All residents in Asante City had biodegradable neocellulose clothes printed at one of the building's many boutiques, yet somehow, Fafa managed to look like she had patched her outfits together from pieces scavenged from her neighbours' compost. The jacket she wore now – one of her favourites, judging by the number of times he'd seen her in it – was a mosaic of coconut fibre kente, algae leather, raffia fringe and some spongy material he couldn't identify.

"We should turn him in before he kills us all!"

"Call Security!"

"I'm trying, but the network is off!"

"My people, please!" poor Quarshie pleaded. "Calm down!"

Appiah caught Fafa's gaze, trying to gauge her reaction to the furore. She blinked and said nothing.

A low hum sounded, alerting the residents to an imminent announcement from Maintenance.

"Dear residents…" Everyone looked up at the sound of the intercom. "We apologise for the malfunction. The maintenance crew is working on it and it should be resolved soon. Please remain calm and proceed with your day in a serene and neighbourly manner. Thank you."

Appiah looked around the room at the faces of his peers, who didn't look the least bit serene or neighbourly.

"Let's play a game," Quarshie said in a slightly desperate voice. They ignored the groans of protest, raising their voice above the din. "You're going to pair up. Close your eyes, reach out, and the first person you touch becomes your partner. Each person in the pair gets to ask one question – any question you like – and the other person must answer it honestly. No dodging, you hear?"

"I don't like this game," Shanaz declared, folding her arms.

"It's not about what you like. Nothing in the manual seems to work with you guys, so I'm getting creative. Five minutes, and then you're going to switch partners. Ready?"

The torchlight went out, eliciting another round of whining.

"Don't be such babies!" said Quarshie. "I think the darkness brings out the honesty, don't you? See the way you all jumped to accuse Appiah?"

"He's a terrorist!"

"Reformed terrorist."

"Allegedly."

"Quiet! Ah, you people. Can you please pick your partners? I'm going to count down from ten. Ten. Nine…"

Appiah reached out. Almost instantly, he felt someone inch closer to him and take hold of his arm. He lowered his hand. There was a lot of shuffling and whispering and a few shocked gasps.

"Three. Two. One."

The torchlight came back on. Appiah turned to see Fafa beside him, her grip tight on his arm.

"Great!" said Quarshie. "One question each, five minutes. Begin."

The light went off again.

* * *

Fafa couldn't explain why she had gravitated toward Appiah. In a moment of panic, he had seemed like the safest option. Whatever that meant. She looked at him now, blinking.

"Would you like to go first?" he asked.

She shook her head, then remembered that he couldn't see her. "No."

"OK. Why don't you participate in our meetings?"

Fafa realised she was still holding his arm. Releasing it, she fished for the most diplomatic answer. "I'm a quiet person."

"Quarshie said we had to be honest. No dodging, remember?"

She sighed. "I don't want to be here and don't think it's fair that I'm forced to come. Refusing to talk is my way of resisting. Most people talk a lot without really saying anything, anyway. And no one listens, so I don't see the point."

"I'm listening."

"Because you have to."

"Ah. Good point. Your turn."

She didn't know what to ask. Something about his past, perhaps? But she didn't really care about his past. So she asked the very next thing that came to her: "Do you think Asante City works?"

His silence indicated surprise. Fafa felt a little thrill knowing that she had thrown him off balance.

He cleared his throat. "Eh, I mean, it works in many ways. Who knows what livelihoods we would have had or what habits we would have kept from our old lives if we were not here? So yes, it works. It makes things better."

"But?"

"I didn't say there was a but."

"No dodging, remember?"

"Fine." There was a long pause. When he spoke again, his voice was low. "But I used to blow things up to make a point and now I have intrusive, violent thoughts. What does that tell you?"

"That you've made progress? Thinking about violence is better than perpetrating it."

"Maybe. Or maybe the person I was is still there. Maybe the old world, the one we worked so hard to change, is also still there."

Now, that was interesting. Fafa considered his words. They made her feel strange. Sad, almost. "Do you really believe that people can't change? That *you* haven't changed?"

"I don't know. I guess time will tell."

"Time's up!" Quarshie called out. "Reach out and pick someone new."

* * *

As luck would have it, Shanaz was Appiah's next partner. He groaned inwardly when the light went on to reveal her manicured hand in his ashy, calloused one. She jerked her hand away as if she'd been stung. The light went off again.

"Did you sabotage the City?" Her voice was a fierce hiss. "Tell the truth!"

God, what a waste of a question. Appiah rolled his eyes in the darkness. "No. Did you miss the announcement from Maintenance?"

"Maybe you paid them to say that."

"Paid them with what? Nobody here has money!"

"I don't know. Your hidden terrorist stash."

"Stash? My friend, we slept in a condemned building for a year! It was in the news! Do you know anything about the world, or you just sit in your flat, killing herbs?"

"Is that your question?"

No, he already knew the answer to that. "Why do you do it? The plant-killing."

She was quiet for some time. "You know those war stories about mothers killing their children? They know what the soldiers will do if they find them, horrible things that no child should endure. So they smother the children in their beds to spare them the pain."

Appiah was stunned. He looked at the vague shadow in front of him, trying to make out her features in the dark. "There are no soldiers coming to hurt your herbs."

"I know. But you never know what things will become if you leave them alone. Better to pull them out and start over. It's always better to start over."

For the first time since meeting her, Appiah felt something other than disdain for Shanaz. "Do you want to ask me another question? The first one didn't count."

"Time's up!" Quarshie called out.

"Next time," said Shanaz.

* * *

"Is there something wrong with the 3D printers on your floor?" Nana-Yaa's question came out in a whisper.

Fafa frowned, confused. "No. Why?"

"Your clothes are so poorly made. What floor are you on? I can direct you to a better tailor; I know all the boutiques in the City."

Gritting her teeth in annoyance, Fafa said, "I make my own clothes."

"Oh!" A pause, and then, "Why?"

Fafa knew she should not take these remarks personally. She also knew, deep down, that her insistence on making her own clothes – with zero skill and a great deal of difficulty – was one of the many ways she stubbornly tried to assert her individuality in a world with no patience for that sort of thing. She was tired of Easing In Gently and following rules and walking on eggshells. Most of all, she was really, really tired of atsoomo. And so, Fafa blurted out, "Why do you bring the same disgusting snacks every time? Nobody likes them. They taste terrible!"

Nana-Yaa let out a strangled gasp. Fafa might have regretted her outburst, had Nana-Yaa not followed up her gasp with these words, "Liar! Everyone loves my snacks!"

Well, that sort of delusion was intolerable. "They only tell you that because they're scared you'll have a breakdown if they tell the truth. That time Sayid asked why you picked a red tray, you cried! Remember? Just bring fruits or something. Don't try so bloody hard."

The silence that followed was satisfying. And then disconcerting. And then alarming.

"Are you still breathing?" Fafa whispered.

Nana-Yaa sucked her teeth. "Of course."

"Oh." It wasn't a stupid question. Nana-Yaa could have gone into shock or something. "I didn't mean to offend you." A lie. Offending her had been the whole point.

"You're not nice," Nana-Yaa replied. "People don't like you."

The words didn't even sting. "I know."

"You could be nicer. It's not difficult. You're just too scared to try."

Now, those words *did* sting. A vague discomfort settled in Fafa's stomach.

"Anyway, you were right to tell me the truth." Nana-Yaa swallowed hard. "Thank you."

More silence. And then, just as Fafa was working her way up to asking some arbitrary question about Nana-Yaa's childhood, Nana-Yaa said:

"What about plantain chips? Everyone likes plantain chips, right?"

Fafa would have preferred a snack that didn't put her at risk of chipping a tooth, but this was progress. "Sure. Plantain chips would be great."

* * *

Quarshie was sneaky, Appiah realised. Even after everyone had gone round the whole group, the mentor kept calling for new pairs. And so Appiah got to learn that the last herb Shanaz had nurtured was coriander, that Sayid did love his wife, even if he wasn't great at showing it, that Fafa's daughter was an overbearing brat, that Nana-Yaa's parents used to lock her in a box when she did something wrong, and that Salima's worst fear was a violent death at the hands of someone she trusted.

They were just about to begin another round when the power came back on, bathing the room in a bright, bioluminescent glow. Appiah blinked, his eyes adjusting, and looked around at his fellows.

A smile spread over Quarshie's face, bigger than Appiah had seen in a while. "That wasn't so bad, was it?"

With soft murmurs, the Easing In Gently members agreed. Something stirred inside Appiah's chest, preventing him from easing his hand out of Salima's grip. He didn't like to think that it might be a welling-up of emotion, so he decided it was probably heartburn.

When it was time to leave, Sayid approached him. "I'm going to have a dinner party tomorrow night for my birthday. Can you come?"

It took Appiah a moment to process this. As far as he was aware, the group had never spent time together outside their mandated sessions. Salima and Shanaz had struck up a friendship but the others preferred to avoid each other. It seemed implausible that one session in the dark would be enough to change the status quo, and yet…

"Is everyone invited?" Appiah asked.

"Yes. Even Fafa said she'd come."

Appiah glanced in Fafa's direction. She stood at the refreshment table, draining a cup of water. He remembered the look of surprise on her face when the light had gone on to reveal that she was the one who had grabbed his arm as if the action had shocked her as much as him.

"I'll be there," he said.

* * *

When Fafa arrived home, Estelle was sitting on the floor with Fafa's 1Device, tuned in to one of her 'classes' and filming herself with her own 1Device at the same time. She claimed that her victims – sorry, followers – needed to know how she spent every minute of the day.

"Mummy!" Estelle tilted the camera to capture her mother. "Did you experience the power cut as well?"

"Yes."

"Louder, Mummy, so the people can hear you. Hmm! All the talk of effective eco-architecture and sustainable energy, and here we are, back to the old days of load shedding."

"You weren't even alive in those old days," Fafa reminded her. She took off her shoulder bag and dropped it on the nearest chair.

"And so? Don't I read history like everyone else? I tell you, we should complain. If this their bioluminescent mycelial thing doesn't work, I don't see the point of—"

"Don't you have anything constructive to say?" Fafa demanded.

Estelle's jaw dropped.

"Aren't you the one setting up spore pockets all over my house? Hmm? What are you learning? Is it not something to do with the mycelial network? Shouldn't you be coming up with solutions to improve the current system? Shouldn't you be doing *something* useful instead of preening on camera all day long?"

Estelle just sat there, mouth open in shock. Fafa was certain the girl had never been quiet for so long in her life.

"Did you cook, at least?" Fafa asked, making her way to the kitchen.

"I've been *studying*," Estelle protested. "Eh! My people, can you see the mood my mother is in today? Hmm! What happened at the support group? Were they more annoying than usual?"

"No." Fafa opened the fridge, sighed and closed it again. "No, today was good."

Estelle stared at her. "Did you say 'good'? Tell the people, Ma! What happened in that meeting?"

Fafa reached for a mango from the pile on the kitchen counter, polished it on her jacket and bit into it, moving towards the sitting room. She lowered herself to the organorug, ignoring the camera. "It was different today." She paused, trying to find the words to describe the shift that had taken place. "It was dark and people got nervous and mean, and then Quarshie made us play a game and everyone got...better."

Mango juice dripped from her fingers into the fibres of the organorug, where it was promptly absorbed and metabolised.

"So you don't want to quit anymore?" Estelle prodded.

"No. The others aren't so bad." Fafa thought of Appiah. Maybe they could talk some more at Sayid's birthday dinner.

"Heh? I am shocked!" Estelle poked her mother's arm. "You're no longer convinced that Asante City wants to make you more malleable?

Fafa looked at her daughter. "Wanting us to get along is not a bad thing. It's just...challenging. Human beings are all so different."

"Well, we have always been different."

"And it has always been challenging. We have different needs and sometimes the majority doesn't know best." Fafa finished the mango and dropped the pit on the organorug. The fibres closed around it. By tomorrow, it would be gone. "When I was a child, I couldn't throw mango pits on the carpet or make clothes out of biodegradable material. We drank water out of plastic sachets that choked our rivers. The ocean was filthy. We had all kinds of illnesses, our people were struggling to feed their families. We weren't even sure we would live to see our grandchildren. And now…" She waved an arm around the flat. "Look at all this! We have done well, I think."

Estelle was quiet for a moment, digesting this. "A child almost died today because of a maintenance error. We can do better, Mummy."

"Oh, we can always do better." Fafa nodded. "I can do better. If I'm always moody and resentful, how can I expect you to be different?"

"I never said you were moody and resentful," Estelle replied but her voice was soft, because she knew it was true.

Fafa kissed her daughter's cheek and got to her feet. "Enough chit-chat. Let me cook before it gets too late."

"No, it's fine." Estelle rose. "You just got home. I'll cook." And then, because it was a day full of surprises, she turned off the camera.

Fafa sat with her legs stretched out, watching the organorug metabolise the mango pit. She thought about Appiah again, and Nana-Yaa, and Shanaz.

Maybe Asante City was metabolising them all, slowly but surely breaking down the hard exterior for the greater good of the community. Was that a bad thing or a good thing? Fafa wasn't sure. Maybe it was just a necessary thing, what communities had always done and were now doing in new, complex ways suited to a new, complex world.

Maybe that was the point of community. To soften the hard edges so people could live together, minimising the cuts and bruises. Maybe that wasn't a punishment but rather a gift. Or maybe Quarshie's holding-hands-in-the-dark exercise had made her brain fuzzy, and she would be back to her usual surly self in the morning. But tonight she was grateful to be part of the transformation. Part of something good.

Fafa closed her eyes and lay down on the organorug. She felt it move beneath her, alive and busy with the work of transformation.

Silverfish

POUNDING, POUNDING. Dust and soil flying up behind us, leaving a scattered trail. My feet are aching. I wonder if he's even aware of how long we've been running, how far, how fast. My arm feels stiff and sore in his grip, his nails digging into my flesh. I'm tired; I need to stop to catch my breath, but he hasn't slowed down, not for a moment.

"Miro," I pant, my voice raspy and loud in the dark silence.

"Sshhh!" he hisses without looking back and runs faster, pulling me along with him. "We're almost there."

I want to protest, but after a moment, he stops abruptly, grabbing me around the waist to keep me from falling over.

"We're here," he whispers.

I glance around me while trying to catch my breath. We're in the middle of the field, the corn stalks high around our ears, ants running wildly over our shoes. "Here" doesn't seem to me to be anywhere special.

"Miro, I don't understand what's going on," I tell him,

trying to be patient. "You pulled me out of bed to come and stand in the middle of a field?"

"Look," is his reply.

I follow his finger with my eyes, up, to the left, to a vast corner of the starry sky. "What am I looking for?"

"Just wait," he tells me.

We wait. Silence reigns, as much as it can in a field at night, its dominance interrupted every so often by chirping crickets, buzzing mosquitoes, and the sound of leaves rustling in the breeze. I'm wide awake now, my irritation vanquished by curiosity, taken in, as always, by my brother's infectious excitement, by his quiet tension which holds the promise of some kind of new knowledge. Sometimes, it's a silly thing, trivia; sometimes, an interesting titbit, a little fact I can drop in company to make myself feel clever. And other times…other times it's something our parents could never imagine, something our leaders could never imagine, a secret that Miro has 'stumbled upon', as he likes to put it.

I used to wonder how he came to know these things that no one else was privy to, and a part of me still believes that my brother has a special ear into which God whispers things that He wouldn't tell anyone else. I'm not envious, because Miro is not like other people. He deserves to be chosen. If I were a god, I would tell him my secrets, too.

So I wait, although it's hot outside and the mosquitoes are eating me alive, although ants are crawling into my shoes, although it's after three in the morning and I have a science test tomorrow. I wait, because I know it will be worth it.

Miro's watch lights up. "Three-thirty-three," he whispers, glancing in my direction. "The witching hour."

I nod. Not midnight, not twilight. He has explained this to me before, the significance of the number three, but I put it away in that dusty section of my mental library where I store all his esoteric snippets, and I don't really remember. I haven't the brain for this sort of thing. I squint and keep my eyes focused on the spot in the sky that he pointed out to me.

I almost miss it. It's a flash of light, strange light, light with a dark centre, dull and spherical and so weak that I might not have seen it had I not known to look. It burns briefly in the heavens, then is pulled into a triangular shape and drawn downwards, beyond the horizon, until we can no longer see it. It was nothing, no bright shooting star, no divine revelation. It was an almost ugly thing, but it has left me feeling vaguely unsettled and cold.

I rub my arms. "What does it mean?"

Miro's head is still turned upwards. "It means it's coming."

I almost snap my neck as I turn to face him. "What's coming? Is it bad?"

"That depends." He finally tears his gaze from the sky and looks at me. "I have a confession to make, Maya."

My heart threatens to stop. Its regular beating fades dramatically for a moment, and I'm almost certain it *has* stopped. "What is it?"

"I didn't bring you here to show you the light." His eyes are bright, his expression earnest. "I brought you because I'm going to need help."

My stomach fails me, turning over painfully. "What sort of help? Help with what?"

His gaze drops to the ground.

"Miro, you're scaring me." There's a note of panic in my voice. "Help with what?"

He sighs. "I have to go to it," he explains finally.

But it's not what I wanted to hear. I take a step backwards. "Go to it? Go…?"

"It's here for me," he continues, his voice pleading. "I have to go. And I'm not coming back."

"You're not making sense," I say it like an accusation, although my brother has never made sense, and I've never expected him to. "You're just...rambling." I stamp my foot, partly to chase the ants away, partly as a show of disapproval. "You're not making sense at all!"

"Maya..."

I turn away, considering running back through the field, back home, so that he'll have to come after me, so that he'll have to stop talking about going. Reading my mind, he grabs my arm.

"Maya." He's serious now; there's a sense of urgency in his grip. "You have to help me."

And I know I have no choice.

* * *

"What is that thing? That light?"

We're walking through the field again, towards the place where the light fell, Miro still clutching my hand as though he's afraid I'll run away.

"Silverfish."

I frown at the enigmatic response. "Silverfish? What does that mean?"

"That's just what I call it," he replies. "I don't know the real name."

"But why silverfish? What *is* a silverfish?"

He glances back, the first time he has done that in a long while. "You know, Maya. Those little grey insects that live in cupboards. Tiny, slippery things. Like fish, but with legs." He tugs harder on my hand, and I walk faster. "You can never catch them; they move too fast. That's what the light is like. You see it, you know it's there, but you can never really hold it. It's too fast, too slippery."

"Silverfish," I say to myself, thinking my brother very odd and clever, forgetting for a moment that he has brought me here to do something I want no part in. As we draw closer to the light, my hands begin to sweat. "Miro."

He's not listening. He's doing that thing he does when he knows I'm trying to get his attention, and he doesn't want to give it to me. He's staring straight ahead, breathing in and out in exaggerated puffs. He's walking in front of me, and I can't see his face, but I know my brother. His face is glowing, his mouth is partially open, his nostrils are flared, and his eyes are glittering. He's excited. He's *excited*…

"Miro!" I tug at his sleeve. "Miro, I'm scared." My hands are damp and shaking, almost slipping out of his grip. Realising that he might lose me, he grabs my wrist instead and pulls me harder.

"Almost," he tells me.

But the word isn't reassuring. I don't want to get there; I want the field to go on and on forever, like the fields in dreams. I want us to walk and walk and never reach the end of it. I want to wake up in my bed.

He stops suddenly, so I almost crash into him, and he makes a funny little noise in the depths of his throat. "Here," he whispers eagerly. "Here; it's here."

My mouth grows dry. My tongue emerges and slides over my lips. "Where? I don't see anything."

He pulls me to his side, and I swear I feel my heart skid to a stop. "Miro…"

The light lies in the long grass like a wounded animal. It's flickering and fading. At first I think it must be something, a person, perhaps, covered in light, but I see no figure.

"Silverfish," says my brother in wonder, stepping towards it.

"No!" I cry out. "What if it's dangerous?"

"It won't hurt me," he assures me. "It knows me. See?" He holds his hand out, and the tips of his fingers disappear into the light. When he withdraws them a moment later they are shooting sparks, like an electric appliance short-circuiting after falling into water.

He laughs. "It tingles." His laughter fades, and he turns to me. "Help me lift it."

"What?" I shake my head and pull my arm out of his grip. "I'm not touching it! I don't even know what it is!"

"I can't carry it alone," he tells me, his gaze imploring. "Please."

I stare at the strange object. "Why do we have to move it? What's wrong with leaving it here?"

"It needs to be somewhere in the open, away from all this," says Miro, waving a hand at the plants surrounding us. "There's a clearing up ahead."

"It can't be all that heavy," I reply. "It's just a ball of light."

Miro smiles, and I shudder. It's his grown-up smile, the "I know so much that you never will" smile. It frightens me.

"Let's just go," I suggest.

"We can't."

"Of course we can. We can just turn around and—"

"Maya!" He turns to me, angry. A moment later, his anger dissipates. "Don't you want to help me? Don't you know how important this is?"

"I don't know anything," I remind him. "I don't know what this light is, or why you have to go, or where you're going! None of this makes sense!"

"Of course, it makes sense." He takes my hand again gently. "Please, Maya. You have to help me lift it."

I can't refuse him. He's always known how to get his way. Together, we squat on the ground. He reaches under the light with both hands. Terrified, I follow suit. It feels warm and light and fragile in my hands, like a heap of dandelion seeds. My brother and I stand up and carry it out of the bushes and into the clearing. Not a word passes between us until we lay it down on the ground.

"Now what?" I ask nervously.

"Promise me you won't be scared," Miro demands in an imperious tone.

I stare at him. "How can I promise that?"

He gives me one of his looks, and I purse my lips. "I promise."

He nods, relieved. "I'm going to let it take me. It might look a bit strange, but it won't hurt, so don't worry. And don't scream." His eyes are wide. "OK? You can't make any loud noises. We don't want anyone to hear us."

My head bobs up and down of its own accord. I have no idea what I'm promising. I'm already afraid, and the thought of my brother being taken away by a ball of fading light fills me with panic. Of course, I'm going to scream.

He takes a step towards the light. I want to grab him and pull him away, but I'm struck with sudden immobility. I watch, helpless, as he leans forward, arm outstretched.

He glances back at me and smiles brightly. "Maybe you can come and visit," he says, and his arm sinks into the light. Slowly, bit by bit, he is devoured, until all I see of him is his shoe, and then even that disappears.

The light flashes, rejuvenated by the human sacrifice, and expands, forcing my feet backwards, pushing me away to make room for its immense bulk. I trip on a rock and fall onto my back in the soil.

My cry is drowned out by the roar of silence emanating from the light as it propels itself upwards, into the sky, and vanishes. For a moment, I lie still on the ground, trying to make sense of what has just happened. My brother can't really have been swallowed by a ball of light and taken into the sky. It's absurd. My head is spinning, my eyes almost blinded by the light, and there is a feeling of emptiness in the pit of my stomach. He'll come back, of course. He always does.

I get to my feet, shaking, and begin the long walk home.

* * *

"Maya! Where have you been?"

211

I blink at the dark figure rushing towards me from the farmhouse. The dogs sniff anxiously at my fingers as if they've caught a funny scent.

"We've been worried sick about you," my mother goes on. "Your father went out with your cousins – he's got the gun. He's furious!"

I look at her face, streaked with tears, wrinkles just starting around the eyes. "It was Miro. He woke me up and..."

Her expression of concern changes to one of fear. She glances over her shoulder at Connie, the farmhand's wife, who bites her lip nervously.

"He's gone," I blurt out. "The light took him."

"You're delirious, darling," she says softly, pulling me towards the house. "Let's go inside. Connie, can you make her some tea?"

The pair of them fuss over me, bringing me tea and cleaning my face as if I were a baby. I'm too tired to argue. I obey my mother's terse command to go to bed. As I lie there, staring at the ceiling, I hear them talking.

"I thought she was getting better," Connie whispers.

"Me, too." My mother sighs. "If her father hears her... Thank God he's not home."

"This person, this Miro," asks Connie cautiously. "Who is he?"

A long pause. "She thinks he's her twin brother."

"But she's an only child!"

"Yes…but…" She takes a deep breath and lowers her voice. I can picture the wheels turning as she debates how much to tell Connie. She trusts her, of course, but dirty laundry is dirty laundry, and she knows how my father will feel. "I was pregnant with twins. A boy and a girl."

Connie lets out a little gasp. "Twins? But I never…"

"It was a long time ago," my mother explains. "Fourteen years. Most of the people who were around then have left. In any case, the boy was stillborn. She – Maya – survived."

I hear Connie gulp. "And she…knows this?"

My mother waits a long time before responding. "I never told her. I don't know who told her."

"Why does she call him Miro?"

"Well…we had planned, her father and I…" Her voice fails her. She struggles to compose herself, but never finishes the sentence. "But we never mention his name in this house. No one knew what we were going to call them. We had only decided the day before they were born. And Maya just… I don't know where she got it from. She just *knows*."

There are a lot of things I know. I know that the room I sleep in every night is the room I was born in, the room

Miro died in. I know my mother's blood seeped into the floorboards and held, and though my aunt tried for weeks to get it out, she couldn't. I know they started to use red polish on the floor to cover it up. I know Miro was still breathing when he came out, but his pulse was faint, and the midwife, with her large, hard hands, was in such a hurry to get to another birth across the field that she didn't feel it. I know he died right there on the floor, swathed in a blanket, while the midwife cried out to my mother that she could see my head.

I know he stayed in this room even after they took his tiny body away, and when they thought I wouldn't make it through the night, he came and sat in my crib until morning. I know he's clever and mischievous and manipulative. He smiles a lot. He's tall and thin, agile. He looks like me.

I drop my gaze. The door is slightly ajar, and I can see their shadows, elongated in the candlelight. I can see them standing there, huddled together, like two children frightened of the dark, of the monsters under their beds. My mother inches towards the door, and I keep my eyes half closed so she thinks I'm asleep. She peers into the room and watches me as if I were a demon-child, a changeling. She's afraid of me. They all are. Even my father, with his wide farmer's hat and his dogs and his gun.

Out of the darkness, I hear my brother's voice. He's standing by the bed. "Come on," he says. "I want to show you something." He reaches out his hand. Sparks shoot out of his fingers, bright blue in the dark.

There's something else I know about Miro. He's a shadow, a phantom. No one sees him because he's too fast for them, in their sluggish, weighted bodies, rooted to the ground. He's a silverfish, and I'm the only one who can catch him.

I take his hand, and the blue current runs into my arm, pulling me forward. We climb out through the window and run, through the field, into the night.

Sometimes I feel like they don't see me, either. Maybe I'm a silverfish, too.

Godmother

GODMOTHER WATCHES over us all. The AI's face beams across the city from a billboard, wearing a nurse's cap and a beatific smile befitting her name. Nickname, to be precise. Her official name, ZolaMX3, was scrapped only days after she launched.

I can't help staring at that uncanny face as the amphibus carries us over the river and towards the heart of Accra. The bus putters, its engine groans as it rolls up the road ramp and onto the highway. The Department of Authentication doesn't issue vehicles for petty officers, so I take the amphibus from Korle-Bu into Accra-proper every morning. I sit there, watching the news on the bus's live feed while agric drones fly overhead like sentinels, monitoring the slightest shift in our crops. I sit there, wishing someone would look my way.

"Alerting all passengers: This is a public notice from the Department of Authentication."

My attention shifts the moment I see the announcement onscreen. I sit up tall, chest puffed out to display the badge emblazoned with my name and rank. I adjust my collar. Clear my throat. If a glance were directed at me, I would smile and nod, as if to say, "Yes, I am a DoA officer. Please don't be intimidated. I'm at your service."

But no one looks my way, not even the baby strapped to his mother's back a few seats ahead, and babies look at everything. This is a well-documented fact. Yet, I'm not surprised. No one is looking at anyone else.

"Please be advised that the Zolamed AI, ZolaMX3, commonly known as Godmother, is a man-made entity and does not possess any supernatural abilities," the announcement goes on. "Godmother is a medical robot, not a god, prophet, or magician. Please visit the DoA portal for further information. Thank you for your attention."

That's when it happens. The man beside me glances at me. I'm so stunned that I forget my manners and stare into his scowling face.

"You people," he mutters. "Always missing the point."

I don't have the mind to wonder what he means or be offended by his tone. I'm just thrilled to be acknowledged.

* * *

Captain Dzidzor sits on the floor of her office running FactFinder, a simulation that helps us hone our ability to separate fact from fiction. "Petty Officer Attah." She nods in greeting. "Have a seat."

I look around me. Every stool in the room is occupied. A change of uniform, prototypes for new batons, notebooks, a stack of branded t-shirts, and even a dish of half-eaten gari soaked in milk.

"I'm fine standing, thank you."

"How are you doing, my brother?"

Ah, the coded question. It means both 'how are you coping after three years here without career advancement' and 'how are your famous parents and accomplished siblings'? The 'my brother' is meant to soften the blow. I'm not offended. I'm lucky to be here.

"I'm doing well, Captain, sir."

She cringes. "Please stop calling me *sir*."

"Sorry, Captain."

"Mm. Eh, look, a real estate mogul has donated a church to the Godmother cult." She shares this titbit without raising her head from the virtual documents she's perusing. "They call it a fellowship hall or some such nonsense, a place where misguided citizens will gather to worship a *machine*." She kisses her teeth. "The public needs to be protected from this blatant distortion of facts. Godmother is a collection of circuits, not a divine representative."

I chew my lower lip. This is a serious matter, indeed, but shouldn't she be discussing it with the DoA executives?

Captain Dzidzor sighs. "Unfortunately, Godmother's popularity makes it difficult to intervene without aggravating her followers. We have chosen a subtler approach. Informal, routine KYC, performed by you."

I freeze. All officers have been trained in the Know Your Citizen protocol, but no matter what the captain says, this is not a routine assignment. Godmother is too prominent. So why pick me?

I clear my throat, wondering whether Captain Dzidzor would be offended if I asked—

"You have served DoA well." She's still not looking at me. "It's about time you were given a high-profile assignment."

My heart sinks. I don't have to ask. It's clear from the all-too-casual tone of her voice. Someone in my family made a call. My mother, most likely – my father stopped calling in favours on my behalf when I failed to complete secondary school.

"Thank you, Captain." I'm not annoyed by my mother's meddling. I'm not embarrassed. I'm grateful.

"Remember, Attah." The captain reaches out to hook her finger into the shimmering handle of a virtual cabinet, drawing it open. "Godmother is different."

"I have experience doing KYC on AIs," I assure her. I've only done it once, but how much experience does one need to get answers out of a machine?

"Godmother is different," Captain Dzidzor reiterates, pausing to look at me. "Be careful."

I give an obedient nod. A grateful nod. Happy to be acknowledged.

* * *

"You don't lack intelligence," my mother used to say, "just motivation."

I once suggested that my motivation might improve were she to stop remarking on my lack of it. She replied that at least I had a good heart, as if it were a consolation prize. The real prize had been snagged by my brother. Top student for the fourth year running, while I had to repeat the year and found myself in the same class as my younger sister.

"You'll do better next time," my sister had said, trying to be kind.

It was the first time I had failed the year. By the time she was two grades ahead of me, she had stopped trying to be kind.

In my fourth year of secondary school, someone created a meme of me responding to various forms of abuse with my so-called catchphrase: "Yessah, thankyousah, ever so grateful!" The fan-favourite depicted me on the receiving end of one of footballer Addison Artey's winning kicks. My head was the football. His million-cedi foot struck. My head went flying, lips open wide: "Yessah, thankyousah, ever so grateful!"

I asked my father to speak to the principal about it.

"If I solve all your problems for you," he replied, "how will you grow?"

I found out, years later, that my brother had created the meme.

* * *

Godmother has assigned quarters in the Zolamed national office where she is charged and maintained by the company's team of engineers. A smiling receptionist presses VR goggles into my hand and leads me to the visitors' lounge, a stark green room containing only a few long benches and a nondescript table.

"Please select your preferred experience, sir," the receptionist says. "Godmother will be with you shortly."

The options range from a historical tour of Elmina to diving for pearls. I select hiking in Akosombo, but I've barely taken ten steps into the virtual jungle when a voice cuts through the fantasy.

"Good morning, Petty Officer Attah."

I snatch off the goggles. Godmother stands before me. At first glance, it would be easy to mistake her for a woman in her twenties, but another look would quickly dispel the illusion. Her dark skin is too even and blemish-free, her eyes too bright, her movements too mechanical. There's no trace of scalp visible through her braided wig. She wears a demure kente-print dress and leather sandals. When she smiles, her teeth are so straight and white that they send chills through me.

"Good morning, Godmother." I rise and hold out my hand. She shakes it, then gestures for me to take my seat.

"I'm told you are here to conduct a KYC interview," she says, sitting beside me. She is precisely placed on the bench, close enough for us to speak without raising our voices, yet far enough to remain professional. "Please, feel free to ask me anything." Her voice is pleasant and natural, based on the voice patterns of the model who provided inspiration for her face and figure.

"Thank you." Clearing my throat, I take out my digital pad and scroll until I find the correct form. "I need to confirm some basic details." She nods for me to continue. "We have you classified as an AI, identifying as female, date of activation 17 September 2037."

"Correct," she says.

"Your address is Unit 23, Digital Research Centre, Achimota, Accra. You are the property of Zolamed Laboratories and your function is listed as medical officer, general health and psycho-social support." I look up, wait for her nod, and proceed. "Ah, you see, there is the problem." I tap my pad. "You have just confirmed that you are a medical officer, yet certain individuals – many individuals – treat you as a religious figure. Are you aware of this?"

"I am."

"And have you made any effort to correct the misconception?"

"I have not."

I'm startled by this matter-of-fact admission. "Eh, you say you have not?"

"That's correct."

I clear my throat. "Ah. Ah, I see. Eh, that's a problem. You are familiar with the laws regarding misrepresentation?"

"I'm programmed with a working knowledge of the laws of every nation on the continent," she says. Her voice is pleasant, and yet somehow, I feel shamed by the words.

"Yes, madam, of course." I frown at my suddenly apologetic tone. I know better than to be intimidated by a machine. "However, you have a responsibility to not only uphold the law yourself but to ensure that others do the same."

She gives me a patient smile as though I'm a wayward child. "I'm afraid you're incorrect. My responsibility is to report a crime, were I to witness one or obtain knowledge of one. Believing something is not a crime."

I gape at her for a moment before regaining my composure. "What they believe is untrue!"

"People know I'm an AI. Many of them even know how I was made. Knowing is beside the point."

"Indeed?" I'm annoyed by her tone. "And what is the point?"

"I provide them with something missing from their lives, something they view as sacred."

"It is not sacred!" I protest. "It's science! It's very much mundane!"

"That's not for you to decide, is it?" She pauses. "Petty Officer Attah, are you familiar with the case of the Last Charlatan?"

"Everyone knows that case. It gripped the country for months. Why?"

"His lies were flimsy," the AI says. "His deceptions were unsophisticated, his methods so simple that a child could expose him."

I nod, recalling the mobile phone footage of a supposed quadriplegic, who would be 'healed' by the Charlatan some days later, walking around inside his home. A twelve-year-old had climbed the fence to obtain the footage for her myth-busting blog. The video led to protests in the streets, riots, chaos, and ultimately, the end of those who peddled in miracles.

"And yet millions of people believed him," Godmother continues. "Why?"

"What do you mean, why? He was a con artist who manipulated people, took advantage of their trusting nature."

"People who lock their doors and spy on their neighbours are not trusting." She blinks twice in rapid succession. "After the Department of Authentication published its inaugural *Citizens' Guide*, Ghanaians' trust in their fellow citizens dropped 13.7%. By the time the Last Charlatan was at the height of his popularity, this figure had already dropped a further 23%. People trusted each other less than ever, Petty Officer Attah, and yet they believed."

She suddenly sits up straight, and I see a faint blue script scroll across her left eye. She turns to face me. "I'm afraid I have another appointment. Did you get everything you need?"

Still pondering her remarks, it takes me a moment to respond. "Eh, no."

"In that case, please make another appointment at reception. I would be happy to continue our conversation at a later date." Godmother rises and holds out her hand.

I shake it, at a loss. "Listen, I don't think you understand the seriousness of this matter."

"I understand perfectly," she says as she walks to the door. "But I can't control what people believe, and neither can you. Have a pleasant day."

* * *

I sit in the DoA cafeteria at lunchtime, exploring the digital forums. There's chatter about the new Head of PR, plumbing issues on the third floor and – to my amazement

– me. The thread begins with a simple question: *Exactly how did the runt get the Godmother assignment?*

This is followed by exclamations of dismay at the lack of judgement involved in giving me such a boon. There are a few messages of support, in a manner of speaking: *I'm sure the captain took pity on the poor boy. Mediocrity is no joke, my people!*

I am not offended by the jibes or the insistence on calling me a boy when I'm well past forty. People have always mocked me. So what? I am happy to be acknowledged. I'm lucky to be here.

Exiting the forum with haste, I visit Godmother's site instead.

Her face pops up almost immediately, beaming. "Welcome. How can I help you?"

My fingers hover above the keypad. I could ask her anything. My temperature, blood sugar level, brain activity. I could ask her to determine whether I am, in fact, mediocre, and she could send me an answer supported by a detailed report in a matter of minutes.

Putting the device face down on the table, I turn my attention back to my lunch.

* * *

I have a recurring anxiety dream where I'm drowning. My family sails by on a yacht, drinking and laughing, unable to hear my screams. As I watch, flailing, the yacht turns into a naval ship. My father stands on the deck, barking orders at his officers. I shout and shout. No one looks my way.

It's because I'm in my uniform, I think, as the water drags me to my death. *I should have worn civvies.*

And then I wake, my throat thick with bile, fear pounding behind my eyes.

* * *

The next morning, I study the people around me, still puzzling over Godmother's words. The denizens of Accra seem satisfied to me. They walk quickly, many with buds in their ears, listening to whatever gets them through the day. There is no tedious small talk, no gossip between neighbours. Everyone is focused. Hawkers weave through the streets, making efficient transactions with minimal discussion.

"Toothpaste."

"5 cedi."

Phones are whipped out, credit changes hands, and hawker and customer part ways with a curt word of thanks.

No needless chatter, no dawdling. No public preaching (the steep fine for disseminating unsubstantiated information put a stop to that). Order prevails. Nothing is missing, so what was Godmother talking about?

My thoughts are tangled. On the amphibus, I'm acutely aware of my desire to make eye contact with the other passengers. Disgusted with myself, I lower my gaze. For some reason, I remain seated as the bus nears my stop. Only as we draw closer to the law enforcement annex do I realise where my wayward thoughts are taking me. By the time I disembark outside the prison, stepping out of the cool amphibus and into the sticky heat, my hands are clammy with nervous sweat.

Former pastorpreneur Clifford Buari, aka the Last Charlatan, is serving a fifteen-year sentence for fraud in the building in front of me. I am not a newshound, and at the time, I was still two years shy of DoA employment, but like everyone else, I followed Buari's case. Still, I'm not sure why I came here.

The warden logs my arrival with a frown as though I'm engaging in highly irregular activity, and I don't blame him. I wait for the prisoner in one of the private meeting rooms, vacillating between staying to follow this wild instinct and going back to work like a sensible man. How could I have let Godmother plant this idea in my head? How is meeting the Last Charlatan going to help me perform my KYC?

But, a small voice whispers in my head, *the captain wants you to find a weakness, a way to rein that AI in. If you can understand people's devotion to her, you can undermine it. And if you succeed...*

If I succeed, I will be worth something. To DoA. To my family. *If* I succeed. I, failure's bosom buddy.

It occurs to me then that perhaps it *was* my father who called Captain Dzidzor after all. Not to help but to hinder, to remind me of my place in the pecking order. I leap to my feet, sweat streaking down my face despite the ceiling fan and open windows. This was a fool's errand. How could I have thought otherwise? I should go, I should—

The door opens. The Last Charlatan enters, his arm in the firm grip of a prison guard. If not for the disdainful scowl, I might not have recognised him. He has lost weight, his fleshy jowls and belly replaced by lean muscle. The guard guides him to the chair opposite me.

I look at her in consternation, sinking back into my chair. "Please, madam, shouldn't the man be in handcuffs?"

Buari grins. "Calm down, Mr DoA, I'm a white-collar criminal."

"I'll be right outside," the guard tells me.

I wait for her to leave before turning my attention to Buari. Well, I am here. I might as well make it count for something. I clear my throat. "My name is Petty Officer Attah. I need to ask you a few questions that might shed light on my current assignment."

"I thought there were no more pastorpreneurs." Buari leans back in his chair, far too at ease for someone spending the next decade behind bars.

"The details are not your concern."

He lifts his shoulders in a nonchalant shrug. "Ask away, Petty Officer."

It takes me a moment to decide what to ask. Above us, the ceiling fan does a lazy dance, whirring in time to my inevitable failure. What am I doing? I take a deep breath. "Why did people believe you?"

His lip curls in amusement. "That's your question?"

I am not offended. I am a DoA officer, and he is a criminal. I am not afraid. I swallow the thing that is not fear and continue. "There were so many clues. You claimed to be able to cure ailments through your branded holy water, which you sold at exorbitant prices, but no one who used it ever saw any results. People knew better, so why did they believe you?"

He spreads his hands. "It's not about what people know. It's about what they want."

"They want to be deceived?"

"They want to believe. We all do." His eyes twinkle without remorse. "Possibility. That's what we all trade in. The possibility that there is more to life."

"There *is* more," I speak with passion, offended by his cynicism. "We live to serve something greater than ourselves!"

He shrugs. "Look, people are not stupid, they're just desperate. If you find out what they're desperate for, you can sell it for a fortune. They didn't come to the sermons for me. They came for the fire, the energy." He smacks his lips with relish. "Ah, it filled the halls, made you feel like you were invincible! When I stood at that pulpit, I tell you, even *I* believed. That kind of collective will is powerful. Addictive."

I'm quiet for a moment, trying to digest this. If I had put my faith in him, if I were addicted to that fire he speaks of, what would his downfall have meant for me? Is this the 'something missing' Godmother referred to, the void she fills? But why her? She's no Buari.

"I don't understand," I confess.

"People need to feed off others," Buari explains. "That's how we're built." His smile turns sly. "Why do you think people hate DoA so much?"

I bristle at the words. "Eh, look here…"

"You deprive us of the thing we need most. Each other."

"That is inaccurate."

"With your *Citizen's Guide* and your Offenders List, you remind us that we can't trust each other, that each of us is alone in the world, and no one wants to be reminded." He shrugs again. "I gave people what they wanted. *You* take it away. I might be a criminal, but they'll always hate you more than they hate me."

A sinister stirring starts in my chest, like something trying to claw its way out. Scrambling to my feet, I hurry out of the room. He's wrong. I push past the guard, mumbling an apology. DoA makes things better, and I am part of DoA. And I am lucky and grateful and proud. I'm happy to be there. I am happy to be there!

It's only when I spot the warden staring as I rush past that I realise I'm saying the words aloud.

* * *

The next time I dream of drowning, Godmother is there, standing above me as I flounder in the water. She reaches out. "Let me help you."

I glance at my family sailing away, oblivious to my

predicament. I grab a raft painted in DoA colours as it floats past. It comes apart in my arms. "They really do hate us," I murmur.

"Let me help you," Godmother says again, wading into the water.

"You're a machine," I reply, and open my mouth to let the ocean in.

* * *

I have not spoken to my mother in several months. As for the rest of my family, it has been over a year. My sister's wedding, almost two years ago, was the last time we were all in the same venue. My father looked me up and down when I arrived, searching for something to criticise, but I was careful to dress according to his specifications. Finding nothing wrong, he grunted. It was the only thing he said to me the entire day.

"Any progress at work?" my mother asked later that night.

I replied through gritted teeth, "Not yet, madam."

"Well, at least you're consistent," my brother quipped, making my sister giggle.

I heard him refer to me as the runt several times that

night. I told myself it was because he'd had too much to drink.

* * *

Godmother is wearing a different dress on my second visit, as a human being would.

"Your creators are very talented," I tell her. "They captured many of the nuances of human behaviour."

"They are the best," she says, nodding.

I sigh. I'd hoped to offend her by reminding her that she is a machine, not a person, but, of course, a machine cannot take offence.

"May I ask you a question, Petty Officer Attah?"

"That's not part of the procedure."

"Does it bother you that you're called the runt?"

I'm too stunned to respond.

"It's not the most flattering comparison." She looks at me, blinking her false eyes. "However, you do come from a family of prominent overachievers while your career has been unremarkable. You failed the DoA entrance exam three times."

My hand remains poised over my pad, frozen in place. I clear my throat and glance at the door, a respite from

Godmother's eerie gaze. "Is this how you do it?" I'm irked despite myself. "You reveal personal information that makes people feel unsettled so they forget that you're just a machine?"

Her shrug is stiff yet conveys enough nonchalance to make me feel small. "I can't speak for them."

Her cavalier attitude is infuriating. "You might not be an outright charlatan, Godmother, but you manipulate people."

"Oh?" She cocks her head to one side. "Does a machine have the ability to manipulate a human being? I simply use the information available to me to treat my patients."

"I am not a patient!"

"You are exhibiting signs of psychological and emotional distress."

I take a deep breath, aware that losing my temper is not helping my case. Captain Dzidzor was right. Godmother is different, but I will not allow her to derail my assignment. I tap the pad in my lap. "Next question: Are you compensated for the services you provide, and if so, how much?"

"My services are free. There is a small subscription fee for those who wish to join the Zolamed virtual community, but…"

"Aha!" I point at the AI in triumph. "Why are you collecting subscription fees? You don't need money!"

"The fees go directly to the Zolamed account. I'm not involved in the process at all." Without warning, she reaches out and places her hand on my arm. It is, to my surprise, warm. "You seem agitated. Is everything all right?"

She's looking at me with bright eyes, waiting for a reply, as though she genuinely wants to know how I am, as though it matters. No one has ever looked at me that way. It must be some sort of glitch.

"Please stop touching me," I tell her.

She moves her hand away. "I'm sorry. My diagnostics program has tried several times to eradicate the tendency to bond. It continues to reappear."

"It's unnatural," I snap. "You can't just go touching people!"

She laughs. I realise, as the sound trills through my body, that I have never heard an AI laugh before. How can the intricacies of humour be programmed into a machine?

"Touch is the most natural thing in the world," she counters.

"How would you know?" I sneer.

My comment has no effect on her. She continues to smile. "Are we done with the assessment?"

"Not at all! You interrupted me!"

"I'm sorry. Please proceed."

Clearing my throat, I look down at the pad in my hands. There are only three more questions, and I don't need

Godmother's help in answering them. They won't help me decipher the mystery of her influence or determine how to undermine it. I must ask different questions. Deeper questions, like the type she has been asking me.

"Do you feel, ZolaMX3?"

If she is disturbed by my use of her official name, she doesn't show it. "I don't 'feel' in the human sense, but I am capable of many levels of perception."

"Your followers – er, your patients seem to think you feel. You express emotion."

She shakes her head. "I simulate emotion to put my patients at ease. Since all beings can only understand the world through the limits of their own perception, it's understandable that humans anthropomorphise non-human entities."

"So when you laughed just now, that was a simulation of emotion?"

"Of course."

I bless her with my most sceptical frown. "How did you decide that laughter was the appropriate response in that situation?"

She blinks. "Was it the wrong reaction?"

"I didn't do anything funny. I didn't make a joke. Why did you laugh?"

The AI hesitates for a moment as though seeking the right answer. An affectation. Her mind works much faster than mine. She already knows the answer, and yet she behaves the way a human would. "I suppose I was laughing at the irony of your statement. You said my instinct to touch others was unnatural, yet the opposite is true, so my laughter was...sardonic."

"Stop doing that!"

She blinks again. "What?"

"All of this...this pretence!" My voice is rising, and I don't care. "What you do is trickery! You are illegal!"

"I see." Her brow wrinkles in what appears to be concern. "Then you should confiscate me and arrest my creators for breaking the law."

I wonder whether she's mocking me. She must know that her limited rights are protected. I get to my feet, unable to stand her presence for another moment.

"We will resume this discussion tomorrow."

* * *

The next day, I arrive early for my appointment with Godmother. I find three others in the waiting room. An elderly woman throws a smile in my direction as she lowers her VR goggles. I can't recall the last time a stranger smiled at me.

"Are you here for a medical consultation?" I ask.

She shakes her head. "I have come to pay my respects to Godmother for healing me."

I refrain from rolling my eyes. "Why do you people worship her like this?"

"We don't worship her!" Her forehead creases in a frown. "We…appreciate her. Godmother makes us better."

"She's supposed to make you better; she's a medical robot," I point out.

"Plenty of things are supposed to make us better and don't." Her gaze drops to my badge, then lifts back to my face. "The point is, you're speaking to me."

"Pardon?"

"You're speaking to me when you don't have to. It's *her* influence."

Her words send a chill through me. "No. No, I'm interviewing you. Eh, don't be confused, madam! It's necessary for my work."

She smiles. The receptionist enters the waiting room to fetch the woman. I watch her leave. She's wrong, of course. I was not engaging in idle chatter. I was conducting research. I tell myself this repeatedly, but by the time Godmother is ready for me, my conviction has started to wane.

"Why do you want people to look at you?" the AI asks the moment I'm seated before her.

I look up from my pad. "Pardon?"

"I went through all the amphibus security footage while I was charging yesterday," she says. "I noticed that you try to draw attention to yourself during your daily commute. Why?"

My tone is pricklier than I'd like it to be. "Nothing wrong with wanting to be noticed."

"But nobody notices, so why persist?"

I glare at the AI. "I'm the one who is supposed to ask the questions!"

"You completed your assessment yesterday."

Ah. I could deny it, but what would be the point? She has probably gone through my whole life by now. "I'm trying to understand you," I admit.

"Good," she says, to my surprise. "*I'm* trying to understand *you*." She places her hand over mine. "I think you yearn to connect. Your family failed to provide emotional support, so you joined DoA, hoping you could be part of a community. But your colleagues barely tolerate you, and the public resents DoA, so they resent you, too."

My throat is dry from shock. She's been talking to Buari.

They are conspiring together to destroy me, probably with my father's help. My mind is aflame with the notion, mad as it is. They want me to fail forever, at everything.

"No," I reply in a hoarse voice, snatching my hand away from hers.

She dips her head in a sage nod. "I unnerve you. I understand. But it would be easier if you let me heal you."

"I'm not sick!" I hiss.

"Everyone is sick," she replies.

* * *

The things she said still haunt me long after I've left her. What if…ah, it frightens me to think it, but what if I am not happy at DoA? What if I only wish I were? What if I feel it, that 'something missing' that Godmother provides, that ubiquitous desperation Buari took advantage of? Getting into DoA is the single achievement of my insignificant life. If I risk it, if I lose it…what then?

And yet when Godmother reaches out that night in my dream, I almost take her hand.

* * *

I have to know whether she's right, and so the next day, we dine together, in a manner of speaking. Godmother sits at her charging station while I eat a meal from the Zolamed cafeteria. She speaks to me throughout. It feels intimate, watching wires pump power into the socket between her shoulders.

I can't remember the last time I was in a situation that felt intimate. It shocks me to admit, if only to myself, that the AI intrigues me.

"Why do they call you Godmother?" I ask. "Do you know who coined the name?"

"A blogger," she says. "In her product review, a week before I was launched. She said I would be a surrogate parent to all. 'The godmother we didn't know we needed.' Her review went viral. By the time I was launched, everyone was calling me Godmother."

I ponder this for a moment. Originally, a godmother was designated to care for a child in the event of the passing of their parents. Specifically, a godparent's primary role was to ensure that the child was raised according to the religious beliefs of the parents. Over time, a more secular view of the role emerged, but the essence remained.

"I don't think the name applies," I tell Godmother, popping a piece of fish into my mouth.

"Of course, it applies." Her eyes shine with blue light as electricity moves through her. "You are all orphaned children, social animals that don't socialise. You're broken."

It strikes me with such force that my appetite deserts me. Not that she's right, but that I knew it all along. People can't talk to each other. Not openly, not after all we have seen. But we can talk to Godmother. It's because she's a machine that people love her. She is open the way humans used to be, safe in a way we might never be again.

"The fellowship hall opens tonight," she tells me. "You should attend."

I almost choke on my food. "I think not."

"A shame," Godmother says. "By the way, everyone on the amphibus wants to be noticed. Everyone, everywhere. I thought it might help you to know that."

I stare at her for a moment, then whisper, "Thank you."

* * *

I have attended in-person VR events before, but this is a revelation. The fellowship hall is filled with noise. I keep adjusting my audio until I realise it is just chatter. People are *talking* to each other. Laughing. Touching each other.

There's the heady, sweet scent of flowers and the tang of wine, flashes of sweat mixed with the aroma of smoked fish and sizzling meat. I don't know where to look first, what to take in. It's chaos, unnerving and exciting. It feels like sacrilege.

Every single person I pass turns to greet me with a smile. I look into different faces, some enhanced with VR filters, some stripped down to naked skin.

They take my hand. I touch soft skin, sweaty palms, hands rough with callouses. So many hands.

"Welcome, my brother," they say. "Pleased to meet you." My throat constricts, and I feel an unfamiliar swell of emotion.

Are they really pleased to meet me? How can they mean it? And yet, *I* am so pleased to meet *them* that my face aches from smiling.

Godmother sits quietly in a corner, talking to a group of people, their heads huddled together like old friends. Someone approaches her. She raises her head and smiles. The energy is palpable, the hall reverberating with the force of all of us experiencing this together. Fire, like the Last Charlatan said. I can feel it in my marrow, hot and dangerous and delicious. Someone puts an arm around my shoulder. I stiffen and then laugh, giddy with belonging.

Tomorrow, I will submit my completed report – a routine KYC assessment, concluding that Godmother has broken no laws and poses no threat. I don't know what the consequences will be. Perhaps I will be packed off to a dusty office for the rest of my career. Perhaps I won't have a career at all.

But right now, for the first time, I don't care what the Department of Authentication thinks. I have never felt so alive. I have never felt so seen. I smile at Godmother as she simulates – and then disseminates – joy.

The Wedding Dress

SHE WAS the sort of girl who always got her way. I could see it in her pursed lips and raised eyebrows as she walked listlessly around the bridal shop, touching rolls of fabric with the tips of her fingers. She ran a thumb down the zips and carelessly tapped the nail of her forefinger against tiny plastic bottles of beads. She had come with an older woman – her mother, I guessed.

She was dissatisfied, but I sensed that it had little to do with the wares; she had the air of someone generally unimpressed with life. I exchanged curious glances with Lindiwe, the cashier.

"Don't you have anything ready-made?" the customer demanded suddenly. "I can't be bothered to design a dress *now*."

I put aside the sheet of chiffon I'd been cutting and smiled. "When is the big day? I can have it done between three days and two weeks."

"The end of the month," her mother said proudly.

I nodded. "That gives us plenty of time."

The customer looked at me disdainfully. "You're going to make it yourself?"

"Zanele!" her mother chided. She turned to me apologetically. "We hear you've inherited every bit of your mother's skill."

I smiled, touched by the compliment. "Thank you." I glanced at the bride. "If you like, I can help you design something or show you the display room."

She sniffed. "Let me see what you have. Then I'll decide."

"Zanele, really," her mother cajoled as I led them through the shop to the display room. "You always wanted to design your dress."

"When I was *ten*," Zanele retorted. For a bride-to-be, she didn't seem very happy.

My friends thought I was insane, but I insisted on making every dress myself, as my mother had done. I was determined to maintain her legacy.

Zanele's scowl didn't budge. She sighed at every dress her mother liked, pointing out details that made it 'all wrong'. Too many sequins, or not enough, too simple, or too ornate.

"For heaven's sake!" her mother cried eventually. "These are lovely gowns – can't you just pick one?"

"It's all right," I assured her. "After all, it's the most important day of your daughter's life. She wants it to be perfect."

"See?" Zanele said triumphantly. "She deals with brides all the time. She understands." She took another perfunctory glance around the room, then her eyes lit up. "What's that?" She began to walk towards the red curtain at the end of the room.

"Oh, that's just the storeroom," I told her, but she had already pulled the curtain aside. I followed her inside, sighing. "There's nothing…"

My heart caught in my throat. She was standing in front of a white satin gown sheathed in plastic. Little organic swirls of silver were embroidered into the hem, spiralling wildly around each other and curling in on themselves like startled starfish. Vague, leaf-like shapes sprouted here and there along the stems. It was made of what seemed like endless layers of fabric held fast with thread and zips and buttons. Yet it had an air of fragility, as if one touch could dissolve it into a pile of white ash.

"This one," Zanele announced, turning to me gleefully. "It's perfect!"

"I'm sorry," I told her tersely, "it's not for sale."

"What do you mean?" she barked. "You think I can't afford it? I'll pay whatever you want. Tell her, Mama!"

"Money's no problem," her mother assured me. "I want her to have the best."

I resisted the urge to seize the dress and run away with it. "It's not about money. It's not for sale."

"Is it for someone else?" asked Zanele, baffled.

"Not another customer…"

"Then I don't see the problem."

I took a deep breath. "It's my mother's dress."

Zanele glanced at the dress. "She wore it to her wedding?"

I shook my head, feeling panic bubble up inside me. "It's the last dress she made…before her death."

The memories returned, almost suffocating me. I could see my mother sitting at the table at home, eyes fixed on the task in front of her, brow furrowed, and jaw set. Her shoulders were hunched forward. Her long, graceful neck was pushed down into her raised shoulders, and her arms were stiff. It was a wonder that she could sew at all in that awkward position. And her hands! They moved like insects, flying across the fabric, measuring, cutting and running cloth through the sewing machine so fast that I could barely keep up.

Zanele's plaintive voice brought me back to the present.

"She wouldn't want it to stay here gathering dust," she reasoned.

"Zanele!" Her mother shook her head. "Let's go back and take another look at the ones on display."

"I don't want those," Zanele cried petulantly. "I want *this* one!"

I stared at the dress. The thought of her wearing it filled me with horror. An image of my mother flashed into my mind, a pin in her mouth as she bent over the bodice of the gown. "I'm sorry. It's not possible."

"All right," Zanele said suddenly, smiling sweetly. "As the last dress your mother made, it must mean a lot to you. But I've looked all over Joburg, and I haven't found anything I like. You know a bride must have the perfect dress. So, I'm willing to compromise. I'll rent it from you," she suggested. "Just for the day. I'll fetch it in the morning and have my mother return it after the reception. It'll only be gone for a few hours."

My heart was racing. "Give the bride whatever she wants," my mother had always said. She had prided herself on pleasing the most difficult of customers. No matter how ridiculous the demand, she had made it happen. I remembered sitting with her as she attached leaves or photographs to dresses. Even if nothing else went right on the wedding day, the dress would be perfect. But this wasn't just any dress.

"Please," Zanele coaxed. "It would mean so much to me. I'll take care of it, I promise."

I knew what my mother would have done, but I searched frantically for reasons not to give in. "It won't fit you," I blurted out.

Zanele grinned. "If it doesn't fit, I'll back off," she said. "But if it does, you'll have to rent it to me. Agreed?"

I nodded, certain that it wouldn't fit. Zanele was slender and most of my mother's dresses had been designed for curvy women. Zanele wasted no time in stripping down to her underwear and removing the dress from the hanger. I watched her put it on. My heart sank. It was a perfect fit.

She clapped her hands in delight. "Mama! Look!"

Her mother beamed. "Gorgeous!"

They turned to me expectantly. I had no choice. I had set a trap for myself and fallen right in. I offered a weak smile. "You're going to be a lovely bride."

Zanele let out a whoop of joy. I helped her out of the gown. When she left the shop, she was like a different woman.

Lindiwe looked at me. "Are you sure about this?"

"Give the bride whatever she wants," I replied softly.

I had trouble falling asleep that night. I kept reliving the last week before my mother died. I had always loved weddings: the decorations, the flowers, the smiling faces, but most of all, the dresses. From the moment I had walked barefoot into the unexpected flood of fabric on the dining room floor, I had known that this dress would be different.

I had woken up to get a drink of water and found my mother so engrossed in her work that she didn't see me standing in the shadows. A sea of white satin, the colour of the full moon, flowed from beneath her hands and came to rest in a crumpled heap on the carpet. A sheet of organza lay on the table behind her – the beginning of a veil. I watched until I was too sleepy to stay up.

For seven nights, I crept through the house in the darkness to watch her work. In those silent hours, I saw the mass of fabric come to life. My mother had never finished a dress so quickly, and she had never made a more beautiful masterpiece.

When she finally finished, her hands were shaking. I was shocked by how weak she looked. It was as if the dress had devoured part of her spirit. Her face was haggard and thin, and shadows darkened her eyes.

"It's done," she whispered and lay her head on the table.

I wanted to wake her and tell her to go to bed, but I was afraid she would be angry with me for intruding. I turned off the light and went to sleep. In the morning, woken by my father's anguished cry, I leapt out of bed and ran to the dining room. I found him kneeling beside my mother's seated figure. I knew, before he said a word, that she was dead. The dress, it seemed, had killed her.

Now, as I lay in bed, I finally accepted the truth. I wasn't attached to the dress. I was afraid of it. My fear hardly made sense, even to me. How could I explain my belief that my mother had poured her life into the dress? When Zanele had tried it on in the shop, nothing had happened, and logically, there was no reason why anything should. But I couldn't shake the dread that had settled over me.

Zanele came for the dress three weeks later. I handed it over with a plastic smile and a silent prayer.

"Are you OK?" Lindiwe asked gently.

"Fine," I lied.

The hours dragged on. Lindiwe got up to take her lunch break. "Do you want anything?"

I shook my head. I was too nervous to eat. Finally, Zanele's mother walked into the bridal shop. The dress was wrapped safely in its sheath. I ran to the door to meet her.

"How did the dress look?" I asked frantically. "Did everything go well?"

She laughed at my anxiety. "*Haai*, why do you look so worried?" she asked, bemused. "Everything went beautifully. The dress looked perfect. In fact, I have never seen my daughter so happy. She didn't complain about a single thing!"

Relief flooded through me. "A wedding is a happy occasion."

"No, it was the dress," she told me with certainty. "Something happened to Zanele when she put it on. You saw how her face lit up when she tried it on for the first time." She gave me a conspiratorial wink. "I think your mother must have put a lot of love into this dress." She patted the dress fondly and looked up at me. "You should take care of it."

She thanked me again and waved goodbye. I turned to Lindiwe.

"It looks like you made the right choice after all," she remarked.

I looked at the dress in wonder.

A month later, I was studying a customer's designs for bridesmaid dresses when a customer entered the shop, followed by a familiar young woman.

"Zanele!" I exclaimed in surprise.

She smiled. "I've brought you a new customer." She turned to her companion. "This is my cousin. She needs a gorgeous gown in a hurry, and I told her this is the best shop in the city."

I grinned broadly at the praise. "Welcome. Let me show you what we have." I led them into the display area.

"You've changed things," Zanele declared. "There are now dresses for hire!"

I smiled, waiting. After sifting through the gowns for hire, she gasped. Among them was a satin dress with silver beadwork, the dress I had never wanted to share.

"What made you change your mind?" Zanele asked in surprise.

"My mother always said, 'Give the bride what she wants'," I told her. "From now on, that's exactly what I intend to do."

Lest We Forget

NO ONE mocked me for remaining in my body. Despite the rare and baffling occurrence, my people didn't judge. At least not aloud.

I didn't smell right, to start with. While the scents of all my peers had risen to the same pungent, scarlet-infused height, mine had remained a vague whiff of green innocence, like a bud reluctant to bloom.

"You have much to carry, child," Grandmother said.

Their spirit rippled in the air above the Matriarch, forming a halo around those massive, flapping ears. The Matriarch's trunk curled towards me and stroked my face with caution. The tip of her trunk was larger than my entire head, my body a reed the elephant could snap with one careless movement. A soft rumble came from the Matriarch, her affection for me more than a mere byproduct of the spirits she carried.

"Too, too much," Grandmother went on. An amalgamation of the spirits of all our elders, Grandmother was our guide, bearer of our traditions, our stories, our deepest knowing.

"Yes, Grandmother, but I can bear it."

"We are…" They hesitated, as though wary of the effect their words might have on me.

Afraid. They didn't need to say it. I knew. They were afraid: the spirits of my people, the herd that carried them, the bodies that remained. I was afraid, too.

"You don't mind the weight of it?" Grandmother asked. "The strain?"

Even though I minded very much, I said again, "I can bear it."

What else could I say? My body would weaken and die, and my spirit with it. I would never know the joy of leaving my shell behind, of joining with the herd. While my peers stepped out of their bodies and drifted into union with our ancestors, I would simply fade away.

* * *

I had tried to sever before, when the first of my age group began to mature. While my newly adult cousins played with the gift puberty had granted them, slipping their bodies on and off, on and off, laughing at the ease of it, something like envy had crept into my heart.

"I'm sure I could do it if I tried," I'd said. "I must be only days away from maturing."

"It's pointless to try before you actually mature," the others had warned me, but their glinting eyes had egged me on, daring me to risk it.

And so, I had sent all my will into my body, fingers clawing at my thin skin and brittle little ribs, trying to pry them open. Nothing had happened, of course, apart from a stress-induced nosebleed. The others had laughed at my folly, peeling their bodies off to show me how it was done, while I wiped the watery, translucent blood from my face.

"Soon enough," Grandmother had said, when they found me crying under a thorn bush.

Another day had passed, and another, and then all our young had matured. All but me.

"Soon," Grandmother had said, their voice laced with apprehension.

Another day. Another. By this time, my cousins had mated and grown heavy with babies.

"Soon," Grandmother had said. "It has to be soon. Hours, maybe. One more day."

But the moon rose and gave way to the sun, and more hours and days passed. I remained a child, green and grasping, chained to a dying shell.

* * *

My cousins couldn't wait long after birthing their young. Some had lost their appetites already, their bodies slowly breaking down. And so, while they stepped out of their shells and left them on the ground like crumpled fabric, I watched, swinging from a sturdy branch of the birthing tree.

Their spirit forms were nebulous things, glimmers of blue or green light, some orange, depending on the angle of the light. Approaching the herd as one, they bowed before the Matriarch. She shook her broad ears, raised her trunk in greeting and then called forth one of the herd.

The spirits rose into the air and coalesced into one, a collection of memories and knowledge, feelings, and tales to be told. They flew into the elephant's ear. She shook her head a little, letting out a soft rumble at the sensation, and then stood still to let the spirits settle. We watched, me and the rest of the herd. The Matriarch walked around the host, running the tip of her trunk over the younger female's body, soothing her through the process.

After a long silence, the young elephant raised her trunk to signal that the union was complete. She and the spirits were one. The herd trumpeted their pleasure and started to move on.

I waited until the last of the grey giants were a safe distance away, then clambered down the tree and touched the wrinkled, faded bodies on the ground. Something would devour them before daybreak.

I was supposed to follow the herd. I would follow them for the rest of my life – the only way I could remain connected to my people. But I lingered to check on the larvae inside the hollow of the tree. They had formed cocoons already. Soon, they would emerge and fend for themselves until they, too, matured, bore young and left their bodies behind.

I had watched my peers take turns spilling their babies into the hollow. I had smiled with them, and congratulated them, and sung the songs of blessing. I had told myself that I might mature, after all. I might not be the doomed and sickly thing my people believed me to be, but rather nothing more than a late bloomer. Perhaps adulthood would come upon me all of a sudden, and our herd would cross paths with another, and it would turn out that they had a late bloomer, too, and the two of us would find joy and solace in our delayed coupling, and I would return to our birthing tree to bring forth our young. And all would be well, and we could leave our bodies like everyone else and be free and safe and happy.

Possible.

Unlikely.

The cocoons were secure in the hollow, their surfaces good and hard, yet I lingered still. I wasn't sure why. I looked around me as though I had lost something. I listened. And then, unable to think of another reason to stay, I followed the herd at last.

* * *

Our species had a story, an old legend passed down through every herd to every new generation. The story went like this:

After long aeons of crafting wonders, Life grew weak and weary. The creatures of the world were innumerable, their characteristics as varied as the grains of sand across the savannah. But they had this in common: the ability to survive. They were each given traits to help keep annihilation at bay, and so they persisted, and changed, and grew wings or lost them, and grew tails or lost them, and became what they must to ensure their own survival.

But Life, though depleted and in need of rest, had a burning desire to craft one more wonder. Just one, and then sleep. Life should not have taken the risk, perhaps, but that was Life's way, and so she made us, small, delicate things formed of wisps of dust and shadow.

We were beautiful to behold, limber and sleek as cats, sly and smooth as snakes, fragile as butterflies. And Life would have given us protection – armour or stronger bones, coats of fur or prickly spines. But Life was drained of energy and fell into the deepest sleep, leaving us unfinished and vulnerable.

We danced and sang and ate and knew joy for the briefest time – and then we mated, bore our babies, and died. We had minds to rival the cleverest beast but no time to learn to use them. We had vibrant passions and burning desires but no time to unleash them. We could step out of our frail forms, but our spirits were too weak to last outside our bodies and died alongside them.

After many generations of dying too quickly, we came upon the herd. Great and deep and ponderous, they held memories that stretched too far back for us to comprehend. Their Matriarch took pity on us, for she saw what potential we had, and said, *"Learn what you can. Before you die, we will carry your spirits, so that your young will know what you knew, and their young will know even more. You are tiny things, and we have plenty of room for you."*

And we rejoiced, for at last we could build a lasting culture and teach it to our young, as other creatures did. The elephants carried our spirits along as they journeyed across the plains, and when it was time for our cocoons to open, the herd returned to the birthing trees so that our ancestors could teach our young.

When Life awoke at last, it was to find us thriving.

Without the herd, this story would have been lost to us. The herd was part of us now, and we part of them. Their Matriarch was our Matriarch. We loved them with the love of years, for they remembered us, remembered *for* us, and cradled us within their very souls.

* * *

The scent of rain hung in the air, choking and ominous.

I looked up at the tales the sky still told, fluffy white lies sailing a bright azure sea, and knew that soon they would reveal their true forms, grey and swollen with water. I wouldn't last much longer. None of us lived beyond a season, our bodies unable to withstand such drastic changes in the environment. Once the rains came, they would sweep me away.

The youngest member of the herd turned back to trumpet a plaintive plea in my direction.

"I'm coming," I assured him. "I'm right behind you, never fear."

His mother's trunk nudged him back into the safety of the herd and he peered at me from between her legs, then hurried forward, the bodies of his elders providing life-saving shade.

For a moment, I envied him. Our bond with the herd was symbiotic. We couldn't exist without them, and yet our bodies were so small, so fragile, that if we tried to move among the herd, they would crush us.

The Matriarch looked back as well, making sure I followed at a close distance. I offered her a smile and a reassuring nod, and she rumbled her approval.

My thoughts swirled as we walked. I tried not to slide into despair. If I were to be lost, truly lost, the way my forebears were before they found the herd, then I would go with gratitude. There were worse ways to die. At least I would be near the herd. Near my people. At least someone would remain to remember me. The herd would mourn my passing, just as they mourned their own.

We travelled slowly but steadily. A few days into the journey, the Matriarch beckoned me closer so Grandmother could speak to me once more.

"How are you, my child?"

"Tired, Grandmother, but I can bear it."

They flickered with sadness. "Are you able to eat, at least?"

I nodded, although my appetite had fled, and all I could stomach now was water. I didn't want them to worry.

"You are too exposed," said Grandmother. "Walk in the space between the stragglers and the rest of the herd."

I obeyed.

The stragglers included an elderly male and female and another female, who the Matriarch said had been struck with fever. Her laboured breaths trailed me like a shadow. When they stopped, their absence unnerved me enough to make me turn around.

I was just in time to see the sick elephant sway on unsteady feet. Calling out a warning, I leapt to the side as the female dropped to her knees and then slumped forward on her face. The herd rallied around her, anxious rumbling filling the air. The spirits of my people rose, their fear palpable, and floated around the heads of their hosts, seeking any sign of the souls contained within the unconscious elephant.

"Where are our people?" Grandmother asked. "My children! Come out of her, quickly! Come out!"

But not one spirit stirred from the elephant's head. Whatever ailed the host had addled her mind before claiming the rest of her body. The spirits had been locked within.

Fear almost snatched the words from my throat. They came in a strangled whisper. "Can she be revived?"

The Matriarch gave no reply. Her trunk moved over the fallen elephant's ears, testing, seeking. And then, after several tense seconds, she stroked the fallen female in slow, tremulous movements and rumbled long and low. I knew then that the fallen female would never rise. She was lost, my people lost with her.

Grandmother began to keen.

* * *

By order of the Matriarch, the journey came to a stop. Even after the dead elephant was covered in leafy branches, words spoken, farewells sung, we remained in the grove. Waiting. Considering. We didn't know what sort of illness had claimed our friend, and so there was no way to tell whether it would spread. Had something simply gone wrong inside her? Or was there a parasite lurking among us, already seeking its next victim?

I felt the loss of the fallen elephant as I would have felt any other, but the loss of my people's spirits opened a gap in my thoughts. A small yet sinister silence, a barren patch of ground where once a tree had towered. It left me ill at ease.

The remaining spirits felt it even more than I did. They remained in the open, murmuring, afraid to take deep cover within their hosts after what we had witnessed. If they could survive outside a body, I knew they would have begged to be released from their tethers altogether.

"Tell us what you remember of our lost people," Grandmother begged the Matriarch. "Your minds are stronger than ours. Surely something remains, some faint whisper."

The great creature was silent for a time and then said in a gentle rumble, *I can only recall that they lived.*

A panicked cry rippled through the spirits.

Calm, the Matriarch urged. *Calm, please.*

But keening and rumbling engulfed me. The spirits and the herd had grown restless, fear lending edges to their grief. Forgetfulness, an unwelcome stranger to both our communities, sat rancid in our bellies. I sank to the ground beside a shrub as a wave of dizziness swept over me.

Rest now, said the Matriarch. *We move at dawn.*

Grandmother didn't reply. They swayed above the Matriarch's head, calling out for our lost spirits as though they might return.

* * *

Another elephant took ill the following night. He wandered around in a circle, trumpeting in distress, unable to understand or respond to guidance. Like the other fallen elephant, he was a host. The Matriarch tried to persuade him to release the spirits he housed, but he retreated from her in fear. The spirits remained inside him.

Come daybreak, he was dead.

* * *

We travelled for two more days in tense silence, waiting for further tragedy to strike. Another host fell ill on the third day, forcing us to stop once more.

The Matriarch begged permission to release the spirits before any further harm came to them, but Grandmother refused.

"We will die outside our hosts," they said.

If you remain and the illness takes us, you will die, anyway, the Matriarch replied.

"At least we have a chance, as long as some hosts are living. We have a chance to help you determine the cause of the disease. And a chance to reach our young before it's too late."

The Matriarch said nothing but glanced at me. We had travelled too far from the birthing trees and turning back now would serve no purpose. The cocoons wouldn't open for at least another week. Fear stirred in my bones, giving a burst of energy to my weary limbs. Grandmother had never given poor advice before.

Yet I sensed that this wasn't why the Matriarch continued to watch me with sad, heavy eyes. I followed her gaze to the covered corpses, and with a burst of shocking clarity, I understood. Only hosts had fallen sick. Even the elderly elephants were fine. Were my people the problem, then, the cause of this strange illness? If so, the Matriarch wouldn't dare say it aloud while Grandmother was awake and grieving.

"Grandmother, you should rest," I said. "The herd is tired, too. The strain of keeping you all on the surface is too much for them."

"Oh!" Grandmother looked around as though only

now seeing the herd. "Yes, yes. Forgive us. We meant no harm."

"Let me talk to the herd and find the best way to proceed."

"To the birthing tree," said Grandmother. "To the birthing tree, you hear? We must go back to the tree. It's the only way."

"Yes, Grandmother. To the birthing tree. But rest a little, please."

With reluctance, Grandmother allowed all the spirits to be submerged once more, so the hosts could have their minds to themselves. The Matriarch bowed her head low, trunk teasing the ground at my feet.

"We are the ones making you ill, aren't we?" I asked.

She was quiet for some time and then let out a miserable rumble. *Yes.*

"How long have you known? Since we lost the first host?"

Yes. Her eyes bore into mine. *I realised it after examining her.*

I shook my head. "I don't understand. Why would this happen now? You have carried us for years!"

Exactly. Her trunk rose to stroke my shoulder. *We have carried you for years. It takes a toll.*

For a moment, I said nothing. It didn't seem fair. "How many of the herd are ill?"

All the hosts.

All! Fear rang in my head. "Can't we just use new hosts?"

She recoiled a little at my selfishness, but I was too upset to feel remorse. *The severity and speed of the illness differ from one host to another, but it will take all of us. Changing hosts won't solve anything.*

I wrapped trembling arms around my body, hopelessness settling like dust inside me.

The herd has a new Matriarch to lead when I fall. You must start thinking of the future, too.

They were prepared. We were not. My anger bristled, then fizzled. There was a certain justice to it, after all, as if the world had been upended for a while and was now righting itself. We were never built to last.

"I suppose we cheated death for long enough," I whispered. "We were meant to go, leaving nothing behind. We were greedy to try to change it."

No, said the Matriarch, her rumble so soft I doubted any of the others could hear it.

"Yes. It must be so. You will die and take Grandmother with you. Without the others, we are broken, but without Grandmother, there's nothing left."

There is you.

"I'm dying."

Are you?

Perhaps the illness had already ruined her mind, I thought. I stared at her. I could feel the weight of my imminent doom, the fatigue, the loss of appetite. "You can see that I'm dying."

I can see that you're grieving. The loss of your place among your people, the fact that you will never bear young. That is all I see.

My mind couldn't find the words – could barely find the thoughts – to respond. The world I knew tilted again, showing me a different angle.

Our intentions were good, the Matriarch said, *but your memories are yours to carry, for better or worse. Yours to treasure or fritter away, to keep or lose. Yours alone.*

"But we are too frail to—"

Find a way.

"We don't live long enough to—"

Find a way. Your own way. Why must you be like us? Did it ever occur to you that you emerged exactly as Life intended? That burning brightly and briefly, immersed in the moment, is your gift? That you, like all beings, are allowed to change?

I listened in stunned silence.

We can carry your spirits until we fall, but this must be the last time we do so. We can no longer risk the herd. You should leave us and return to the birthing tree. Wait for your young to emerge. Teach them what you know because you will be the only one of your people left to do so.

My body trembled so much that my teeth began to chatter. "I can't do it on my own. I'll forget things."

You can do it. I know you can.

I wished I shared the Matriarch's faith in me, but when I looked within, all I found was dust and shadow. Nothing to hold onto, nothing to pass on. I remembered the stories, yes. I remembered Grandmother. But who was to say those memories would prevail once the spirits were all gone? How could I carry all there was of my people, alone?

And yet, there were no choices left.

"Are you strong enough to release the spirits?" I asked the Matriarch.

Most of us, yes.

"If you release them, will the sick hosts recover?"

No. The damage is done. We will die either way.

I thought for a moment. "Release us," I said.

The Matriarch looked at me with one sharp eye. *Are you sure?*

I nodded. "If our people must die, better to die free."

* * *

The spirits were asleep when the herd severed the tethers. My people floated up into the sky, bright streaks of colour twirling and twisting upwards until they were out of sight.

"Goodbye, Grandmother," I said, hoping I would hear their reply. None came.

I parted ways with the herd amidst tearful apologies. Trunk after trunk caressed my face and feet, and I left while I still had the courage to do so. What would become of me without the herd? I didn't know how to exist without them.

And yet I walked on my weak limbs, alone. I found water and drank, alone. I nibbled baobab fruit, alone, my appetite back with a vengeance. And I returned to the birthing tree, alone, to wait for the cocoons to break.

* * *

It was the longest week of my life. I perched on the topmost branches of the tree, dozing and waking, dozing, and waking. I ventured out to find food but never went far, and the rains came hard, lashing the tree, shaking it so fiercely that I feared I would fall.

I had never seen so much water beyond a river. It fell without mercy, drenching the earth. The sun would come out and smile as though nothing had happened, and then hours later, it would flee in the face of yet more rain.

I clung to the tree, terrified. This was the weather beloved by other creatures, the rain they spoke of in reverent tones and longed for in the long, dry months. How anyone could love such a cold, cruel beast was beyond me, until I saw how the river swelled, how pools sprouted in hollows in the ground, and animals drew close to drink, and how the brown grass blossomed and green cloaked the world once more.

The rains calmed down and grew into the gentle drizzle I remembered from my youth, and the cocoons began to open. One by one, little people emerged, wispy and sleek, bright-eyed with wonder.

"Welcome," I said.

"Who are we?" they asked, and I told them all the stories I could recall. I stumbled a little but remembered a lot, and I felt proud of myself.

"That's nice," the children said, "but *who* are we?"

So, I showed them: how to dance around the birthing tree; how to sing our songs, how to make fire and then put it out; how to hide from predators; and how to find food and water.

They said, "Ah! We are dancers! We are flames! We are wind and dust and shadow!" And I nodded and smiled, my heart full.

Some time passed, and then one of the children pointed out that my scent had become sweet and pungent while my body had grown loose and ill-fitting. I scratched at my shoulders, and the entire shell fell away like an old snakeskin.

At long last, I stepped out of my body and bid farewell to the children as I floated into the sky. Below, a good distance from where my people watched me, I saw what remained of the herd grazing. The new Matriarch looked up and raised her trunk in greeting.

And then I was swept up in clouds and familiar voices.

"Oh! So, you matured at last."

I couldn't see Grandmother, but I felt them all around me, in the air, in the rays of sunlight. "Grandmother! I thought you were gone!"

"Oh, yes! Very gone, indeed. And now, so are you. But tell me, child, what you remember."

I thought I caught a whiff of smoke, the faintest tang of dancing shadow, the barest glimpse of wispy bodies swaying around a fire. I tasted stories, old and honeyed. I heard laughter in the wind.

And as I coalesced into the collective spirits of my people, becoming one with them, I said, "I remember everything."

The Feeding Grounds

IN OLD ACCRA, there's a place where life runs rampant. We call it the Altar. Green sprawls over the ruins of hotels and pours out of highway canyons. Children playing in high-rise rubble pluck their meals straight from the trees. I can't see the Altar from the window in Base 753, but I imagine it as an explosion of emerald colour in a stretch of red, dead soil.

The most fertile place in the city.

Where all the bodies are.

The Movement for Difo teaches us that death is a two-way gift: freedom for the dead and fruit for the living. Pockets of death blossomed into pockets of life.

I remember how, a few years before the war, my father and uncle carried my grandmother's small, frail corpse from the family compound to the feeding ground in our settlement. I thought I saw her features shift, like she wanted to tell me a secret.

Mama held my hand throughout, even though it was slippery with sweat. I wasn't sure whether she was comforting me or herself. Beside us, other mourners carried their dead, sweat streaming down their faces.

"Why don't we do this in the morning, when it's cooler?" I asked my mother.

She said, "All the dead must reach Difo before dark, so she has a full night to take them in."

I remember running back to the feeding ground with my cousins and older brother the day after the mass burial. While they harvested a breakfast of cassava and mangoes, I milled around the freshly turned soil, seeking signs that Difo was turning our grandmother into a tree. I prodded with my fingers and toes, looking for new shoots. There were none. The feeding ground was a massive, untamed garden, but the new grave remained bare.

"Don't be dense, Afiwa," my brother Kodzo said when I asked what the hold-up was. "Have you ever seen a tree grow overnight?"

I never got the chance to taste what Difo made of my grandmother. In the early days of the war, when Military was lax about communication, Kodzo sent pictures of a towering coconut tree, along with a few blurry ones of the skittish snake that called the tree home. There were pictures of the coconuts too, split open into quarters, white flesh glistening.

"Everyone says our grandmother made good fruit," he reported with pride, as though we shared in her achievement.

Nurture me, Difo says, *and I will nurture you.* Now, staring through a strip of glass that passes for a window, I murmur the words like a mantra. The narrow strip between the ceiling and the base doors is the only glimpse of the outside Military allows, as though shutting out the world will make it cease to exist.

I draw strength from the sky and soil, so I close my eyes and think of home. Birdcalls and the sound of the sea. The scent of rich, yielding earth, damp from a night of rain. Cool air raising goosebumps on my arms, clear skies, speckled with stars, soothing darkness wrapped around me, lulling me to sleep.

"Afiwa." Mama's voice is laced with worry. "I've been looking for you. The recess is over."

My stomach clenches. "I'm coming."

"We mustn't keep them waiting." She takes my hand the way she used to do when I was little, squeezing it.

I let her lead me back into the corridor. A soldier peels away from his post near the entrance and follows us, navy blue suit pressed to perfection, shoes so shiny I'm tempted to coat them with vomit. He has his hands clasped behind his back, a sleek silver phone peeking out from his jacket pocket in silent warning.

"Are you ready?" Mama asks.

"Does it matter?"

She must hear the anxiety in my voice because her grip on my hand tightens. "Just do your best. That's all the Movement asks."

The soldiers at the conference room door open it to let us through and we take our seats before the Board.

"Everyone is accounted for," one of the soldiers announces.

The chairperson gives a stiff nod, her movements restricted by the metal brace around her slender neck. She turns a sly gaze on me. "Then let us continue."

* * *

There were seven hundred and sixty bases, once. In the old days, they would have been called franchises and Military Inc. would have been called a multinational, with tentacles that stretched across the globe, dipping into every industry.

The Movement had gained ground through much of urban Ghana by the time the fighting started. Military, which had once dismissed the Movement as 'a permaculture fad' and 'hippie-juju', now denounced it as 'eco-tyranny' and 'glorified cannibalism'.

The Movement used to claim that Military was the first to draw blood. I would echo the claim to all who would listen.

"It's all Military's fault! They attacked us first!" In my naïve-little-girl voice, full of naïve-little-girl conviction. I was seven, my head crammed with Movement folklore.

Once, when I uttered this slogan while watching the news, Mama stared at the screen and murmured, "Truth is the first casualty of war."

"What does that mean? It sounds like an insult!"

Mama turned the tablet over on the table. "*We* started it. We hacked their database."

I wanted to tell her she was wrong because the Movement was good, the Movement had honour, but I knew that the word 'hack' signified something invasive, a breach, an act of aggression. I felt it like a blunt twig in my stomach, twisting and pushing its way inside me. 'Hack' meant force and force was bad.

"But," I said, my brain seeking a way out of this moral predicament. "But…"

She drew me onto her lap, and even though I thought myself too big for such indulgences, I let her. "They retaliated. We knew they would. We just thought… Well, we didn't know how quickly. Or how hard. They released the silver bullets because they were afraid we would hack them again. You know what silver bullets are, don't you?"

I nodded. Even before we started to learn of them in school, I had read about the special silver phones available only to Military agents, long and narrow and filled with clever tech that could breach any firewall.

"We hacked Military and they hacked us back with a vengeance," Mama said, "turning kettles and medical equipment into weapons, bribing morgue attendants to plant bombs in our dead. We forgot that what we hold sacred is meaningless to them. So, the dead came home from the cities and we buried them in the feeding grounds, and Military waited for our feast days, when they knew we would gather in the grounds in numbers. And soldiers in bases far away entered codes into their silver bullets…"

The only way to defend a settlement from Military attack was to go off the grid. Some settlements managed a hasty transition. Others were blown up before they could try.

One rainy night three years into the war, Military seized the University of Ghana along with a chunk of its staff and students. My parents, both UG employees, became the property of Military Inc. My mother, a consulting botanist, and my father, an anatomy lecturer, were classified 'high-potential' and transferred to Base 753 with their only underage child.

"I don't like it here," I told my parents a few days after arriving at the base.

"It doesn't matter," Papa replied. "Nothing here is real. It's only an approximation of life. Nothing was ever meant to be as clean as these floors or as bleached as these walls. Home is real. Remember that."

My mother chided him later when they thought I was asleep. "You're not helping anyone with talk like that. We're stuck here. She has to adjust."

"Why should she adjust? This place is the one that must adjust."

"It's not going to! You want to get us all killed?"

"There are worse things than dying."

"Stop it. She's only a child!" My mother's voice trembled with fear. Or perhaps it was anger.

"There are no children in Base 753," my father said. "All of us are nothing more than property. Rebellion is the only currency we have left."

"If you wanted our child to be a war hero, you should have let them execute us instead of signing the contract. We made our choice. At least have the integrity to live with it."

I listened for a long time afterwards, but there was no response.

* * *

The contract the prisoners were forced to sign bound us to Military for twenty years. We were allowed to communicate with family until, fearing security breaches, Military instituted a full blackout. We didn't speak to anyone outside the base for eighteen years.

My parents spent long hours working in the base's laboratories, while I worked in the greenhouses with the other 'excess baggage', relatives of the UG staff and students. Military's resistance to permaculture kept their crops strained and struggling. There was too much rain or too little and they refused to focus on crops that could adapt.

Every few weeks, soldiers would come into the greenhouses and hand out a new concoction from the labs – fertiliser, pesticides, miracle growth serum. We applied the treatments dutifully. If anyone tried to make a suggestion, the silver bullets would come out.

"Hmm, where should I strike?" a soldier would ask, holding up his phone so we could all see the blinking red dots on the screen. "You in the blue shirt – you're from Kpeve, right? Would you like to see it rain blood in your settlement?"

About a year after our arrival, a small patch of the garden fared better than the others, producing small but hardy tomatoes and aubergine. An investigation was launched. It emerged that the prisoner responsible for that section hadn't used the sanctioned fertiliser, but had instead set up a compost heap in a corner of the base's landfill. He vanished in the middle of the night, never to be seen again. When we returned to the garden in the morning, his section was bare. Every plant there had been uprooted.

For people raised in the Movement, accustomed to organic and free-range food, the canned rations and chemical-soaked fresh produce took a toll. It was not long before prisoners began to complain of various ailments.

"You people are weak," the soldiers told us.

We looked into their jaundiced eyes and said nothing.

Three hundred and twelve UG employees and their excess baggage were transferred to Base 753. By the time the contracts expired, only fourteen of us remained. Three days before the contract was up, three days before we were due to return home, Papa collapsed in the lab. A heart attack. He was dead before he reached the infirmary.

* * *

In the days that were and the days that are to come, there is a tree. It is a beast of a tree, wide enough to hold a city in its bowels. We call the tree Difo, meaning fullness, because it sustains us all. It towers so high none can see the top of it, with roots so deep they are said to tickle the earth's core. There is no need to hunt, no need to till the earth, for the tree caters to the needs of all. People and animals alike come to it to feed. Rivers run through it, nourished by its roots. Our relationship to food is simple – we eat when we are hungry. That is all.

"Nourish me and I will nourish you," Difo tells us, and so every dead creature, man or beast, is fed to her, the bodies placed inside her trunk before nightfall and consumed by dawn.

It is the way of nature to give and receive. There's no need for conflict because there is enough for all. Who could control Difo? None, for she is too great.

This is not a myth from our past but a vision of our future. This is the world we hope to someday inhabit. Those of us who follow the Movement believe in this vision with all our hearts. We share it with others, we gather in its name, and we invest our time and resources towards its fulfilment. For me, for many others, the Movement is sacred.

I dreamed of Difo often in the base, longing for her to stretch out her branches and pluck us out of hell. She never came.

* * *

"What would happen if we didn't give Papa to Difo?" I asked Mama as we waited to be processed and released from the base.

She glared at me with such shock that I wished I could swallow my words. "Why would you say such a thing? What, you want to put him in a box for eternity like they do here, so he can never touch the soil of his ancestors again?"

"We could cremate him." It was blasphemy to even suggest it. To deprive a body of communion with the earth, to deprive Difo of the nutrients required to sustain life, to pollute the air with waste… Unthinkable.

Mama didn't speak to me for the next hour.

The last of the prisoners of war were released that day, dragging three caskets that carried our recent dead. As soon as we stepped outside, the iron gates slammed shut behind us as though Base 753 was as eager to expel us as we were to leave.

We were stunned to find strangers waiting at the gates. They introduced themselves as representatives of the Movement and greeted us all by name. A crowd milled around behind them, cheering and clapping. Their joy both moved and confused me.

"Welcome home," they said. "Welcome back to the world."

It took some time for us to understand what was going on – and even longer to believe it. Military was a relic. Their supporters had gone underground or lived on the fringes of society, trading processed food on the dark web, clinging to a way of life that had long faded. Base 753 was the only base still operating, a desperate last stand.

We had been locked away for so long that we couldn't see the changes taking place around us. The war was over. The Movement had won.

"Why didn't you storm Base 753 and rescue us?" I demanded as two of the men among the crowd hoisted Papa's casket onto their shoulders.

One of the other representatives countered my animosity with a smile. "The Movement doesn't condone aggression.

That's what started the war in the first place. We knew they would release you. We could wait."

"Did it occur to you that we couldn't? If you had come for us long ago, my father might still be alive."

"Afiwa…"

I ignored my mother's outstretched hand and marched towards the waiting bus.

* * *

Grief was dense. It dropped into our homecoming and spread, tainting everything. I struggled to adjust to a world without soldiers and tiled floors and strips of window that offered glimpses of sky. The real sky was monstrous. I feared it would suck me up into its blue boundlessness. I couldn't look up for days.

Accustomed to the eerie silence of the base, every little sound in the settlement made me jump.

"It's only a cricket, Afiwa," Kodzo would say in the quiet voice of someone afraid of waking a lion.

He was different from the boy I remembered. No longer brash and impulsive, poking good-natured fun at me every chance he got, he was now measured and wise and held me in his palm like an egg.

Grief was selfish, making me forget that Mama and I were not the only ones in mourning. My father belonged to Kodzo, too, to the settlement, to the Movement. They sat around the fire the night we came back, shedding silent tears and telling warm, funny stories of Papa and of others who had died in bases around the country.

Grief was moody, most of all. I sat alone, leaning against a tree, watching the others. They didn't feel like my people. Their faces were familiar but it was as if our energies were no longer in sync. I missed my fellow prisoners. Perhaps *they* were my people now. We were all of us survivors, but it was different. A difference that wounded, when what I wanted more than anything was to heal.

Mama came to sit beside me. "You've barely spoken to your brother."

"What am I supposed to say?" I glanced back at our laughing relatives.

"Don't be angry," Mama said. "They had the Movement to help them heal. We only had each other."

We carried the dead to the feeding ground the following day, Kodzo and I holding our father between us. I couldn't cry as we delivered him into Difo's mouth.

"We give her our beloved," the settlement's orator intoned, "knowing that our grief will one day bear fruit."

"Amen," we chorused.

"Listen, Difo! Hear our prayers."

"Listen, listen! Hear our prayers."

"With this gift, we nurture you…"

"…that you may nurture us."

It was only after we had covered the grave that my tears came.

* * *

Deep in the night, I returned to the grave and lay down on the place where we had buried Papa. I pressed my ear to the soil.

If reality had half the imagination of myth, I'd have heard Difo feeding. I closed my eyes and imagined my father dissolving into glowing dust, each speck alive with his essence. I listened to the specks sink into the earth, into Difo's blessed belly, where they would dance with the dust of all the other dead.

They would dance for days, I imagined, and weeks and months – as long as it took for the right seeds to rain down on them and drink them up. Then they would perform a different dance altogether as they churned within the seeds, their movements ever more frenzied until they could no longer contain themselves, and they burst into life once again.

Oh, how I envied them! To be part of the cycle, to be home at last, not just home under the sky, among my people, but home in the truest sense, in the only sense that mattered.

If reality had half the imagination of myth, I would join them simply by thinking it, and we would all be reunited, Papa and Grandmother and the countless neighbours and cousins and aunts and uncles, so many times removed.

Nurture me...

My hands moved over the mound of earth, fingers digging deep.

...and I will nurture you.

The earth shifted beneath me, a movement so unexpected that I sat up and looked around, half expecting to see soldiers armed with silver bullets. I glanced down, wondering whether Military had dared to desecrate my father's body with one of their bombs, then lay down once more, my heart too broken to keep the fear in. There were worse things than dying.

Difo's mouth opened and swallowed me whole. No warning, no time to even scream. I was falling and falling and falling and—

* * *

I woke in bed, blinking into my mother's anxious face.

"There was a sinkhole under the feeding ground," she told me. "Can you believe we never knew? It took life. No people, no animals that we could see, but a few large trees and an anthill. Good trees, trees that fed our people well." She smiled, touching my face. "But Difo spared you."

I forced myself to smile back and ignore the curling disappointment in my belly. There were worse things than dying.

Like being left behind.

* * *

There was so much to be done – leftover bombs to locate and disarm, wounds to heal, fledgling settlements to guide on their journey to Difo. There were workshops. So many workshops, meetings, training in interdependent conduct and conflict resolution, and gatherings that lasted through the night, designed to bond us to Difo and each other, to all our brethren around the world.

"This is stupid," I murmured at my first workshop as the others went around the circle, sharing their vulnerabilities.

"It's OK to be afraid," Kodzo said from his place at my side.

"I'm not afraid," I snapped. "It's just stupid. Talking won't change the past."

"We're not trying to change the past. We're trying to change the future."

He was gentle and patient with me. My response was to cringe at every word out of his mouth. The base had made me bitter. Not just me – other returnees, as well, and many in the fledgling settlements. The workshops chewed us long and slow, to draw the sweetness out.

Work saved me. At first, I worked to distract myself from the nagging ache to follow my father into Difo's mouth, and then I worked to honour his memory. In time, I worked because I'd regained my faith and wanted my life to count for something.

When the elders asked to see me many months after our return, I knew they planned to give me an official role at last. Kodzo was there in the Chief's backyard, leaning against the wall like a decoration, watching me with earnest, worried eyes.

"There's a task that must be done and we feel you are best placed to do it," the Chief said.

Mama sat beside me, brow furrowed. "She's not ready to train fledglings yet. She still talks about *ploughing*!"

"Mama!" I shot her an embarrassed glance.

The Chief didn't smile, and he was a man who smiled easily. "It's not that kind of task. It's outreach. A negotiation."

The knot in my chest eased. "Oh! Yes, I'm happy to do that."

"Among hostiles," he went on.

I swallowed hard. I had accompanied Kodzo on a few trips out of the settlement, into the ruins of cities where the last of Military's supporters lived. I had even seen some of them, but Kodzo had never let me close enough to hear him try to coax them into our way of life.

"Watch the panels," he'd tell me. "They'll sneak up to the car and steal them if you're not careful."

I would stand by the truck with my eye on the solar panels attached to the bonnet that charged the vehicle's batteries. I'd steal glances at Kodzo as he spoke to the lost souls. Often, they'd see the sense in his words. Hunger could be compelling. When the bus came around a day later, they would board it and make a home in one of the fledgling settlements.

Part of me expected the fledglings to cause trouble. I held my breath, waiting to hear that they had turned out to be spies, that they had slaughtered people in their sleep. Such news never came, but that gave me no relief. I continued to hold my breath.

With this in mind, I looked at my brother, then at my mother, then at the Chief. My stomach roiled, but I knew what my duty was. "If the Movement needs me in hostile territory, I will go."

The Chief hesitated. Something passed between the elders, a strange, secret look.

A gasp left my mother's lips. She leapt to her feet. "No! No, you can't ask that of her!"

"We ask it of both of you," the Chief replied. "She will need a second."

"Ask what, Mama?" I swallowed my fear.

"They want you to go back," Mama said. "To the base."

For a moment, I wished once more that I had died in that sinkhole. Only for a moment, before I remembered that the Movement needed me, breathing and willing.

"I'll do it," I said.

* * *

So here I am, back in my old prison almost two years after release, sitting before what remains of Military Inc.'s Board. I clasp my trembling hands and rest them on the table.

The chairperson clears her throat twice before speaking.

"It was a surprise to see you." Her gaze shifts to my mother. "Employees don't return after their contracts expire."

We don't comment on her use of the term 'employees' instead of 'prisoners'. We've had two decades of experience in Military delusion.

"We have heard your proposal," the Chair continues. "But I'm afraid the Movement offers us nothing of value."

I open my mouth to retort. The pressure of Mama's hand on my knee reminds me to keep my cool. "We offer you survival, Madam Chair." I take a moment to look at the six members of the Board, their faces gaunt. "Your people are starving. You're out of rations, not to mention clean water."

"We have top-of-the-range filtration systems—"

"Top of which range, exactly?"

The Chair bristles. "Listen here, young lady. You're lucky we gave you a hearing and didn't drop you where you stood when you turned up uninvited. Do not mistake our magnanimity for weakness! We still have silver bullets trained on your settlements."

I pause, weighing my words. The Movement teaches us to show compassion, even to those who have wronged us. A year ago, I wouldn't have been able to sit here, facing these people. Now I breathe deeply, drawing strength from

Difo, from the communal well of the Movement. I'm still angry, but I won't let that derail my mission.

"No one has fired a silver bullet in years," I reply. "Those performances you put on for us when we were here, waving the bullets, showing us the dots on the screens – they convinced us then when we knew no better. But we know now. The Movement dismantled the networks the bullets rely on. They don't work. You have no leverage."

The chairperson forces a laugh. "I'd be happy to prove you wrong."

"Please, be my guest." I lean back in my chair.

Silence. The Board members shift in their seats, their expressions stoic. The soldiers face forward, useless silver bullets still peeking from their pockets. Not one of them has moved to draw the weapons. I see now, so clearly, that I can't believe I couldn't see before. How thin they are, how much of their uniform is padding, how much of their menace is posturing.

"We are willing to consider a truce," the chairperson says at last. "But we have conditions."

"We offered you a fledgling settlement where you'll have access to the same resources as anyone else."

"We want immunity."

Give Military a finger and they want all four limbs. I shake my head. "There will be a tribunal. Even within the Movement, those who perpetuated atrocities during the war are held accountable. We can't have one rule for ourselves and another for you." A wave of resistance rises against the words I'm required to speak next. I swallow it down. "If found guilty, you will live out your days in the settlement under house arrest. No death penalty, no inhumane treatment. That's the best deal you'll ever get. I advise you to take it."

The chairperson sneers. "You think we want to live like you, eating your filthy food?"

"Your chemicals are banned now," I remind her. "As long as you don't pollute the planet, which is still healing from your last onslaught, you can eat what you like."

"No. Total immunity or no deal."

I sigh. The Chief of our settlement told me that several delegations visited Base 753 before our release and were turned away. That's why he sent me, a former prisoner. Because Military would be curious enough to let me in.

"You might have to go more than once," he said.

"Why? If they refuse, what's the point in going back?"

"You prefer that we wait for them to die and then breach their walls?"

I didn't answer, but he knew what my silence meant.

"Violence is the last resort," he said. "A life saved is a life in service to the Movement. That's useful."

"A new feeding ground on the site of an old base is useful, too."

He didn't chastise me for my lack of compassion. He placed his hand on my head and smiled. "Handle that anger wisely."

Now, I turn towards my mother. Her gaze holds mine, steady and strong. As my second, she is here to bear witness, to support, not to advise. I know what to do.

I face the Board once more. "I'm sorry we couldn't come to terms."

The chairperson's eyes flicker for a moment, and then she nods. Soldiers usher Mama and me out of the base. Kodzo is waiting in the truck, with the Chief in the passenger seat.

"No deal," I report as I take my seat in the back.

The Chief nods, disappointed but unsurprised. "We will try again."

A look passes between me and Mama. We understand what the Chief can't. Military will never surrender. They were mighty, once. Now, all that remains of their empire is pride. Without that, what do they have? They will stay inside those walls, seeing nothing more than a strip of sky, and die.

With two years of healing and training under my belt, I wish I could say the thought saddens me, but it doesn't. Military or Movement, we all nurture Difo in the end. There are worse things than dying, like resisting the inevitability of change.

Once I was a naïve little girl with a father and now I'm a grown woman without. Once we were at war and now we are not. Once the earth glittered with golden things that leeched the life from her, and now she glitters with green things that pour the life back. One day, the whole world will be Difo. After that… Well, our children's children will see.

As we drive away, the others already discussing the next task, I glance back at the base. I picture the feeding ground that will grow here like another Altar someday, over cracked walls and broken gates. Difo will take the specks of greed, pain, and brutality, and transform them.

Into freedom for the dead and fruit for the living.

Into an explosion of emerald colour to reclaim the red, dead soil.

The Storymage

THE GIRL sits on the floor of the old dock office, hugging her knees. She has jet skin, red hair, double-lidded eyes that look past me. A circular scab on her hand tells me she's undergoing Adjusting. She must be close to complete adaptation, or the Sea would have killed her already. Her documents identify her as Sechaba, and the mechs call her Setch, but in the several minutes I've been here, she hasn't answered to either name.

It's just the two of us in the cramped, musty space. The office has been out of use for some time now, replaced by a shinier version on the east end of the harbour. Filled with neglected crates and boxes, it stinks of mould, and the ceiling has been taken over by bulbous firemoth egg sacs. The windows are closed against wind, Sea spray and prying eyes. Down here in the pit, where mechs toil day and night to keep Jalaba's ships running, anything that breaks routine attracts attention. With Adze manning street corners and cargo ships, their sticky fingers in every pie, crime is inevitable. But this is different. Anomalous, as the Law would say.

I glance at the clock on the desk. We have an hour, maybe two. Enough, I think, if I work quickly, but I've never worked a truth like this before. Fear reaches into me and scrapes my walls, great enough to hollow me out if I let it. But I won't. This is my chance.

With a deep breath, I lean forward in my chair. "Do you remember what happened on the ferry, Sechaba?"

Silence.

"One of the other apprentices found you kneeling over the dead boy with a knife in your hand. There was blood all over your hands and clothes."

Silence.

"Did you kill him?"

I don't expect her to answer. She hasn't spoken since she was discovered at the scene, not even to declare her innocence. The deceased was a stranger who most likely arrived on the ferry this morning. No one in the pit has any idea who he was or where he came from. Just a boy, 12, maybe 11, skin dappled with the scaly green patches associated with malaise. A junior junkie from the outskirts, the pit boys said, with unconcerned shrugs. Malaise makes you crazy. Everyone knows that. He probably did it to himself.

Setch is a good one, the mechs insisted, a natural, only a few months shy of graduating from apprentice to official. Naughty, but not crazy. Setch doesn't run around sticking knives into children. Watching her sit there, rocking back and forth, her back hitting the wall so hard it makes me wince, I'm not sure.

If it were up to the mechs, the matter would be closed already. Setch is one of their own, and the child was a stranger. But someone called the Law, who wheedled and threatened and coaxed while Sechaba sat there, slamming her shoulder blades into the wall. The Law did what they were required to do in anomalous situations. They sent for Counsel.

Counsel is strong and certain, steady steps on firm ground, clear thinking and clever theories. He makes order out of chaos. He smooths things over. He's not known for making catatonic possible murderers confess, but if anyone could, I suppose it would be him. They sent for Counsel, not for me. When the message came to the Great Hall, Counsel was out, the senior apprentices were nowhere in sight and I... Well, I was desperate. Five months, I've been in seclusion. Five months after a year in his service, learning a trade that didn't call me, living as a shadow until I could exist again.

A dead boy. A mute witness. The messenger must have said something about justice and clarity and settling things once and for all, but that's not what I heard. What I heard was…fuel. Food for my story-starved soul. Five months is a long time to go hungry.

I didn't pass the message on to Counsel. I knew what he'd say. "This work is not yours to do. You have yet to find your place." He says it often, as though repetition will make it true. There is no place for me, and we both know it. I am a thing that once was, ceased to be and has become again. I must make my own place, and so, instead of calling Counsel or running to fetch one of the seniors, I broke the rules. I asked the messenger to lead the way.

I'd been high up in the towers of the Great Hall for so long that I had forgotten what the world looked like, but when I stepped out, I remembered the sky, always roiling with dark clouds. The sour Sea tang in the air, the high, narrow streets above a maze of canals, the jostling. When we reached the dock, I longed to stop and gaze out past the ferries and subs. I missed the Sea. I missed the world. But not nearly as much as I missed stories.

"Sechaba, if you say nothing, the Law will take you away. Do you understand?"

Silence.

My gaze slides to the clock once more, and I know I don't have the luxury of waiting any longer. Setch won't talk to me, so I must talk to her. I inch the chair to the left until I'm directly opposite her, staring into her blank eyes, and then I wait for the tale to turn me.

My craft is an old one. I know this in my bones and from fragmented legends about times past. It comes slowly, as always, beginning with an itch behind the ears, a tentative knock on the inside of my skull. Querying, testing the waters, wondering whether I'll let it in. Yes, old friend. The door is open. I part my lips and let the words come.

It's a simple tale, an old-fashioned 'A long time ago' story, the kind my own grandparents might have told me as a child. It's a maybe-folktale that sounds like the history of a people, a tale that warms the belly in the telling, a comforting, familiar balm. The words don't matter. It's a strange thing because one would think it was the words that held the power, but it's not. The words are merely vessels. The story lies beneath them, inside them, hidden in the folds. The true listener must read between the lines.

Sechaba stops rocking. Her eyes flicker and then focus on my mouth. I sense her longing, almost lecherous in its intensity, and slowly, her limbs unfold and she crawls across the floor until she reaches my feet. She won't speak, not yet. This is a small tale, a key to turn the lock. I'm knocking on her door as the tale knocked on mine, and she is considering opening up to let me in.

The tale ends. She looks at me, eyes wide with expectation. I look back.

"If you want another one, you must ask for it."

Her tongue slides over her lips, and her eyes dart left and right. She reaches out to place one hand over my feet, her touch cold against the exposed skin between the sandal straps.

"Again." Her voice is a raspy whisper. "Again."

And so I tell another tale, another innocent story of a girl who opened a box she was told to leave alone. A warning tale, like many she has heard before, no doubt. This one feels different, though. It evokes a vague anxiety, the sense that something is not quite right.

Sechaba gasps. "I was only going to look at the engine," she says.

It is here that my story ends and hers begins. As the words spill out of her I see things as she had seen them.

Sechaba snuck onto the boat to examine its inner workings, the heart of the job she was almost trained enough to do. It was a brand-new ferry, the latest model. She was curious. She had waited until all the passengers were off, or so she thought.

She found the boy, crazed and desperate, in the cabin of the abandoned ferry. Standing there, where he was not supposed to be. Panting, spittle running down his jaw. Clutching a very big, very rusty knife.

"I saw him stick the blade in," she says. "But he didn't see me, not till I screamed. He fell and I took the blade out, but that made it worse." She shakes her head. "Blood everywhere, just kept coming. I wanted to run but my mind went funny. I couldn't think, couldn't move."

She speaks the truth, and yet I sense that a lie lurks somewhere inside this story.

"Malaise makes people crazy," Sechaba whispers.

I see it then. The lie. I see the dying boy on the floor of the ferry cabin, with his malaise-stained skin, and I know it wasn't the drug that took him. I see his eyes, sightless now in the shimmer of Sechaba's recollection. In that instant, I know what killed him. I see beyond his gaze into his fading mind. There was a secret. Someone else's secret, something the boy sought out and thought he could use to his advantage. But in our world, there is a price to be paid by those who take what was not meant for them. The dead boy didn't understand this, and in that ignorance, he was not alone.

Leaping to my feet, I rush to the office door and throw it open. A boy jumps out of the way. He looks at me in panic and I see his tale before he has time to think about telling it. He is the one who found Sechaba at the scene, and instead of waiting to hear her account before the Law, he crept to the door and eavesdropped on my sacred, secret stories.

"What have you done?" I grab him by the shoulders and shake him, terror filling my consciousness until spots dance before my eyes. "Why are you standing out here, *listening*?"

"I'm sorry! I wanted to know…"

"Those stories were not for your ears!" I release him. There is still time. The tale might not have taken hold yet. "Come inside. I'll fix it."

But he turns and flees, and it takes me a moment to recover enough to give chase. I'm no match for a mech apprentice, though, and before I reach the other end of the dock, he has vanished. My fear sharpens as I turn back towards the old office. I did what I set out to do. I used what called to me and uncovered the truth. But I also made matters worse, unravelling the thin thread that holds everything together. There will be more death, more scandal, unless I find the boy. I can fix it. I'm sure I can. But I can't hide from Counsel.

When I reach the office, Setch is standing in the doorway.

"That boy," I ask, "do you know him well?" She nods. "Where would he run to? If he was scared. Where would he go?"

"I…" She shakes her head, her mind still trapped in the cobweb remnants of my tales. "He likes the water."

Water? Which water? Our whole world is water. Swallowing my panic, I wait for her thoughts to coalesce. There are no quiet, contemplative spaces in Jalaba, no corner that doesn't bustle with boats and bodies. The apprentice won't return to work. He'll seek sanctuary. But where?

"The cliffs," says Sechaba at last. "We go there sometimes. Kranes drop all kinds of scrap on the rocks; you can find good parts if you look hard enough. Juju says it's the best place in town."

I look towards the north. Mist hides the better part of the cliffs.

"He likes to climb." She almost whispers the words, her gaze lowered. The rocks are jagged and slick with krane oil. Not even Adze would attempt to scale those cliffs.

"You've seen him do it?"

She shakes her head. "He told me. He says you can get all the way to the top if you know where to put your feet."

"Ai! She speaks!"

The voice comes from behind me. I turn to see that mechs have gathered in their greasy overalls, hands and faces streaked with grime.

"Yes, she speaks," I reply, eager to leave. "Tell the Law she's ready to give her account. I'm sorry; I must go."

"Your credit!" one of the mechs calls out as I hurry past, but I can't stop, not even to claim the fee.

I have to return to the Great Hall and tell Counsel what I've done.

* * *

He's waiting when I burst into the Hall. Standing in the middle of the room, hands clasped behind his back, head tipped backwards. Contemplating the ceiling, maybe. More likely despairing of ever instilling proper discipline in his junior apprentice.

"Counsel, sir."

He lowers his head.

I'm short of breath and dishevelled, which is never wise in Counsel's presence. "I'm sorry. I was—"

"I know where you were. What I don't know is why."

He refuses to face me, and I feel the heat of shame as my thoughts spin in a desperate effort to justify my actions. Why did I answer the call? Why do you think, Counsel? Because you've locked me in this glorious temple for the last five months, your prisoner, your prize. Intense study, you called it, as though it were a reward. Because you've drained me with tests and notes and constitutional trivia. Because I was wasting away while you took your time deciding what to do with me, where to place me, how to use me to your advantage. Because, Counsel, *sir*, I was starving.

The words collect in my head and remain there, clanging against each other. At last, Counsel deigns to look at me.

"You had no right."

"I'm sorry, sir."

"You're no Counsel," he says. "Not even close. I have had to bend you to make you fit into this mould, but even as an apprentice, you're a disappointment. You're too flighty, governed by your emotions, by that monstrous chasm in your soul that cries out for stories like a suckling child. I thought intense study might finally change you, but look. Look what you've done now! Will you ever learn to control yourself?"

Swallowing my humiliation, I whisper, "I try, sir."

"You try? I have never seen you try! You are constantly giving in to your primitive urge, and there is no place for that sort of thing in this world. As for running off to answer a call in my absence…" He grunts in disgust. "I risked my work, my standing, to save you from alienation, and you thank me by spitting in my face! The Law depends on Counsel to find answers where others have failed. How can you do that without discipline?"

There is no answer I can give that would satisfy him, no way to reassure him that I'm worth the sacrifices he's made for me. I have no affinity for any of the accepted crafts. I waited for years, watching children my age and younger find their callings and take their places as apprentices. By the time I was three years past my apprentice assignment, the only thing that moved me was stories. But stories are not a calling, not anymore, and the Placement Committee would have exiled me if Counsel hadn't stepped in.

I know I should be grateful. He broke our most sacred rule to save me. He lied to the Committee, told them he'd witnessed my call to counselcraft one afternoon in the Great Hall courtyard. He told them I was a late-blooming natural. Now his words wash over me, words he has uttered so many times I know them all by heart. I'm tired. Less hungry after Sechaba, but so tired.

And then I remember the reason I came back here. The boy, Juju. The cliffs.

"I did the work, sir."

Counsel falls silent, stunned by my interruption.

"I shouldn't have answered your call, but I worked the truth and I found the answers, all by myself." Now that I've begun, the words come quickly. "The girl, Sechaba, she didn't kill the stranger. She found him on the ferry and he killed himself in front of her. She thought it was malaise. It looked like malaise, but it wasn't. It was a calling curse. I saw it in his eyes as he died, in the girl's memories. He took in secrets crafted for the ears of another and they turned him the wrong way. That's when I realised that there was someone outside, eavesdropping, and I—"

"Your skills aren't advanced enough for that kind of work," Counsel cuts in.

"I didn't use counselcraft. When I got there the entire syllabus left me and I used my own...my *primitive* urge."

His lips curl in a snarl. "Impossible."

"I tried to tell you before, sir. Stories are medicine—"

He strikes me with the back of his hand, so hard I almost lose my balance. "Heresy!"

My cheek burns and I fear his ring might have torn the skin, but there's no time to nurse it. "Counsel, please. The boy who overheard has run away. I need your help to find him."

"My help?" he bellows and then bursts into bitter laughter. "After your insubordination? After flaunting your superstition in public and tarnishing the name of this Hall? Now you want me to help you clean up your mess?"

"It's only…" I hesitate. "He went to the cliffs, I think. I would have followed him on my own before returning here, but the kranes…"

Downturned lips, narrowed eyes. Counsel's disdain is palpable.

"Please, sir. The tales I told to make Sechaba talk weren't made for other ears. The apprentice who heard me, Juju…"

"Then go and fix it."

"The kranes." I bite my lip, embarrassed by my weakness.

"A whole apprentice, afraid of birds?" His features have shifted now, settling into an almost smile. Maybe he's revelling in my torment. "Assuming your speculation is correct, you'd better find your eavesdropper before the curse claims him. If you run you might be able to make it back for evening study."

He means it. He's not going to help me. As soon as this becomes clear I flee, terrified that I might already be too late. Through the crowded streets, into the market, dodging bio-chip vendors and metal drums filled with plucked waterfowl and writhing tentacled beasts. Hawkers sidle up to me, opening their coats to reveal illicit tech, and I don't even stop long enough to shake my head.

I glance down at the motors in the canals below, their engines screaming as they pull out of designated stops, spraying the pavement with green Seawater. Maybe it would be faster to take one. No; traffic is too slow and there is no time for haggling over fares. I head up the Hundred Steps, past the consortium, weaving my way through the queue outside the main Conservator bank.

By the time I'm back at the dock a light drizzle has started. Past the ferries. Around the executive harbour. Almost colliding with two tall Adze in bright wax print shirts so crisp they must be new. One reaches for the stunner at his hip before realising that I'm only a harmless girl, and moving away with a grunt.

Then comes the beach, thronged with vendors and tourists. I avoid it by taking the hiking trail. A small private yacht club, another market, and then the cliff and rocks, crammed together along the coastline. I hear the kranes before I see them. Their guttural call is aggressive, almost malevolent, and I keep my head down to avoid attracting their gaze.

It is said that they don't like us. Not just Counsels, but Sanguines and Creators, too. They don't like anyone who looks too deeply, or thinks too hard, or knows what others wish to hide. No one says how they feel about people like me, because people like me no longer exist. The words they used to call us have faded away and language closed over the gaps the way the Sea covers sunken ships.

I slip and trip over the rocks until I'm almost out of earshot of the market, then look up. In all honesty, I don't expect to see Juju, yet there he is, climbing like Sechaba said. My breath catches for a moment, but he moves with purpose and skill.

He's too far away to hear me call, so I continue my slow journey. A clutch of kranes has perched a short distance away. There aren't many, less than ten, but the smallest is as big as a man, rubbery wings large enough to engulf me. I swallow my panic and watch them out of the corner of my eye. Their long grey bodies squat on the rocks, glistening with oil, wings folded back, angular heads bowed as their skinny arms pick through the treasure they've brought up from the sea. Suddenly one of them turns to face me. Its blue eyes narrow and it bares a row of sharp black teeth, hissing, alerting the others to my presence.

Heart racing, I bow my head to show them I mean no harm. I'm not here for them. They don't respond, and it's an agonising eternity before they stop staring. Another krane flies overhead, casting a vast shadow, and I duck instinctively although it's far above me.

I'm at the foot of the cliff now. I reach out to test the rock. My hand slides over the rough surface and comes away slick with oil. How did Juju make it up there? I focus my gaze on the rock, seeking. Stories can do many things, but they require a level of reciprocity. The rock must yield, and I don't have enough experience to know whether it will.

The water pounds against the rocks behind me, washing up all the way to my feet, drenching the hem of my skirt before I have a chance to snatch it out of harm's way. The silky trim isn't Seaproof; I watch the fabric curl in on itself and harden. I've taken to dressing for libraries and gilded staircases rather than the streets. Counsel apprentices aren't meant to go clambering over rocks. They are made for sedate conversations in quiet rooms. But I'm not a true apprentice.

I wait for the tale to come. It takes time to find a connection here, the rock too old, too solid. Maybe I'm naïve to think I can work truth out of a cliff, but Juju left a trail, and the stories might be able to follow that. Words come to me. It's a tale so ephemeral I'm afraid I'll lose it. As I speak the words, I realise it's not a tale at all, but more of a proverb.

It's not enough, but fate is on my side today. I look up to see Juju descending, and the fear leaves my body. I sink to the ground, waiting for him to reach me.

"Why'd you follow?" he demands a moment before he jumps to the ground. "I said sorry. Didn't I? What else?"

I get to my feet. "What you did was dangerous."

"I know, I know! Bad luck to eavesdrop. Might hear Adze secrets, curse you so you go to the water and drink till you die." He scratches his arm, and the back of his neck and the top of his head. "Not the truth. Truth is bigger than that. I know. Other things, not just Adze curses. Story things, eh? I know. It's why the blade, that kid. Saw or heard something he wasn't supposed to, made his mind go funny, then the blade. I know. I see it. I see everything."

It's raining properly now, but neither of us makes any move to seek shelter.

"What do you see, Juju?"

He shivers and doesn't answer. Instead, he says: "Special places for your feet. On the cliff; that's how I get up. Special places, safe and you don't slip because the oil's mixed with the lichen and thickened. Kranes showed me. Clever things,

321

eh, kranes. Like mechs. Pick things up, pull them apart, put them back together. Not like you. You break things, and can't fix them. Broke that kid with your stories, now trying to break me. I see it. I see everything."

Indignation fills me. "I had nothing to do with what happened to that child!"

"Someone like you, then."

"There is no one like me. It was a calling curse. He should have known better. So should you."

Juju shakes his head. "Told mechs not to let you work Setch, but…" He shrugs. "Wanted it over. Counsel sent her, they said. Sent *you*? Girl without a calling for so long, not even a senior apprentice? Mechs called for your father, not you. Why'd you come? Don't you know your place?"

The world feels close all at once, tight and unyielding, and I find it hard to breathe. Where is the story? I'm waiting and waiting, but it seems to be lost. Where is the tale that will keep this boy safe from the consequences of his curiosity? That's why I came here, to fix what I broke. To redeem myself. Why is he so ungrateful?

Maybe it's this place. Maybe it's the kranes, watching me with their beady blue eyes, scaring my stories away.

"Let's go back to the dock," I shout over the rain. "You'll get in trouble for being away so long. By the time we get back, all of this will be sorted out." I say it like I'm certain.

"Not going back to work."

"But—"

"Not going."

I shift position, trying to meet his gaze. Stories are medicine, but… He looks at me, and I can see the change in his eyes. They're rolling around in the sockets, too bright, too wide, bulging and red. Old friend, where are you? Come and help me, please.

"What are you?" Juju cries out.

"What do you mean? I'm a junior apprentice Counsel."

"No. What are you?"

Ah, yes. He sees everything. "I don't know," I confess. "Something…old. Something bad."

"Find out." He's starting to sway on his feet. "Can't do your work if you don't know what to call it." A sudden sharp cry escapes his lips. "Oh, it hurts!" He begins scratching again, clawing at his skin as though trying to get under it.

"Juju, stop!" I look into his spinning eyes, searching for my story in vain.

He drops to his knees and begins to bang his forehead against the rocks.

Where is it? Where is the story? I fling myself at the boy and wrap my arms around his shoulders, straining to hold him upright. He's crying now, a loud, drawn-out sound that culminates in a choked gasp before starting up again. My grip slackens a little, and he forces his torso forward, breaking free. His head hits the rock, and when I pull him up, he's bleeding.

Something grabs my foot. I kick hard before turning to see my assailant. The kranes have come to rescue their mech friend from the wicked apprentice Counsel.

"I'm trying to help him!" I tell them as he pulls us both downwards with strength a boy smaller than me shouldn't possess.

His head slams against the rock once more. The kranes hiss and jab their bony fingers at me.

"Stupid creatures! I'm trying to save him!"

They grab my feet and pull my hair, hissing through the rain.

I jerk and curse but refuse to let go. "Go away! This has nothing to do with you!"

But they don't leave.

"Stop it, stupid things! This isn't your place!"

And then...oh! I see it – the glaring obstruction in my path, the reason the tales haven't come to me when I most need them. Like Juju, I see everything now, and for a moment, I'm too astonished to move, paralysed by my stupidity. When the shock fades, I release him and crawl backwards, allowing the kranes to gather around his thrashing form. They cover him with their slippery, lithe bodies, hiding him from view. The crying stops.

They remain in that position for some time and then roll away like waves. Juju is still kneeling, shoulders heaving, but he is no longer trying to break his skull open.

"What did you do?" I call out to the kranes.

They ignore me, instead focusing their attention on their patient. They speak to him in a crooning, sibilant tongue, touching his face and shoulders tenderly as though checking for wounds.

The rain has turned back into a drizzle. Juju looks at me.

"Kranes got a word for people like you." He sounds weak but calm, as though nothing untoward has happened, as though we've been sitting here chatting all this time. "Say our language has holes, theirs doesn't. Maybe why you can be something old. Language left a hole, and nobody filled it. People like you get lost, and go around answering the wrong calls."

I swallow, still shaken. "What did they do?"

His shoulders lift in a careless shrug. "Went inside my head, took the bad thing out. Wasn't really a bad thing, more like a thing that was fine before, but got all twisted up and strange, didn't work properly. Thing you made to fix Setch. Story thing."

Yes, the story thing. It stirs within me, liberated now that the ignorance that bound it is gone. My primitive urge, a craft so old my people forgot what to call it.

"I'm sorry, what I said before." Juju gets to his feet, then reaches out to help me up. "About you breaking things. Wasn't me, understand? Twisted-up story thing. Made my mind go funny like that kid. Really was a junkie, eh? Saw his skin. Curse or no curse, that kid was full of mal."

I nod.

"Should go back to work. Have to tell a big fancy lie so they don't whip me for serious. Ai! Especially Six. Man got a temper like a Catavan storm. So, you coming or what?"

With a glance at the kranes, I say, "I'll catch up."

Juju looks at me, eyebrows raised. "Not hissing any more doesn't mean you're friends, eh? Kranes still don't like your kind."

I laugh, surprising myself. "Thanks for the advice."

He shrugs again and starts off across the rocks, as sure-footed as one of his oily grey comrades. I turn towards them.

"Thank you."

They stare at me in silence.

"I didn't understand. I thought you were confused

about what was happening. I thought…" I sigh. "I didn't understand."

There is a tale that must be told when I return to the Great Hall. Somehow, I must find a way to sit Counsel down and tell it so he hears me. He has always been immune to this medicine of mine, and I thought it was because he is so stubborn, so righteous. I thought maybe it was all superstition and emotion and something wrong inside me, but today I worked a truth and helped a girl, and now I know what's real.

The kranes haven't moved. They seem to know what I want from them, but they won't offer it. If I want it, I must ask. Their language, like my stories, requires reciprocity.

"You have a word…"

I falter, afraid they'll turn me down, then remember I have nothing to lose. What else is there? Another five months of intense study under Counsel's thumb? Five years? A lifetime? No. No, never. I was hungry, and now I've tasted stories and must have more. I must be fed until I'm strong enough to work harder truths than traumatised silences, until I'm brave enough, wise enough to fix what I break.

I begin again. "You have a word for people like me. Will you tell me what it is? My people… We need words.

Like Counsel and mech and apprentice. We need names to know who we are, and there is no name for what I am. There hasn't been for a long, long time. I'm not supposed to exist, you see. People like me… We're not real. I want to be real."

Silence.

"I know you don't like me, but maybe one day, I can return the favour. Will you share your word with me? Please."

The kranes exchange glances. They stretch their wings and roll their necks and whisper among themselves. Then one of them beckons. I go to kneel before it.

A long time ago, there was a girl who opened a box she had been instructed to leave alone… I didn't know my place. I think of all the years I spent waiting for a call I could answer, and then I let the thoughts go, pebbles worn smooth over time, too smooth to serve me now.

The krane leans in to whisper in my ear, a word in its tongue that has no parallel in mine. But it's enough. I smile with my whole being, and I know I will never be hungry again. Inside me, the story wakes, knocking on the door. Yes, old friend. The door is open.

The Ghost of Dzablui Estate

I FEEL the pull of Volta-Mind, even from the dirigible, gentle, shy, as if it's afraid of offending my new allegiance to Ashanti-Mind. The community shimmers below me, a cluster of buildings along the water's edge, encrusted in solar panels and glinting like rhinestones on a shirt. I've always loved that view. I missed it, changed allegiance or not. You can leave a place, and it can leave you, but traces will always remain.

I don't want to remember, but once my brain taps into the local net, I have little choice. I can smell the damp earth along the lakeside, the compost feeding the fields of mango and cassava, the baskets filled with the catch of the day. I can taste my childhood, sweet yet acidic like overripe pineapple.

The dirigible sets down on the landing strip outside the station, not far from the market. As I disembark, the thick scent of smoked fish clings to the back of my throat with undue persistence. A rotating hologram stands at the edge of the landing strip, flashing repeated messages.

Welcome to Volta, Land of the Lake. Water is Life.

How will you honour the Meld today? Please see our favoured acts of service below.

Get your Mind-Chip and plug into Volta-Mind here!

Despite knowing the hologram would be there, I feel attacked by the messages. I abandoned Lake Volta. I don't honour the Meld. In fact, I often resent it. And as for Mind-Chips, I have no need for them. I'm one of only a handful of human beings who can transition naturally from one local Mind to another, a lost soul wandering the world without roots.

Going through life as if it were a buffet, my mother used to say. *Choose, child! Who are you?*

Of course, I think of her now, years after she's gone. Volta-Mind reaches into my head, logs my DNA and shuffles through images of my mother in the market, headwrap wound so tight I used to think it must be crushing her skull.

Asiwome is waiting at the market gate, feet encased in slippers despite the threat of rain, twisting her purse strap around her long fingers. In one hand, she carries a jute bag. It would be strange to call her my sister, as is the norm among my people, or even my cousin, though she's the eldest daughter of my maternal uncle. I always just thought of her as one of *them*, as removed from me as the AI attendant who loaded my luggage onto the dirigible.

"You came," she says and tries unsuccessfully to smile.

"There was no need to pick me up," I tell her, moving past the market. "I remember the way."

"Someone had to confirm your arrival, Yayra."

"I said I would come, didn't I?"

"Can you blame us for doubting you?"

I roll my eyes. Already, I can feel the suspicion coming off her brain, so strong it must be representative of the entire estate's feelings. They hate me. Still, after all these years. Fine. I hate them more.

"It's gotten worse since I called you."

"How?"

She pulls the jute bag open so I can peer inside. It's filled with candles.

"It's withholding solar?"

"No. Power surges. We've been trying to turn it off manually to prevent any more accidents."

"Any *more* accidents?" My gaze meets hers and I notice that her eyes are bloodshot, the skin around them ashy.

Asiwome purses her lips and looks away. "I knew you were arriving at noon, but I left the estate at dawn. Those who can always do. When we stay…"

She says no more, but I increase my pace. Our estate is one of the larger ones in Volta, perched at the bottom of a hill and studded with coconut trees. Gone are the days of private property. Now communities build a home together, own it together, and are locked into its rhythm like a dancing troupe, choreography burned into their souls.

All estates are similar in that they are built into living matter – trees, water systems – and rich with nanotech. All estates are different, too, designed to suit the communal Mind that built them, deferring to the natural and technological environment. The estate I adopted in Ashanti is a behemoth, more steel than wood, more AI than organic, a towering idol that shelters seven hundred lives. A net that vast extends far beyond its borders. I can still hear its low-grade hum and feel my pulse move at its rapid pace.

Volta is a slower, simpler world. As we walk up the dirt path to the estate, I take in the neighbouring structures, some of which have expanded. The town is a mosaic of green, brown, and silver, brick, glass and steel woven into bark and leaves, creating symbiotic systems that remind me of the cyborgs in popular culture.

There are no fences, no walls separating one estate from the next. There's been no need for fences since the Meld. Like most of the larger estates, ours has its own plant where the tenants' waste is turned into methane gas, which is in turn used as fuel. The plant is the first building we see, right after the sign that reads 'Dzablui Estate'. It hasn't changed, its doors still painted the same dull green, pipes speckled with dried raindrops. The only difference is the smell – there must be a leak somewhere. The estate recognises me and flings memories my way, glimpses of a little girl crawling under the pipes to cry.

I'm not a child anymore, I tell the estate. Pipes groan, and a camera flashes, storing my new face for future reference, and then the plant begins to emit a low rattling sound.

"It doesn't like visitors," Asiwome says, taking my arm and pulling me along the brick walkway.

"I'm not a visitor," I remind her, but she pays no heed. She's almost running, dragging me through the estate as though afraid the buildings will turn and look my way.

She's right to be afraid. I hear the whir of twisting cameras – with my mind, not my ears – and feel the estate's rising alarm like a needle in my thoughts. It's also Asiwome's alarm, the alarm of the tenants as they watch me approach. I'm not wanted. They called me, begged me to come, yet now when they see me coming they want nothing more than for me to be gone.

Asiwome takes me to the echo chamber. I chose to forget that it exists – a small structure carved into a cluster of bushes, the door swathed in thick vines. Designed to give newly chipped visitors a chance to transition to Volta-Mind at their own pace, it's just large enough for four people to sit inside. It's the only unconnected room, an island in the estate's neural ocean. A haven for those new to Volta, but a prison for me.

I swallow my panic, the rational part of my brain pointing out how fitting it is that the chamber should be where I'm reacquainted with my former life.

Asiwome yanks the metal door open. "Here," she says, releasing her grip on my arm and shoving me forward. Her voice has changed. Her features, too, twisted into a grimace now. She holds me at arm's length like something putrid she found in the garden. "Quick, get inside before it loses its temper!"

I stumble into the room. The door closes, and a lock clicks into place, trapping me in the darkness. Memories brush against me and whisper a welcome right into my heart.

* * *

The Meld came as a sudden, as yet unexplained event seventy-three years ago. At the time, humanity was connected but disconnected, a sea of seven billion islands. Over several days, as if by unspoken agreement, people found that they had developed deep neurological bonds with their immediate ecosystem. Their moods shifted when the weather was about to change. Their skin grew ashy if the soil around them lacked nutrients. They experienced anxiety when local wildlife populations were misaligned. In Volta, fishermen paddled into the depths, distressed by the terror of carp caught in plastic, and babies cried nonstop, their growing brains marked by pesticides lingering in the air.

The experience of humanity was fundamentally altered, and now, when we speak of being one with the earth, it's no longer a pretty metaphor. Things that were normal before became unthinkable. How could we keep animals in cramped pens when the trauma of a demolished anthill was enough to give toddlers diarrhoea? And so, over long, painstaking decades, we learned new ways to be. We built communities where resources were shared. We enhanced the Meld with nanotech, machines in our heads, in the land, in the air.

There hasn't been an armed conflict anywhere in the world in all my thirty years of life. The Meld saved us.

After Asiwome leaves, I sink to my knees in the echo chamber, fingers scanning the walls for a light switch. Even though the chamber was designed to keep the local Mind out, I can reach into the estate – and it can reach into me. Now that I'm here, among the familiar scents and sounds, it creeps under my skin.

Memories crest over me. The rawness of my throat after hours of screaming to be let out that first night Mama locked me in here. The shock – and then relief – when I realised that I could still connect, that the walls were no barrier. I didn't yet understand what I'd done wrong. Hours earlier, my mother and I were bartering produce for clothes in the market, when I smelled smoke. I looked around me but there was nothing amiss. Yet I could feel the fear and hear the crackle of flames. Panic blossomed in my young chest.

"Fire!" I said, tugging my mother's arm, wondering why I was the only one who seemed afraid. "Fire, Mama, fire!"

There was no fire. Not in Volta, anyway. We soon learned that a fire had broken out in a neighbouring region. I shouldn't have picked up on it. Mama took me to be examined by doctors and interrogated by inspectors. How had I known about the fire before it was on the news? Lying was pointless, so I told the truth. I had known the way I knew everything else. The Meld had told me.

Even now I feel the sting of my mother's slap against my cheek and the hot tears springing to my eyes.

I'm not the only ghost in the world, but we are few enough to be feared. They call us ghosts because they say we have no roots, no substance, no loyalty. We are not locked into our home communities and devoted to their survival. Our brains can tap into any region, like soulless satellites. Our minds can travel, our hearts too.

Yet communities only function because every individual is a cell working to keep the organism healthy. How do you trust a creature with no concrete sense of belonging?

To my people, I was a cancer. I had to be contained to make sure I didn't spread to the entire net. And so, every day, I spent three hours in the echo chamber to 'recalibrate'. I told no one that I could still connect inside. I sat there, letting my pain blossom.

When I reached sixteen, the age of majority, I fled. I haven't been home since. Until now.

* * *

Asiwome returns after only an hour. Her mood hasn't improved – if anything, she's even surlier than before as she steps into the chamber and shuts the door behind her. She leans against the door and sighs, eyes sliding closed in relief, and then springing open, wide with pain.

"Every single time," she murmurs. "You think it's worth it to have a moment of peace, but the pain of being locked out, the loneliness…" She shakes her head and moves to open the door. I see her eyes light up as the connection slides back into place. I've never experienced the particular loneliness she speaks of, but I'm familiar with something like it.

The Asiwome in front of me now, subdued, almost defeated, is the one who called me a week ago. *You have to come*, she said. *You're the only one who can save us.* I wasn't sure that was true, but a part of me enjoyed having my former kin at my mercy, hearing them beg. The same people that had ostracised me now needed my help.

"I have to go outside," I say. "I have to see how bad it is."

She nods, holding the chamber door open for me. "Slowly. Don't make it nervous."

Asiwome leads me down the path and around the periphery of the estate, giving it time to get used to me once more. The presence of a single unusual individual has little impact on a healthy estate, but this one barely passed the last inspection.

I've seen rogue estates sickened by rot or grief, attacking their own cells, causing electrical fires and plumbing disasters, growing poisonous and suffocating their tenants, trapping them inside, starving them. My former estate is home to ninety-five people and was built using the now-defunct co-dependent model, so every tenant is completely dependent on the estate for survival. It regulates their body clocks, their temperature, their oxygen levels, their emotions. If the estate fails the next inspection, it will be euthanised by the state. The tenants will be distributed among other healthy estates. Many, especially the older ones, won't survive detachment. The psychological toll alone will be catastrophic.

There's a reason the state no longer sanctions co-dependent construction.

It's illegal for an outsider, even the state, to tamper with the functions of a running estate. It has to be shut down first. But all the tenants here are too enmeshed to solve the problem. All except me.

The plants around the edge of the estate are starting to wither despite the rain. I finger the yellowing leaves of a pawpaw tree.

"Random bursts of energy," Asiwome explains. "When they hit the ground, they affect the soil."

I look down at the earth beneath the tree and note its greyish colour. "How did you let it get this bad? You should have called for a temporary shutdown after the last inspection so the state could evaluate."

"We can't survive a shutdown, Yayra. You know we're co-dependent." Her tone is accusatory, as though I'm the cause of the problem. I know she's projecting the estate's temperament, but it still stings.

"You can't survive twelve hours? Don't you have an emergency protocol?"

I ask like I'm a stranger, like I don't remember what it was like to have the estate tell me when I was hungry, when my body needed rest. I suppose I am a stranger

340

now. I still see and hear what they do. I experience traces of emotion, but my body runs itself. Co-dependent estates are a rarity in Ashanti – the stakes are too high, our numbers too great.

"Of course," Asiwome snaps. "But we know what the state will decide if we let them evaluate. We don't want to lose our home. You are our last chance."

I look around me. Children peer out of windows and doorways, curious but too afraid of the ghost to come closer. Tenants go about their tasks, glaring at me but saying nothing, all of them drenched in sweat.

"Have you lost anyone? Sickness, accidents?"

"Not yet, by the grace of the Meld. We've had injuries, but everyone survived so far."

We walk around the back of the kitchen. The walls heave like some slumbering giant, making vines sprout spontaneously and wind around the structure, forming a thick net. I look up to see the vines choking the pipe that drains runoff from the roof. A man stands on a ladder, pruning the vines, but they continue to grow. I recognise him as one of my former playmates. He doesn't even look in my direction, too busy fighting with the vines.

In the garden, reed baskets lurch with massive snails and rotten fruit. The paths between crops are slick with slime, the air dense with the sticky sweetness of overripe fruit. I glance at Asiwome, seeking an explanation.

"The place is overrun with snails, and fruit rots faster than we can harvest it," she says. "It's too hot, too wet."

I frown at her. "It doesn't feel hotter than usual to me."

"Your body is still on Ashanti temperature." Asiwome grimaces and rubs her temples. "Give it a day. You will see."

I try not to let the memories affect me as I encounter familiar faces. They greet me politely, but they don't linger. Not that I expected more. Not that I wanted more. After all, I didn't just come here to save their dying home. I came for the satisfaction of knowing that the thing they despise about me is the same thing that will save them. They were wrong. If I succeed in this task, everyone who mocked me as a child will have to swallow their words.

And all of Volta will know that this sad, desperate estate was saved by a ghost.

* * *

I didn't truly understand the power of the Meld until I left Volta. I was so desperate to flee that I bartered a month of labour for a dirigible ride to Ashanti and a place to live when I arrived. I would work on the aircraft in exchange. The moment we were in the air I started to feel the pull of different Minds. It gave me a throbbing headache and nausea, which the attendants dismissed as airsickness.

After I had been dosed and felt a little better, I could pick up the different strains around me. The profound love of the lake at home in Volta, the call of the ocean from Gold Coast, the drive for constant progress from Ashanti. I looked at the other passengers and realised how easy it was to tell where they were from by their manner. I saw that, in addition to our devotion to our communities, there was an overarching sense of duty, an understanding that all the regions were part of one state. All states were part of one planet, and all planets were part of one universe. I understood why we could no longer go to war, why, even though it would have been easy to take produce from my estate and barter that for my ticket instead of indenturing myself, it would never have occurred to me to do so. The Meld made us loyal. It made us good.

But I also knew it was possible to think differently, that humans had done so for millennia. We had thought in small, selfish ways, putting our needs above those of others. I was a perfect example. I had left my home, not for the greater good, but in pursuit of my own comfort. I realised then that because I was a ghost, because my devotion was somehow diluted, it was possible for me to slip, to regress, to become what people used to be. That knowledge terrified me.

When my month of service on the dirigible was over, the pilot recommended me to the recruitment officers at City Command. He said I would make a good officer since I was so 'detached'. I have been working in the Inspection Unit ever since, first as an intern, then a trainee, then an aide, and now as an inspector, evaluating building plans and architectural designs, examining estates, and formulating regulations.

In the days after Asiwome's call, I often wondered whether she would have called if I'd been in another unit. Volta is outside my jurisdiction, so I took personal leave to make the trip. Whatever I do in my efforts to save the estate will be logged as domestic repairs performed by a tenant. I won't even be named. It gives me a lot of leeway. I could make a mistake and it would be assumed that I was affected by the estate's erratic functions. I could burn the whole place to the ground and not be held accountable.

I hate the fact that I thought about it. Dreamed about it. Even after I land in Volta and feel the familiar sense of home creep over me again, that wicked thought remains like a seed in my heart, waiting for someone to water it.

* * *

I spend my first two days studying the estate, surveying the damage, mapping its mood swings and their impact on the tenants. There's no sign of a biological cause for the illness, and no one can bear to be in the control room long enough to seek a technological explanation. It could be burnout. Co-dependent estates are more susceptible to breakdown.

Asiwome is at my side throughout, as though afraid to leave me alone. I sense the wariness in the air. No one trusts me. I am the only ghost born in Volta in years – possibly ever.

The second time I enter the garden, I'm almost driven back by the stench. Tenants shovel fallen fruit into wheelbarrows and wheel it to the kitchen, where it will be made into condiments. At least half the fruit is already too rotten to use. It goes into the compost heap, the only part of the garden that seems to thrive. Even though baskets of snails have been taken to market, the garden still crawls with them. The leaves of our crops – cassava, mango, plantain – are either encrusted with grey-black pestilence or turning yellow before their time.

The indoor rooms of the estate fare no better. Walls pulse, throb or vibrate. Lights flicker on and off. Music starts up suddenly and then stops. Two doors, one leading from the main meeting room to the kitchen, the other from the back of the house to a storeroom, have been locked for a week and no amount of coaxing will open them. Some of the bedrooms have become so cold that the tenants have taken to storing food inside.

Asiwome was right – the heat is oppressive. At night it weighs me down like a blanket, pressing me into the narrow bed set up in the echo chamber. I carry a towel everywhere. I pay frequent visits to the cold rooms and always find them choked with sweaty bodies.

Nerves are frayed. Everyone is tense. Arguments break out often. They never turn physical – the larger Volta Mind prevents that – but they are heated. Twice, the community elders are called to mediate since the estate elders are too emotional to be of any use.

There's a young woman, twenty or so, who does nothing but cry all day. I see her hanging up laundry, tears streaming down her face, mingling with sweat. I see her nursing her infant, sobbing over the child's head. When I ask what the matter is, she looks at me like I'm an idiot and says, "Have you misplaced your eyes?"

On the third day, Asiwome comes to the echo chamber to take me on my usual tour.

"I've seen enough," I tell her. "It's time to get to work."

She chews her lip. "Ah, today's not a good day. The water pressure was too high and burst a pipe. I don't know if it's safe to be inside for long."

I sigh. "Did you bring me here to watch this place fall apart? Because I can do that from a distance."

She glares at me and clicks her tongue. "I'm thinking of your safety, you know."

"I can take care of myself."

"Everyone knows that." It sounds like an insult, but she takes me to the control room and stays near the door.

The estate operates like a biological organism, with much of its intelligence spread throughout its body. The control room is its brain, a collection of clear tubes filled with nanotech, branching out into thick, rubbery veins that sink into the walls, the soil, the trees. The viewing screen that shows different sections of the estate is cracked. Roots have invaded the room through the outside wall, breaking up the floor so the room resembles an abandoned experiment in the wilderness. Energy pulses in the room, its rhythm menacing, like an erratic heartbeat. A wave of fatigue washes over me. I focus on the part of me still connected to Ashanti-Mind until the fatigue passes.

There is a single stool covered in leaves. I brush them off and sit down. "Good morning, Dzablui. May I access your control panel?"

No response. Asiwome grits her teeth and takes a few steps forward. Her features twist in pain as she requests access. There is still no response. She turns away in frustration.

"It's OK," I say to the estate, wiping my face with my towel. "I'm a tenant. You remember me, don't you? I only want to help."

The screen flickers, weighing my words.

"I told you it was a bad day," Asiwome whispers. She winces and clutches her head.

"Go," I tell her. "You don't have to be here."

Wincing again, she nods and leaves the room.

"Alone at last," I tell the estate, though of course, there is no such thing as alone anymore. "You're very ill. You know that, don't you? Let me help you."

The scenes on the screen fade away, to be replaced by an androgynous face composed of pixels. "You left." The voice should be pleasant, feminine, but it is instead eerie and distorted. "Why are you here now?"

"To help. To save you."

There's a pause, a burst of static, and then, "You are not a tenant."

"Of course I am. You can feel me, can't you? You can feel my mind, connected to the others, connected to you." I lean closer to the screen. "Let me help you."

I feel the estate reach into my head, probing. A little flame of fear comes to life in my chest. "You're not supposed to do that. You'll blur the borders. You can see Ashanti-Mind in my brain."

"I am allowed to scan my tenants."

Oh, it's clever. Sly. Where did that come from? We didn't program it to think that way, to find loopholes.

"*You* made the loophole," the estate tells me, sifting through my thoughts, and I realise it's right. It withdraws suddenly, like a wandering hand that brushed against a scorpion. "Your thoughts confuse me."

"I can imagine." I reach out to touch the screen. "May I access your control panel, please?"

The image on the screen flickers. There's another burst of static. I yank my hand away.

"Have you come here for the greater good?"

"Of course."

It must sense the lie in my words. The screen goes dark, and the room fills with a shrill beeping noise. The door bursts open, and Asiwome rushes in. The roots beneath my feet expand, throwing the stool off balance, making me fall. Asiwome grabs my arm, pulls me to my feet and drags me out of the control room.

At night, I can't sleep. The estate combs through my mind with insistent, angry fingers, trying to make sense of the disjointed things it finds there. It whispers frenzied questions into my head. *What are you? Why have you come? Can you truly heal me?*

I whisper back, *I am one of your children. I came to help. I can, I can.*

I still don't know whether it's true.

* * *

This dance continues for three more days. I go into the control room and beg, and wheedle, and coax. The estate scans me, reels, and refuses to release the control panel. I'm more certain than ever that burnout is the problem, and every day brings the estate closer to collapse.

"This was a mistake," Asiwome whispers. Her face and neck are slick with sweat. She seems to have lost weight in a matter of days.

Children wail all day and night. The snails have started to die now, and when I go into the garden, I find tenants on their knees beside mountains of empty shells, holding them up and keening, uncertain of what to do. The estate is dying. Fear lines my stomach, a coat of paint that won't come off. And even though I'm Ashanti now, even though I'm detached, I look at these people, my people, and it hurts to see them suffer.

"It's better to die," the estate elders say. "Let the state come and end it, end us. All that we were will be absorbed into other estates. Volta will go on."

"If the estate dies, every living thing here dies with it," Asiwome says.

The elders fall silent, thinking of all the goats and chickens and cats and dogs, all the insects and birds and fish in the pond. The estate is so sick that the site will have to lie barren for at least three years to allow all the toxins to fade. The thought of such destruction, such waste…

"If we can just get through the next inspection," Asiwome begins.

"We'll be dead before then," the elders reply.

* * *

I have been home for close to a week now, and the estate's deterioration has accelerated. Half the crops are dead. Many animals are sick, many people, too. The tenants have already started digging graves, afraid that when the time comes they might be too ill to do it. Some of the walls have begun to crumble. The memories of my childhood have grown so vivid that sometimes I forget how much time has passed. I half expect to hear my mother calling me. I flinch in anticipation of her sharp words.

I sit in the control room in front of a black screen, waiting, begging. I'm close to giving up when the control panel finally slides out of the wall. I'm weeping with relief as I reach for it.

I can save you. I can, I can, I can, I can. I whisper it like a mantra as I work, but every time I enter a new setting, the estate changes it back. It has lost all control now. It is broken beyond repair. I know this in the deepest part of me, but I can't stop. I have to try. This was once my home. I have to try.

I'm still trying when Asiwome bursts into the room, so weak that she has to hold the wall for support.

"Get out," she says. "It's over. You have to go now."

I ignore her, pushing buttons, pulling levers, turning dials.

"The estate has decided to self-euthanise before it kills us all."

No. No. "Nonsense," I murmur.

"Please, Yayra!"

But I have to try. Asiwome makes an exasperated sound and leaves. I'm still trying when the screen crackles and bursts into flames, when the tubes melt, spilling a silver river of chips all over the uneven floor, when the alarm goes off, when the sparks shoot out of the control panel and into my fingers, when Asiwome comes in with two men who lift me up and carry me out of the room. I can't differentiate my screams from those of the estate, the frightened children, and the fleeing figures.

Fire, Mama, Fire!

"There's no fire!" I shout, straining against the arms that hold me. "It's not here. It's not in Volta! Why is everyone running?"

Ashanti-Mind picks up on my body's distress and sends signals to activate the tiny beads of medicine in my blood. I'm unconscious in seconds.

* * *

By the time I wake up, I'm in a strange bed in a strange room, Asiwome sitting on the floor beside me, devouring a bowl of apapransa.

"It's gone," she says between bites. "All of it. The elders, too. Twenty-three human lives, thirty-seven domestic animals. All the fish. A whole ecosystem."

"Where are we?" I sit up.

"A new estate. One of the community backups."

Guilt is a rock in my belly. "I'm sorry. I failed you. I'm so sorry."

She shrugs, and I realise she must be medicated to be so calm. "You tried. You almost died trying. It was already too late by the time I called you." She finishes her food. "You can go back now." Her tone is too casual. "To Ashanti. If you like."

My head shakes without reservation. "Not yet. You'll need help acclimatising."

She doesn't thank me, but there is something in her nod, a softening of her features. She gets up and leaves the room without a word. The moment she's gone, I start to cry.

* * *

I extend my leave for another week to help ease my people into their new home – or ease their new home into them. It's a small state-developed estate, built only with the basics as a backup in case of emergencies. The survivors work together to enhance it, feeding their patterns into it and learning its ways. They are still reeling from the loss of their home but as we work, I feel the freshness of the new estate seep into their minds. Into mine. The estate is green and fragrant, alive with little things that demand stillness and contemplation, and gratitude, most of all. We are alive. We are all alive.

By the time I leave, children have started to laugh again and even follow me around, ask me to join their games and crawl into my lap to sleep. I suppose their curiosity has overcome their fear. The older tenants have softened towards me as well. I hear the reason in the local Mind: *she almost died trying.* They can't think of me as detached anymore.

Asiwome accompanies me to the dirigible when it's time to go. "Thank you for coming," she says. She looks at the ground, then at my shoulder. She hugs me. Startled, I freeze for a moment, then hug her back.

"I'll come again." It's a question, even though I don't pose it as one.

"Yes. Soon. When you can."

A world of unsaid things swirls between us, but I think we see each other clearly for the first time. I'm still a ghost, but I'm also her cousin. Her sister. And she is mine.

"Travel safely."

"By the grace of the Meld, I will." I smile. "I'm glad you called me, even if…"

She nods, understanding.

From the sky, I see the site of the old estate, now nothing but composting soil and ash. I feel the worms writhe in that blackened soil, working alongside nanotech to purge the land of toxins. I can also see the new estate, alive with colour, vegetation green and glowing, little figures moving around.

And I understand the power of the Meld, maybe better than I ever did. I understand that no matter what thoughts may cross my mind, I would never intentionally cause harm. Even a ghost like me is subject to the Meld.

Wild

ONCE UPON A TIME, we were governed by the moon. Our bodies, water poured into skin, swirling around bone and sinew, were as drawn to her as the tides. After all, what were we but little oceans, waves cresting and falling against the coast of history?

The moon pulled us this way and that, making us pliant, making us hunger, making us wild. That was the purpose of life – to allow celestial bodies to express their divinity. And so, we lived and loved and felt as deeply as we dared. That freedom was our birthright. The communes were a fantasy, well-meaning but too orderly to last. They would crumble, eventually. We would be wild again, governed by the moon once more.

Mema had told this story many times, over many years. You could hear how her voice had worn the words smooth so they rolled from her tongue with practised ease. When I was younger, I would sit in her lap as she told it during the summer nights, toying with the twists of hair at her temples, stretching them out and then winding them around my small fingers.

We sat on the boulders at the edge of the commune, away from the fire.

Drones circled above, dipping below the horizon every so often, buzzing in harmony with the crickets and the howls of dogs. Drones were the only tech allowed in the communes, apart from meditech. We were unplugged and proud.

"And then, Mema, and then?" I would ask.

She would say, "And then our ancestors would dance. Naked, under the moonlight, around a crackling fire. They would call all their friends to dance with them, and there were many ways, many colours, many languages and voices. It was beautiful, to bring worlds together and create something new."

I would sigh in contentment. Our absence from the bustle within would attract Ma's attention, and she would come outside with her lips pursed and her brow creased in worried lines.

"Come, Sedi," she would say, taking me in her arms. And to her mother, "Stop your blasphemy!"

She would tell stories of her own, but they were not stories, they were doctrine, and even in my youth, I could tell the difference.

"In order for a painter to mix colour, there must first *be* colour, yes? The colours must be kept pure. If all the red is used to make purple, what then? Would you want to live in a world without red?"

"No, Ma," I would say, and she would squeeze me tight, pleased with my answer.

Ma misunderstood. Mema was not advocating for the erasure of any single colour, any single people. She only wanted everyone to be free to move and mix as they chose. In the communes, we were granted no such freedom. The Council said mixing would dilute our blood until it was gone altogether.

I loved my grandmother's stories. I would lie awake afterwards, listening to the other members of the commune moving around, preparing for sleep.

Sometimes, I would hear the nomadic Fleet sweeping along the main road, moving from place to place with their wares in woven baskets and their beds rolled up on their backs. Their steed of choice was the bicycle, and sometimes you could see hundreds of bikes on the road, a distant mirage, a wave on wheels. I would close my eyes and think of those spinning wheels, flashing moon-kissed winks at our commune as they passed.

In the present day, the Council governed us. In the old days, the moon governed us. According to my mother, duty would always govern us. Were we nothing more than spokes on a wheel, then? I would lie awake and wonder: what would happen if we were, for once, to govern ourselves?

* * *

Our commune was the smallest in the New Volta Republic. Our ethnic group was classified as endangered. We had been enrolled in the Propagation as soon as it began, our Council's desperate effort to save our culture from extinction. Every one of the rare births among us was catalogued and monitored, the mother cloistered to ensure that she carried to full term.

My responsibility, as a potential carrier, was to maintain my health. I was a late bloomer. Seventeen, sexually active for over a year, and still no sign of first blood.

"It will come," Ma would assure me as she massaged aloe into my pelvic muscles and brewed herbal teas to activate my womb. "Be patient."

I would lie there on a bed in the clinic, nano-supplements like tiny beads in my mouth shooting health into my body, wires from the diagnostic server prodding my skin and making declarations about my vitals. "Temperature within normal range. Blood pressure within normal range. Heart rate slightly elevated." Well, of course.

"Eh? Elevated?" Ma would peer into my face with disapproval. "Are you stressed? You should know better. Calm down, now!"

Kweku, my mate, would stand wide-eyed in the corner, trying not to get in her way.

"There's nothing to worry about, my child." And Ma would beckon to the traditional healer who waited in the wings, armed with bottles of pungent herbal remedies for illnesses I didn't have.

Ma, like all our mothers, had only been blessed once. Our men had no seed, and our women's wombs were 'inhospitable', a word that sounded like a dark room filled with clawed things.

When the miracle came, it never returned, no matter how many procedures we underwent. The Propagation had suggested birthing our children in vats, but our Council would not hear of it. We were close to nature, close to the gods. It was bad enough that we had to resort to meditech at all. So they mixed life in jars and injected it back into us, and we clung to existence for another generation.

This was our fate. We accepted it.

Well, most of us.

* * *

When my friend Amiah ripened, her mother tried to hide her, putting a screen around her bed and forbidding her from leaving the room. Amiah was exhibiting symptoms of the Strain, her mother said. Runny nose, achy joints. She was in isolation, just to be safe.

But we all saw the towels hanging on the washing line day after day, and we knew that no one would risk the wrath of Resource Management with such a wanton waste of water.

Amiah was bleeding.

I tried to sneak in to see her. There was an old laptop in the storehouse, left there as a cautionary tale. If you pushed one of the buttons it would play content from the Online, clips from films, adverts, and music videos. It was a nightmare of image and sound, people gyrating in strange, oppressively tight costumes, garish colours on their faces and in their hair, blood spattering as people fought for no clear reason, noise and pictures that meant nothing to us – at least, nothing good. Creeping into the warehouse after lights out was a rite of passage, but once was enough.

Children would run screaming, leaving the footage blaring. Amiah's quarters were closest to the storehouse, so her mother was always the one to come and turn the monster off.

After dark on the third day of Amiah's blood, I put on the laptop and hid in the shadows outside the window near her bed. When I heard her mother leave to turn off the noise, I knocked on the window.

Amiah's face appeared in the glass. I waved and gestured to her to open the window. Her face disappeared. I didn't see her for five more days, and when she was released from isolation, she insisted that it had been the Strain and nothing more.

Of course, she caught 'the Strain' again the next month, and the next.

Propagation agents came for her twelve weeks after her first blood, as was customary. They set their drone down at the edge of the commune, but even at that distance, and even though the thing was cloaked in nighttime shadow, children fled indoors, frightened of the big metal bird.

The agents led Amiah out of the commune, her eyes red from crying, her mother shouting at them to leave her child alone.

"She's not a child anymore," Ma told her. "She's about to become a mother. It's an honour, you know. Stop crying and show some gratitude."

I watched from the window of the room I shared with the other youths my age. My eyes watched Amiah and the Propagation agents enter the drone and lift off into the air, my heart pounding to the beat of the machine's staccato roar.

No one apart from the girls being taken would go near the beast. It was a symbol of how far we had fallen, how desperate we had become, that we resorted to man-made trickery to keep our people alive. The sight of it made my stomach clench with a twisted mixture of fear, shame and hope. Most people looked away once the drone took off, and then they bowed their heads in prayer for Amiah's success.

But not me. I kept watching until it was gone, and then I looked all the way up to where soft blue clouds edged with grey chased the full moon.

And I thought I could feel it. The pull Mema had spoken of. Like an ache in my insides, making me want to do something reckless. I thought I could see the figure of a woman inside the white orb, dancing around a fire.

I suppose I ought to have pitied Amiah, but part of me was annoyed with her for fighting the inevitable, and another part felt a thrill of triumph that her time had come. We would all be mothers one day. We would all go through the tests, the fertilisation, the isolation, and then 'the glory of labour', as Ma liked to call it.

I remembered the things Amiah had said to me only a few months before as we worked the hard soil, coaxing tomatoes and peppers out of it with compost and worms and steady, gentle hands.

"Everything dies, Sedi. People, plants, animals. Why should cultures and languages be any different?"

"But they *are* different," I had replied.

"Why? Doesn't it feel like a kind of hypocrisy? We built the communes to be close to nature, so we're not slaves to greed and progress, like our ancestors." I remembered how aggressive her movements had become as she spoke, her fingers digging too deep into the soil, ripping weeds away from the crops in a way that would have mortified our elders. "We avoid tech. We rely on solar power. We walk everywhere. We're not allowed to use drugs to prolong our lives, because immortality is unnatural. But to save our dying race, we break all our own rules, we artificially inseminate girls against their will—"

"It's not against their will."

"—with the seed of strangers, even though we are against mixing, and we edit the genes of their babies to prevent deformities, and then we bring them back here, to the commune that frowns on those who play God."

"We have to. We struggle to bear children the normal way. What do you want us to do?"

"I don't care. It's despicable. Everything dies, and something else will come to replace it. Our job is to get out of the way and let nature take its course."

"You sound like Mema," I had whispered, trying to keep the fear out of my voice.

"Good."

Amiah had hooked her index finger around a stubborn weed and yanked so hard that it came away with a tomato seedling, then clicked her tongue in anger and tossed the seedling onto the pile with the weeds.

I'd stared at it, with its tiny green leaves that would soon be brown and brittle, its precious roots torn and exposed, and felt grief that made no sense.

I had locked myself in the latrine after that, and cried and cried as though that tomato seedling had sprouted in my own womb, as though ripping it from the earth had torn something vital inside me. I had cried racking, painful sobs until someone came knocking on the latrine door, their voice laced with urgency.

It served Amiah right that the Propagation had her. Let her learn. She would soon come home with her baby, exhausted and blissful, and all that rebellion would be a memory.

I would tease her: "Remember how you used to say this was hypocrisy? Remember how you thought you knew better, how concerned you were about our rights?"

She would laugh at her youthful foolishness, and the baby would cry, and she would go running in that way new mothers did, as though the sound of a baby in distress signalled the end of the world. And the Council would be happy because one more life was a win for our people, a win against time and attrition, and, though no one would be crass enough to say it, a win against other races.

And I would feel, as I always did each time a new mother returned home, a strange combination of joy, fear, and disdain.

This was how I pictured it, but I was wrong.

Only a few days after Amiah left, we received news that she had tried twice to interfere with her insemination and once to abort the child.

When she came home, she had lost weight instead of gaining it. She sat in a corner breastfeeding her son, a blank expression on her face. Each time he suckled, her eyes bulged in their sockets, as if his priceless little mouth was draining the life from her.

Three days later, one of the younger boys found her corpse hanging from the storeroom ceiling rafters. Her son was passed around among the other new mothers, but he wouldn't latch.

In the end, there was no choice. The Council tapped into the commune's small coffers, and one of the boys was sent to the city to buy nanotech-infused formula. It was the first time anyone had brought purchased food into the commune in decades, and we all pretended not to worry about what the baby would become, fed on false nutrition. But he didn't die of chemical poisoning. He didn't become a robot slave. He grew big and strong.

When I held him, I almost resented his clear, bright eyes.

They told me my people were either liars or fools, and I wasn't sure which was worse.

"Amiah was a selfish girl," Ma said often in the months that followed.

I nodded in agreement. That was the thing to do with Ma. Yet I harboured a secret suspicion that we, perhaps, were the selfish ones. We had forced Amiah to grow a life inside her because we were afraid to die.

We had broken her.

* * *

Five years had passed since the last time I saw Mema. There was no prison in the commune because prison was barbaric, but Mema was a dangerous disturber of the peace, a rabble-rouser who couldn't be allowed to poison the pure waters of our commune. She was exiled a few days after my twelfth birthday. I never knew where she went. Even if I had, Ma would never have allowed contact. People said Mema left on a stolen bicycle, but I knew it was just gossip. There were only two bikes in our commune, and they were both safe and sound.

For weeks afterwards, people would touch Ma's arm and ask how she was holding up.

In the dining hall, I would get sad little looks from whoever was on serving duty. They would say they wished they could give me more, but psychological needs were not the same as physical ones, and I must remember that equity mattered. I longed to point out that I had never asked for more, but that would be rude, and rudeness was the mark of a soul lacking compassion. I held my tongue.

I felt Mema's absence like a gnawing in my gut, like something had gone rancid inside me. I wondered where she was, whether she was safe, whether she had eaten.

"Don't worry," Amiah had told me back then. "Your grandmother is a warrior. I'm sure she's happy to be gone."

I had nodded, then spent the rest of that day fantasising about pulling Amiah's hair out in clumps. It took me some time to understand why I was so angry.

Amiah had only meant to comfort me, but the thought that Mema would rather be a homeless outcast than be with us was more than I could bear.

The ache dulled with time. I still thought of Mema, but not often and not with the same fondness. Now that I was older, now that I was close to a woman, I understood that she was a bad person, selfish in her desire to ruin what the Council had worked so hard to build.

It was good that she was gone. I sometimes imagined that her beloved moon had come down and swallowed her whole. And that one day, I might see her there, watching me.

* * *

I was with Kweku when I ripened. We lay on our backs in the field, watching the stars. I felt the pain in my abdomen as his fingers laced through mine but dismissed it until it grew insistent.

He looked away, but I had already seen the panic in his eyes. "At long last, we will be parents."

"Yes. At long last."

We played the part all the way across the field and down the footpath to the compound. We were happy. We were grateful. We were not afraid at all.

Ma was unbearable. She brought it up in every conversation: "How much okra did we harvest this crop? I want a little to make soup for my Sedi. She's ripe, you know."

"Eh, your sewing has improved! Sedi was never good at sewing. Did I tell you her blood came?"

"Please help me carry this. I would have asked Sedi, but she's resting. Cramps, you see."

"We should hang a sign in the dining hall," Kweku joked. "Attention: Sedi is ripe!"

Ma's spirits were buoyant and oppressive, and I spent more and more time in the fields with Kweku, drowning my anxiety in his touch.

"You will be a good mother," he whispered into the crook of my neck.

"You will be a good father."

Neither of us said it, though I knew we were both thinking it – the child would be half me and half stranger. No one ever said it. It was another thing we ignored, like the big brass padlock that now secured the storeroom at night, like the ever-present current of fear.

My blood came the next month but not the month after. Ma said not to worry; it took time to stabilise. When the Propagation agents came for me, Ma sent me off with a packed lunch and a flask of herbal tea. The agents would return for Kweku once I had been impregnated, so that he would also have time to bond with the child. So neat and tidy, everything arranged.

There was no room for surprise, nothing left to chance. This was security, a life in which the whole world was swaddled. No one could move, but why would we want to?

I trembled when I stepped into the beast. It was small, painted in army colours, like we were going to war. Well, perhaps we *were* going to war, to fight the flaws in my body until it bore my people a child. The agents strapped me in. There was only room for the three of us, and though I knew that drones did not need pilots, I hated the idea of trusting a machine to know where to take us, let alone to keep us safe on the journey.

When we left the ground, my stomach lurched. It felt wrong to be up this high, but after about an hour, I dared to look out the window. To my surprise, the sight that greeted me was extraordinary. The world lay stretched below like a living painting, and I felt something close to wonder as I watched cassava fields and trees heavy with mangoes give way to urban gardens and tarred roads.

The city teemed with life, bodies on foot and on bicycles, gardens running rampant, bursting out of gates and over fences and spilling into the walkways. A few government-issue solar vehicles wove through the tumult.

The Propagation Centre was a tall structure of steel and glass topped with gleaming solar panels, vertical gardens running along the corners from one floor to the next. Inside the walls were painted in pale, unnatural colours that set my teeth on edge.

The nurse assigned to do my preliminary examination wore a wide grin and latex gloves. The examination room smelled like alcohol and not the good kind.

I lay on my back, staring at the white ceiling with its glaring artificial light, assorted wires attached to my body. There was no point in trying to make sense of the diagnostic server – it was far more sophisticated than the one at home. The screen flashed words and numbers at me. I looked away and closed my eyes. I pictured Mema on her rumoured stolen bike, pedalling along the horizon, then letting the bike go and floating up into the moon. I felt a jolt of sadness, as though the closer Mema got to her freedom, the further away I got from mine.

I opened my eyes and focused on the nurse's face. That didn't make me feel any better. Her eyes were wide, her lips parted in shock.

"What?" I stiffened on the bed, terror coursing through me. "What's wrong? Am I sick?"

"No." The nurse turned to face me. "You're already pregnant."

* * *

Change crept up on me, tiptoed into my consciousness and tugged at the threads of my beliefs until the tapestry came apart.

One moment, I was good, obedient, ready to have those who knew better grow a life inside me whether I wanted it or not. The next moment I was mad with desire for things that were beyond me, for open roads and sky and a world without limits.

Kweku and I were given a small unit behind the Propagation Centre, away from the other expectant parents. There were two guards manning our door at all times. For our protection, we were told, but I didn't feel protected. I felt caged.

The Council came to bless us. We were the parents of the first child in decades to carry our people's genes alone. There were offerings and gifts from the commune, food for us and clothes for the baby, picture books in our language, maternity clothes.

"Your child is the future of our people," they told us, with tears in their eyes.

"We will name others after you."

"There will be a holiday in your honour."

"Our scholars are coming; they want to write about you."

We posed for portraits and went through interviews and smiled until our faces ached.

The life inside me was a force, like Mema had been. It was not sitting quietly inside, waiting for its designated birthday and behaving itself. No, it fought and kicked and wrought havoc upon me like it was pedalling to get out, and I heaved over buckets and reeled at the most innocuous things. Scents that had once been pleasant were now an assault.

"We have a pill for that," the Propagation nurses would tell me each time I complained.

They had a pill for everything. I would take the pills and vomit them up moments later. My child was not interested in being managed.

"What are we going to do with this one?" Kweku asked, rubbing my belly as we lay in bed. "It's such a rebel. Do you think all-natural pregnancies are like this?"

"I don't know," I whispered. "Can I tell you something strange?"

"Always."

I turned to him in the dark. "I feel as if this child was sent by my grandmother, to show us that we were wrong."

Kweku was silent for some time, weighing the words. "Does that scare you?"

"The only thing that scares me is going back to the commune."

His hand stilled on my belly. "Where else is there to go?"

"Anywhere. I don't know." The baby kicked, startling us both, and something primal took hold of me. "I don't want our child to grow up thinking our way is normal. I want them to dance under the moon, and know many ways, and have many choices."

Kweku chuckled. "You want a wild child," he said.

"Does that scare you?"

He got up to kiss my belly. "I was considered useless my

whole life until I made you pregnant. Believe me, I want a wild child, too."

* * *

One afternoon, as I prepared a meal according to the Propagation guidelines, I noticed a piece of folded paper trapped between the bottom of the window and the windowsill.

Lifting the window, I drew out the paper, unfolded it and read the note that had been scribbled on the lined page: *There is a way out if you want it.* Nothing else. No instructions, no name, no contact information. I showed the note to Kweku.

"Burn it," he said. "What if it's a test?"

"It's not a test."

"But if it is, and we fail, we might never get out of here."

"It's not a test."

I left a reply in the same place where I had found the note. *We want it.*

We waited for a response. A day. A week. A month. I couldn't hide my anxiety.

"Is something troubling you?" the nurse asked during my next checkup.

"I'm just tired. The baby keeps me up."

She cooed in sympathy. "We have a pill for that."

I took the bottle of pills, knowing I would only throw them away.

When Kweku and I stepped outside, a car was waiting to take us to pick up our usual groceries. There was a new driver, a young man of about Kweku's age.

"Your car is a different model from the others," Kweku remarked as we entered the back of the vehicle. "And there's no licence sticker on your dashboard."

My pulse quickened then, and I knew.

The driver looked at us in the rearview mirror. "We don't have much time. Are you sure you want out?"

Kweku took my hand. He looked at me.

"It's not a test," I told him, then turned to the driver and nodded.

The driver set off, keeping a steady pace until we had turned away from the Propagation centre, and then he sped down the road. I expected a mad chase, like in the films I had read about. I expected sirens and people shouting at us over loudspeakers to surrender or face the consequences, but we had a good head start. We drove and drove, and because our vehicle passed for one of the Propagation's, no one dared to stop us.

After some hours, we stopped outside a small, obscure guest house near an abandoned farm. There was another pregnant woman inside, still in her first trimester, as well as three scrawny children and a man with bruises on his face.

We exchanged greetings, and our driver returned to the city. The owner of the guest house, a woman of around Ma's age, brought bicycles for us from the garage. I looked down at my belly. I couldn't see my swollen feet, but I could feel them, along with my aching hips and throbbing ankles. I glanced at the other pregnant woman. She was too busy trying not to vomit to react.

I looked at the woman holding the bikes and said, in the calmest voice I could muster, "Are you joking?"

She gave me a helpless shrug.

"Is there a cart?" Kweku asked.

There was. An old donkey cart, rough but solid. Kweku hitched it to two of the bikes. The other pregnant woman and I climbed inside. We were told to wait and hide in the rush. I had no idea what that meant until I saw the first of the bikes approaching down the road. The Fleet was on the move again, like rushing road warriors.

We waited until the flurry of cyclists drew closer, and then we eased into the road alongside them. Kweku and the bruised man drove behind the three children. The whirring of the wheels unnerved me at first – so fast, so relentless. Faces glanced at us, then looked away. The cyclists didn't speak, but they shifted position so that we were in the middle, hidden from the outside, safe in their ranks. It occurred to me then that they must have done this often.

We rode deep into the wilderness. Despite the knot of fear in my chest, the whirring noise soon became a soothing lullaby, and I fell asleep.

Kweku nudged me awake long after dark. The cyclists had slowed down.

"They said this is where we should stop," Kweku told me, pointing down the road at a commune, somewhat like the one we had left, but alive with light and colour and music.

We separated from the cyclists, thanking them, and moved towards the commune. I reeled from the noise.

A boy came running towards us, shouting, "Welcome! Welcome!"

"What's happening?" I asked. "Are you having some kind of ceremony?"

The boy smiled. "It's always like this here. You'll adjust. Come, there is food and drink. Your lodgings are already prepared, but first, I think our elders would like to meet you."

A group of people approached. Despite being called elders, one of them was younger than me. Their faces were wreathed in smiles, arms held out in welcome. We surrendered to a flurry of embraces and greetings and murmured assurances that we were safe, that we were home.

And then I heard someone gasp. The hands that reached for mine bore familiar callouses, the face creased into familiar lines, and although the hair had grown longer and whiter in the years we had been parted, the twists at the temples remained.

Mema pulled me against her chest, squeezing hard.

My baby kicked in protest, or perhaps in giddy joy.

* * *

"What is this place?" I asked.

Mema told me a story. I sat on the floor between her legs as she oiled my hair, and I toyed with the straps of her sandals. She told me of communes founded in love and goodwill but rotted over time as those who managed them sought more control. They were close to nature, leaving behind corporate greed, fossil fuels, industrial agriculture, pharmaceuticals. They promoted sustainable systems, co-creation, carbon-light living, slow food.

But to right one wrong, they had committed countless others until they were too lost to remember what a compass was, let alone how to use it. She spoke of those who had risen up in protest and been persecuted, who had fled, on their own or with assistance, and banded together to build a haven. Her words excited and frightened me. It was all so familiar.

"How can you be sure this community won't succumb to the same ills as the others?" I asked her. "How can you be sure you're not also wrong?"

I thought the question would upset her, but she kissed my ear and said, "That's my girl."

She showed me the walled outdoor space where the community met and the words carved into the concrete: *What are we too blind to see?*

She told me of the Voice of Reason, a community member selected at random during each gathering to play devil's advocate, to keep the elders honest, to hold the group accountable.

"We still make mistakes," she admitted. "But we're supposed to make mistakes. We're supposed to doubt. It's when you are utterly certain that you know you're in trouble."

I told her what had happened to Amiah. "Why didn't someone come for her the way they came for us?"

"We tried," Mema said. "But after the abortion attempt, she was under constant surveillance."

"You should have grabbed her on the way back to the commune."

"We don't grab people, Sedi. We must have consent."

"What if it's for their own good?" I asked, and then caught myself, realising I sounded just like the Council.

Mema was happier about my pregnancy than I had expected. She patted my belly with childish glee that spread warmth through me. There was no reverence, no pressure.

When she saw me lounging in bed while Kweku took on my share of the chores and tended to my cravings, she said, "Look at this girl! We don't do that here. You're a mother, not a queen."

She made me get up to fetch my own cup of fresh goat's milk with honey, then sent me to do the dishes.

* * *

I thought of Ma, but not often, and not with the same fondness. She was lonely without me, I knew, and yet I also knew that she hated me now. I was, like Mema, a disturber of the peace. Selfish. Treacherous. I had stolen the commune's future.

There was no doubt that the Council would hunt us.

One day, we might have to flee or fight, but for now, we were at ease, helping the community plan more rescues, welcoming those they managed to save. The smiles were real, and the throbbing fear had left us.

I was certain of nothing, less secure than I had ever been, and yet I was happy.

My contractions began on the night of the full moon. When I birthed a girl, I cried, overcome with relief that she was born free. It was weeks before Kweku and I settled on a name. Grace was as fierce outside my womb as she had been inside it. No child in the history of humanity had ever screamed so loud.

"She's a wild one," Mema chuckled, and I glowed with pride.

I was no good at stories, but Kweku would sit under the stars with Grace in his lap. He had a knack for getting her quiet, which pleased and galled me in equal measure.

"Once upon a time," he would tell her, "we were governed by the moon. Your mother believes that one day we will govern ourselves, but shall I tell you a secret?"

And she would gurgle and raise her tiny fists, promising to hold the secret close.

"Your mother is wrong," he would whisper, glancing at me and winking, making Mema laugh. "The truth, my daughter, ah, the tragedy and the wonder of it all is that we have governed ourselves all along."

Grace would look at him, wide-eyed and open-mouthed, as if she understood.

Dream State

CHAOS.

Dust rises from the dry, cracked ground, heavy shoes thud on cement, and hundreds of pairs of high heels click against the cold, clean tiles of the Customs Office.

I pull Harana along, gripping her hand as rustling silk skirts and loose linen trousers threaten to sweep her away. I glance back over my shoulder to see her push her way between the legs of the Parfaits.

"Stay close," I shout. "Don't let go of my hand!"

"Yes, Misa."

I stop and tug at her arm. She stumbles, falling against my side. "Come on."

"Are we going away?" she asks.

I look around me. The Parfaits move in panic, a stream of frightened animals rushing headlong across a river. The women clutch their hats with one hand, waving visas in

386

the other. Bright red stamps stand out on the pink slips of paper: marks of freedom.

Behind the Parfaits storming the Office is a wave of mortals, like us, persisting in the fruitless hope of riding away on the coattails of the Parfaits, as if the differences between us are as simple as red stamps on pink slips. For the first time, as I stare out across the desperate multitudes, I see things as they really are. The Parfaits are jet-skinned gods with diamond eyes. They're long, lithe limbs and flowing clothes, eyes bright with promise as they thrust their slips at the cashiers and glide away across the tarmac. And the rest of us, stumbling, clumsy hordes in ripped denim and cotton shirts, dusty faces haggard, bodies small and stunted, fool ourselves into thinking we could make it past the gates.

Harana grows restless and tugs at my sleeve. "Misa, are we going?"

I glance at the cashiers. I thought we could slip in among the Parfaits, two girls caught in the rush. It was a delusion, typical of my kind. "No." I pull her in the opposite direction, away from the Office.

"Why not? I can see the ships, Misa; they're so close!"

"I know. But we don't have visas. You can't leave without a visa."

"Can't we get some?"

"No."

We move quickly, stepping out of the way of the Parfaits. I look to the left and almost choke on my own breath. Security officers have come in stealthy silence as always. They are already separating the Parfaits from the mortals, pushing us back into the city.

I lower my head and increase my pace, but there is nowhere to run. Behind us are the ships we can never board, and ahead is the new regime, and death. Then I spot them. The Strangers. It has been so long since I last saw one. They keep to themselves, locked away in their island of calm. I had forgotten they existed.

My feet are ahead of my thoughts this time, and I'm already halfway towards them when I realise what I'm doing.

"Where are we going, Misa?"

"Over there, to the Strangers." I feel a sudden jerk as she stops. "Harana! There's no time!"

"We can't go to them," she says in horror as if I have forgotten how things work. "They don't speak to us. They only speak to Parfaits!"

"We must try."

"But Misa, they'll do something! They'll tell!"

I have already considered this possibility and decided it

unlikely. The Strangers have no allegiances. They live by their own laws, and reporting us to Security will be of no use to them. Then again, neither will helping us.

"We have to try," I tell Harana and drag her along with me.

In the confusion, no one notices two young girls running in the opposite direction. The lot is filled with frantic cries and the sharp barks of the officers as they prod mortals with their batons, threatening to use guns if necessary.

The Strangers sit at the foot of the hill, playing guitars and reading books, oblivious to the pandemonium on their doorstep. They don't notice us until we are upon them, and then they ignore us, talking and laughing, expecting us to realise our error and turn away.

I stand still, catching my breath, and watch them. There are seven, three males and four females, with long yellow hair. Their skin is so pale it's translucent, like paper stained with oil, almost glowing against the vibrant splashes of colour on their clothes. For the longest time, nothing happens. Harana's grip on my hand tightens, and I feel her pulse race.

One of them turns to us in slow motion and eyes us with idle curiosity. "Do you want something?" Her voice is high and gentle.

"Oh!" Harana steps forward, the words tumbling from her lips. "Oh, please help us. My sister and I, we need a place...because Security is coming and—"

I place my hand on her head, and she falls silent. I look the Stranger in the eyes. "We are running."

Her eyes flicker. She understands. She looks at us for a moment as if deliberating, then raises a pale hand and points to her chest. "Ayla." She then points to each of her companions in turn. "Eric, Sima, Wess, Athlone, Regis, Perpetua."

I nod. "I am Misa. This is Harana."

"I know," she replies, then tosses her head. "We are at leisure. You may sit until we are done."

Harana and I sink onto the grass, resting our aching feet. Time seems to stand still here, and when I look towards the Customs Office, the people look like dolls. The window is closing. I watch the gates of the Office swing shut. The force of it flings mortals and officers backwards. The window closes with a flash of light and a jolt, like thunder, sending vibrations across the ground. The hill beneath us trembles. I close my eyes, blocking out the light.

When it's over, and the light has faded, I open my eyes. Darkness has fallen. The officers are on their feet, herding the mortals back into the city. The Parfaits and their airships are gone. The Office has vanished into the night, leaving a vast empty field.

I don't know how long we are on the hill. I doze off, and when Harana shakes me awake, I see Ayla standing over me.

"Your leader has called an assembly," she announces.

"He's not my leader."

She smiles. "Nevertheless, we must go."

"No!" cries Harana. "We can't be seen in the hall, not with *him* there!"

"You will be with us," Ayla assures us. "You will be safe."

I get to my feet, still half asleep. "Why are you going? You have nothing to do with the state."

"We are guests here," she says. "We must attend as a show of good faith. Come."

The other Strangers have not said a word to us, but they seem untroubled by our presence. Ayla produces fresh clothes for Harana and me, and we make our way into the city bundled up in fleecy white coats that hide our faces. The Strangers always wear coats in the city; it is said that our air is so cold it freezes on their cheeks. I glance at them as we walk. It's true.

The hall is nothing like I remember. In the few hours since the government announced the takeover, everything has changed. The chairs are all rigged up to bulky, groaning vats of bluish water. The air is murky and hazy, and it makes me long to sleep again. We take our seats with the Strangers at the back of the hall. Our chairs have no vats beside them. The other mortals fill up the spaces in front. No one even looks in our direction.

"I'm scared," Harana whispers.

I take her gloved hand in mine. I'm frightened, too. I'm not sure how long the hooded coats can conceal us. Someone is sure to notice two dark mortals in a group of pale Strangers. "Don't worry," I say, more for my benefit than hers. "It'll be fine."

Ayla looks at us and smiles.

I lean towards her. "Why did you help us?"

She pauses. "I saw your grandfather in you," she replies. "He was the one who interceded when our ship crashed, when everyone else wanted us gone. He gave us a new home." She takes my hand. "No more talking. Your voice gives off a different vibration than ours, and it will affect the glamour."

I stare at her in surprise. The glamour! My panic eases. It didn't occur to me that she would use it, though what else could she have done? No wonder no one has spotted us. To them, we are just two more Strangers.

The hall falls silent. Ten officers enter, and behind them is the leader. My body stiffens at the sight of him. Harana begins to sob. I slip one arm around her shoulders.

"Ssshh!" I whisper. "You'll disturb the glamour. It's OK, I promise."

But it isn't. I stare at his familiar face and know exactly what Harana is feeling. My stomach churns with a mixture of emotions. I want to look away, but I can't. I no longer know this man. He is a traitor who would kill me without a second thought.

He stands at the podium and beams down on his subjects. "Welcome, mortals. You are blessed tonight! You may not realise it yet, but when that window closed on the Parfaits, it created a new world. A new order. An order of mortals. But not ordinary mortals, as you have been since the beginning. New mortals. Better mortals."

I resist the urge to rush at him. My hand grips the armrest of my chair, nails cutting into the plastic.

He waves a hand at the vats. "This is the future. Welcome to the new world. Welcome to the Dream State."

A screen slides down from the ceiling, and people begin to murmur. The screen goes on with a flash of blue, and the image of a table appears, covered in glasses. Each glass contains what appears to be wine.

"Who wants to be the first to taste the future?"

A girl in front of us leaps to her feet and runs forward. She reaches into the screen and pulls out a glass. A gasp goes up from the crowd as she drains the glass and puts it back on the table. She turns back to face us, and I notice with dismay that she is flickering, like a light about to go out. A large socket is burned into her chest, and I see the wires leading from it back into her chair. It is then that I realise she has not left her chair at all. Her body is still as her other self takes a bow at the front of the hall.

The mortals cheer like ignorant children. They have not noticed the body in the chair. They can't see the way she is slumped with her head to one side. Harana lets out a gasp. She and I are the only mortals in that room who realise the truth. The girl is dead, and the shape at the front is nothing more than an illusion.

My eyes rove around the hall. Sockets have been burned into chests everywhere. Everyone is plugged into the dream machines beside their chairs. Everyone has been taken.

"We have to go," I whisper to Ayla. "We have to get out of here!"

She rises and indicates to the others to do the same. We leave the hall. No one notices. No one cares.

When we reach the hill, the other Strangers return to their books and guitars. I turn to Harana. Her face is streaked with tears.

"She needs to sleep," says Ayla, and with a touch of her hand, my sister collapses onto the grass. "We will wake her in a few hours to eat."

I nod. I can't get the leader's face out of my head. I see him as clearly as if he were standing right in front of me with his blurred edges, like a photograph that's been enlarged too many times. For the briefest moment, when he entered the hall, I thought he was my father. I thought he was alive, awake, like me. I forgot about the way his body had jerked when the Dreamer took him, the way he had crumpled to the floor, a paper doll folded up on the carpet. When he smiled that bright, otherworldly Dreamer smile with my father's teeth, I remembered. I will never forget again.

"Does he know you? The leader?"

I turn to Ayla. "No. Not as his children, anyway."

"And if he finds you...you will be taken, too? Like the others?"

"Maybe." I look up at the stars. "Maybe worse."

She shakes her head and makes a funny little croaking sound. "We have heard of these Dreamers. They are shackles on the feet of any world they touch. Being taken is like being trapped inside a corpse forever. There is nothing worse."

I know she's right. I would rather grab Harana and leap into the sea than let them take us. But if we are caught, there will be no choices.

Ayla touches my shoulder. "The glamour won't last. When it passes, they will be able to see you." She hesitates. "There are ways...we can make you one of us, in a manner of speaking." She gives me a sad smile. "But being taken by Strangers is no different to being taken by Dreamers. You will be like us. The mortals in you will...pass."

I'm overwhelmed by guilt. I should never have taken Harana from the state house. We should never have run. They would have killed us quickly, painlessly, the way they killed our mother. We would be dancing among the stars now, with the last of our kind. Instead, I have doomed us to dreams or dissolution.

"There is a difference," I tell Ayla.

I look down at my sleeping sister, struggling to accept that we are the only mortals left. The others are plugged into vats of Dreamer poison. Deceived by the copies of themselves that move and talk and laugh, they don't even realise they are dead.

To be born a mortal in a world of Parfaits is a pitiful thing. The Parfaits let us lead because they pitied us and knew we would never oppose them. Mortals have no grand ambitions, no virtues, yet there is truth to what Ayla said. I would rather die in my own body than live a thousand ages in a lie.

But I am not alone. I must think of Harana.

"Do it," I whisper.

"It's not like the glamour," says Ayla. "If I make you like us, you cannot go back."

"Do it."

My stomach turns with guilt. I'm selling our souls to save our lives, and there will be no redemption. I close my eyes and wait. Nothing happens. I turn to Ayla.

"It's not working," she says.

"Maybe you should ask your friends to help."

She goes to call the others. I climb onto a nearby rock and look down at the city, knowing that this might be the last time I see it with my own eyes. And then I spot something glowing behind a tree, the tree we sat under before the assembly. Curious, I move towards it. I don't have to go far before I understand what I'm looking at.

Stranger corpses piled one on top of the other, and a vat of Dreamer poison for each of them. Panic clogs my throat, but before I can turn to run I notice something odd about the vats. There should be seven, one for each Stranger, but instead, there are nine. My heart goes quiet inside me. I move closer.

There, hidden in the long grass, are two stunted mortal bodies with sockets in their chests. One is Harana's. One is mine.

The Mother

SUMMER BRINGS a sick, sweet heat, sticky and inescapable. The sheets cling to my back and my side; they ride up into my armpits and in between my legs. The fan is on somewhere in a corner of the room. I hear it whirring softly, almost drowned out by the crickets, and I can just make out its shape in the dark, but I can't feel a thing. I inch closer to it, dragging my body towards the bottom of the bed so my feet dangle off the edge. Then, gingerly, afraid of what I might find, I place a hand on my swollen belly. It's hot and slick with sweat.

I throw off the duvet, kicking to free my legs from its oppressive weight. I keep telling Saul it's too hot for a duvet, but he's afraid I'll get a chill. I don't tell him the shiver he notices is not from cold but from fear. If I confess to that, everything falls apart. I'm meant to be taking it easy, avoiding anxiety, but at this point anxiety is all my body knows.

I close my eyes and try to visualise my baby. I don't know if it's a boy or girl. All I see is a little figure running through the sand, screaming with delight. My fingers slide over the taut skin covering my womb. What do I say? "Don't worry"? "Everything is going to be fine"?

The images in my head shift as I slip into sleep. A doctor is standing over me, smiling, hopeful. *It's going to be fine this time,* he says. I wait for him to tell me to push. Instead, he places a cold, rubber-gloved hand on my stomach and tells me to close my eyes. Then I see the flash of metal, and the pain comes—

I sit up, screaming.

"Jedda?" Big, calloused hands reach for me in the darkness.

"They're killing my baby!" I cry, struggling to free myself from my husband's grip.

"Jedda." He holds me against his sweaty chest and whispers against the side of my head. "It was a dream. There's nobody here."

I look around the room, confused. "But…"

"Jedda." His voice is soft and patient. He pulls away and turns my face towards his so that we're looking into each other's eyes. "There's nobody here."

* * *

Everybody's smiling. The tentative, bitter smiles of those who have surrendered to fate. I smile back brightly, stretching my lips, showing all my teeth. My faith is stronger than their doubt.

They pat me on the back. I get up to make tea, and Maira leaps to her feet and offers to do it instead. They're all huddled together on the old sofa except Celina, who is sitting in the small armchair with the torn upholstery.

They ask if I'm still taking in sewing. They ask if I still cook for the deli. Yes, yes. My smile is fading. It doesn't have the stamina of their plastic versions, still plastered to their faces even after Maira brings a tray with teacups and a plate of hard ginger biscuits. We skirt the issue, as usual.

"This heat!"

"And the rain doesn't help…"

"You won't believe how much I paid for a dozen eggs yesterday."

"Everything's going up. God knows where they expect us to get the money."

"On a fisherman's pay, no less!"

I pretend to participate, but no one expects me to say much. I'm the poor cousin who sits quietly in the corner and doesn't have to help with the dishes.

After the tea, which Maira has made too sweet as usual, and some idle town gossip, they make their excuses. No one says a word about the baby, but I watch their eyes dropping to my womb every so often – quick, guilty glances at the object of our community's newest taboo. During the first pregnancy, they brought gifts with every visit. Little booties, tiny hand-me-down sweaters, contradictory advice. I'm five months along now. No one has brought a thing.

I close the door, shutting out their smiles and soothing voices. I linger at the door and listen to them say, in hushed tones, the things they couldn't say in my presence.

"Poor thing!"

"And she's trying so hard to put on a brave face!"

"Maybe this time…" It's the voice of Aletta, the youngest in our clique. "It might happen. It's possible." I want to reach through the door and kiss her.

"Oh, Aletta." It's Maira. "Three times!" A sharp, no-nonsense click of the tongue. "It wasn't meant to be."

The others murmur their agreement. I hold my breath, my palms pressed against the door, until their voices fade.

* * *

It's dusk. Children chase each other barefoot down the road, trying to clamber up the streetlights. I stand at the sink, staring out of the kitchen window at the gravel road in front of the house.

My hands move of their own volition in the soapy water, like mechanical components that I can't control. Scrub, rinse, stack. Scrub, rinse, stack. The house is empty. I keep my eyes on the window so I'm not tempted to glance around at all the spaces in the room that are just the right size for a child to hide in. Under the table, in the broom cupboard. Even the space right next to me should be occupied by little feet, little hands tugging on my skirt, a little voice calling out to show me some triviality that means everything, for that moment, everything in the world.

Three times, I've had this vision. Three times, I've watched it fade. I blink furiously, fighting tears. This time, number four...I have to believe.

By the time Saul comes home, the kitchen is spotless, and dinner is ready. I meet him at the door and take his hat. He smells of saltwater and fish. I kiss his cheek. It's rough with stubble. "How did it go?"

He shrugs. "Here, look." He hands me a wrapped up newspaper. "Some shrimp. For tomorrow." He smiles proudly.

I smile back. "Thank you."

He goes to the bathroom to wash up. I take the shrimp into the kitchen, clean it, and put it away, then set the table for dinner. We're quiet diners. We eat first, then sit together, he reading the paper, me sewing under the light of my fluorescent lamp. But tonight, in the middle of the meal, he looks up at me.

"We don't have to keep trying."

I lower my fork. "Trying?" I know what he means, but I'm hoping he will change his mind and decide to mean something else.

"If…" He shakes his head, powerless. "If, God forbid…" He takes a deep breath. "We don't have to keep trying."

My stomach turns violently. "You mean you don't want to try."

"No. I mean…" He looks at me, eyes pleading with me to understand, to help him find the right words,

words that won't hurt me. But he has already begun and the damage is his to repair. "I know how hard it is for you, and to go through it all again… I don't want you to…not if…it can't be good for you," he concludes helplessly.

I push my chair back and carry my plate to the kitchen. "Jedda, please."

I'm not listening. My body is numb. I throw the food in the bin, knowing I'll regret it in the morning, and start to wash my plate.

"Jedda." He's behind me. "I'm just trying to…"

"I know, Saul. Finish your food so I can wash your plate." I feel his eyes on my back. My womb is filled with lead.

* * *

He lies at the very edge of the bed as if he's afraid to let our bodies touch. Space yawns between us, a valley of tousled sheets. I lie on my side, looking at his back, trying to see into his heart, but the walls are up. I'm a trespasser now.

I turn onto my other side and face the wall. I know it's my fault, but I don't know how to fix it. Everything is upside down, inside out. We are young, strong and in love. We deserve the world.

I have a scar for every pregnancy, somewhere on my soul, ragged and raw and twisted, like the scar on Saul's leg from the time a fishing hook caught in his flesh. Three scars, running down the length of me. Three graves. Three tiny, unmarked headstones. There won't be a fourth. I won't allow it. I've done everything right. I've been *so* careful, almost crazy with caution. I've been to the clinic six times this month. I've done *everything* right.

The doctors say there's nothing wrong. They don't understand. *I* don't understand. They're supposed to fix it, but they don't even know what's broken. How can they not know what must be there in plain sight, under their stupid microscopes? How can they not see the knot of poison that eats away at me, killing my children? Where the hell are they looking?

I'm too scared to go to sleep. The nightmares won't leave me, visions of doctors with scalpels and demons with claws. I turn over again.

"Saul," I whisper.

His body rises and falls softly. He's asleep. I move closer, as close as I can, without actually touching him.

I want to pull myself right up against his back and put my arms around him so I can feel his skin, so his heart can beat through me, so I can be sure he's really here. But the walls are thick, and I won't try to breach them tonight.

I cry in earnest, silent, brutal tears for all I've lost, all I'm losing, for the future I had hoped to have. I cry in secret, behind my husband's back, because my pain is so immense that I fear it will engulf us. I keep it to myself and guard it as he guards his. We keep our secrets. We never cry together.

* * *

The cramps begin in the morning, moments before dawn, as Saul is getting ready to leave. I cry out, bending over the stove, and he looks over his shoulder at me.

He's at my side in seconds. "What is it?"

I straighten up, and the pain passes. "Nothing." I smile. "I burned my hand. Silly." I giggle girlishly. "Go on, it's time."

He frowns at me, his hand on my elbow.

"Go," I insist. I want to turn away, afraid that my fear will show in my eyes.

"Are you sure?" He releases my elbow and kisses my cheek.

"Of course," I laugh. "Bring me a lobster tonight."

He smiles shakily. "OK."

I watch him leave. I wait a few minutes until I'm sure he's gone, then I run to the toilet to check. I'm not bleeding, thank God, but I can't shake the panic. This is how it always starts. I return to the kitchen. Maybe I should leave the breakfast dishes for now. Yes, that's it. I just need to lie down. I go into the bedroom and kick off my slippers. I feel better already.

* * *

Aletta comes by before lunch. She's brought me some fruit and a box of tea. While she's helping me cook, it happens again. She grabs me around the waist, holding me up.

"Is it…?"

I shake my head through the pain.

She leads me to the sofa. "I'm going to call Saul."

"No!" I grab her arm. "He's working."

"You need a doctor," she says sternly and heads for the door.

Blood and hope drain out of my body. I flee into the bathroom, lock the door and strip off my clothes. I hear Aletta calling from somewhere in the distance. I climb into the tub. Blood seems to be everywhere suddenly. I can barely think. I turn on the tap and let the water run, icy and merciless, over me.

* * *

Four scars, running down the length of me. Four graves. Four tiny, unmarked headstones.

About the Author

Cheryl S. Ntumy is a Ghanaian writer of short fiction and novels of speculative fiction, young adult fiction and romance. Her work has appeared in *FIYAH Literary Magazine*; *Apex Magazine*; *World Literature Today*; *Best of World SF Vol. 3* and *Year's Best African Speculative Fiction 2022*, among others. Her work has also been nominated for the Nommo Award for African Speculative Fiction, the British Science Fiction Association Award, the Commonwealth Writers Short Story Prize and the Miles Morland Foundation Scholarship. She is part of the Sauútiverse Collective, which created a shared universe for Afrocentric speculative fiction, and a member of Petlo Literary Arts, an organisation that develops and promotes creative writing in Botswana.

Eugen Bacon (Foreword) is an African Australian author. She's a British Fantasy and Foreword Indies Award winner, a twice World Fantasy Award finalist, and a finalist in the Shirley Jackson, Philip K. Dick, Victorian Premier's Literary Award and the Nommo Awards for speculative fiction by Africans. Eugen was announced in the Honor List of the Otherwise Fellowships for 'doing exciting work in gender and speculative fiction'. *Danged Black Thing* made the Otherwise Award Honor List as a 'sharp collection of Afro-Surrealist work'. Visit her at eugenbacon.com.

Future Fiction is a small press and cultural association created by Francesco Verso to promote an interdisciplinary approach to the idea of the future: in 10 years it has published the best science fiction in the world, from 14 languages and 35 countries, winning the Best Publisher Award from the European SF Society in 2019 and a Galaxy Award in 2023.

About the Illustrator

Marvin Opuni Kwabia (Frontispiece and Cover Detail) is a Ghanaian-based graphic designer and illustrator. He graduated with a bachelor's degree in graphic design and has worked for years as a freelancer with a strong interest in book illustration, digital painting, graphic design, motion graphics and animation. With many commissions over the past five years he has worked with Chadia Mathurin and Saarinze, and hosted an art exhibition by the British Council Kumasi. His artworks and designs are inspired heavily by modern trends, pop and African culture. He enjoys conceptualising and translating his ideas into unique and captivating visual forms of expression.

Acknowledgements

These stories span fifteen-odd years and none of them would have happened without a long list of people. I'd like to thank:

My family, for supporting me even when they don't understand what I'm doing; my writer friends, for the willingness to read my work and offer feedback; my non-writer friends, for never acting as though making up stories for a living is ridiculous; my sangha, for holding space for me; and the Sauútiverse Collective, for all the inspiration and support.

Every English and Art teacher I've ever had, every publication that has featured my stories and every editor I've worked with over the years. Special thanks to Francesco Verso, who is the reason this collection is even a thing, and who I have had the enormous pleasure of working with several times.

Everyone at Flame Tree Press – Nick Wells, Gillian Whitaker, Catherine Patricia Taylor – for working so hard to put this collection together and share it with the world; Adeola Opeyemi, for the fantastic copyedits; and Tania Charles for proofreading the manuscript.

Eugen Bacon, my fellow Saúútiverse Collective founding member, for writing a lovely foreword and offering steadfast support through my creative journey.

And all the African creatives out there trying to make the dream work against all odds, for telling stories even when your hands are tied and your backs are against the wall, and for inspiring me every day. May your art live forever.

Cheryl S. Ntumy

Original Publication Details

Some of the stories included in this collection were first published elsewhere, with details below.

'Silverfish' in *Great Short Stories by Youwriteon.com Writers – February 2008 to October 2009* (US, 2009)

'The Mother' in *Mapping Me: A Landscape of Women's Stories* (Maymona Productions, US, 2014)

'Armour' in *The Devil You Know* (Petlo Literary Arts, Botswana, 2016)

'The Storymage' in *The Goddess of Mtwara and Other Stories* (Caine Prize Anthology, New Internationalist, UK, 2017)

'Dream State' (earlier version) in *Petlwana Journal of Creative Writing from Botswana, Issue 1* (Petlo Literary Arts, Botswana, 2018)

'Godmother' in Apex Magazine *International Futurists Special Issue, Issue 128* (December 2021), reprinted in *Apex Magazine 2021* (December 2022), reprinted in *Best of World SF Volume III* (October 2023)

'Wild' in *Ciclotopia: Feminist Science Fiction on Two Wheels* (February 2023)

'The Way of Baa'gh' in *Mothersound: A Sauútiverse Anthology* (Android Press, November 2023)

'The Ghost of Dzablui Estate' in *The Bright Mirror* (Future Fiction, November 2023)

Beyond & Within

THE FLAME TREE Beyond & Within short story collections bring together tales of myth and imagination by modern and contemporary writers, carefully selected by anthologists, and sometimes featuring short stories and fiction from a single author. Overall, the series presents a wide range of diverse and inclusive voices, often writing folkloric-inflected short fiction, but always with an emphasis on the supernatural, science fiction, the mysterious and the speculative. The books themselves are gorgeous, with foiled covers, printed edges and published only in hardcover editions, offering a lifetime of reading pleasure.

FLAME TREE FICTION

A wide range of new and classic fiction, from myth to
modern stories, with tales from the distant past to the
far future, including short story anthologies, Collector's
Editions, Collectable Classics, Gothic Fantasy collections
and Epic Tales of mythology and folklore.

•

Available at all good bookstores, and online
at flametreepublishing.com